25 Ways to Kill a Werewolf

Jo Thomas writes speculative fiction, tending towards dark fantasy. She has taken the advice "write what you know" to heart and, as a result, werewolves now turn up in the strangest places. (None were harmed in the writing of "25 Ways to Kill a Werewolf" but friendly vets were pumped for advice.)

To find out more about Jo, her pack of Hellhounds and her interest in swords along with the odd piece of fiction that doesn't contain werewolves, have a look at http://www.journeymouse.net/

To Keith,

I hope you enjoy this – and can read my writing!

Jo.

25 Ways To Kill A Werewolf

Jo Thomas

www.foxspirit.co.uk

25 Ways to Kill a Werewolf © 2014 Jo Thomas

Cover Art by Sarah Anne Langton
http://www.secretarcticbase.com/

conversion by: handebooks.co.uk

ISBN:
978-1-909348-61-5 paperback
978-1-909348-62-2 mobi
978-1-909348-63-9 epub

.

A Fox Spirit Original
Fox Spirit Books
www.foxspirit.co.uk
adele@foxspirit.co.uk

I'd like to dedicate my first published novel (wow, that sounds good—and pretentious) to the memory of Alice Beck and Jennifer Thomas, as well as to Samantha and Jennifer Jackson, who support me through everything.

I'd also like to thank the awesome Fox Spirit Books team (Adele Wearing and Darren Pulsford) and the Skulk (who I'm too lazy to name individually), as well as offering particular thanks and recognition for the alpha and beta readers: Emma Jane Davies, Dylan Fox, Noel Gayle, Nick Marsh, Helen & Simon McGrory, A Bruce Stewart.

My name is Elkie Bernstein. I live in North Wales and I kill werewolves.

I'm human and nothing special. No quick healing, no super strength, no fantastic reflexes, no mutant powers. Just human.

I get hurt and the injuries take their own time to heal. It leaves me weak and vulnerable so I avoid it. I can't fight a million attackers at once — I don't have the raw talent or the trained skill — so I avoid doing it. I can't read minds or call lightning from the sky so I avoid situations where they would be my only possible line of defence. I'm nothing special.

But anyone who tells you that you have to be special to kill werewolves hasn't been trying hard enough. And anyone who says there's only one way to kill a werewolf needs to experiment more. A lot more.

Method 1: A Stake Through The Heart

I found out that werewolves exist when I was still fifteen, just about a week before my sixteenth birthday in fact. It was too young to cope with what happened but I don't suppose anyone is ever ready for werewolves.

So. The first day.

I woke from a dream I don't remember but it probably involved local golden boy, Ben Lloyd — at that time, they usually did — as my hormones gave me my wake-up call. Yeah, it will have involved masturbation. I'm only human.

I got up, showered, dressed and grabbed a piece of toast on the way out the door. I ate my toast as I sat on the garden wall and waited for Dave. I counted weeds on the lane and wondered whether the potholes were bigger than the same time last year.

'*Bore da*,' I said when Dave arrived.

'Bugger off,' he said back, 'Mornings're never good.'

In those days, Dave was just the boy next door and next door was the farm at the end of the mile long lane. The decrepit ex-labourer's cottage my mother rented belonged to that equally decrepit farm, my mum not being able to afford anything better and Dave's parents not being able to afford to fix up either place. Asset rich, capital poor, what with sharing the meagre profit from a small Welsh hill farm among ten cousins.

'Meet in the copse, tonight?' Dave asked.

Before you get the wrong idea, neither of us was sure about this puberty thing or ready for the pairing up the kids at school were doing. Sure, we had our fantasies but who doesn't?

'After chores?' I asked. When Dave nodded, I added a "Kay."

See, we were both young for our age, really. Skinny and half-formed. He'd not yet had his growth spurt and looked like a drowned rat on a good day. I was half a head taller and not much better to look at. I had no chest then and it still hasn't made an appearance. Most people assumed I was a boy — after all, boys can have bum-length hair these days, it's called equality — until I opened my mouth.

'Staves?' I asked.

One of the entertainments we'd devised was attempting to 'quarterstaff' like the people in the films. I have since found out, of course, that they weren't doing it right, never mind us.

Dave nodded. This was about as in-depth as our morning conversations got. Dave was never an early bird by choice and we only talked at all because arrangements like these could not be made in front of the other kids.

I should probably describe the lane turning from dirt to asphalt, the appearance of a cracked pavement, or the shape of the village as we walked through it. I could talk about the blackbirds calling from hedgerows and skylarks above the fields. I could tell you about how fields smell, even a pasture that the beasts aren't on, and how that compares to the smells around the houses. But these are memories built up over years of taking the same walk. I was paying little attention to it at that time in the morning.

And nothing ever changed, day-to-day. We even got a variation on the same greeting from the others every morning.

'The lovebirds are here!' a girl called out.

Dave turned red and I hoped I didn't. We looked at the bus stop on the other side of the road as if the others weren't there. We both had plenty of practice at this, though I used to do it so I wasn't staring at Ben, who'd been gone for a few weeks by now.

That morning, we found ourselves staring at a stranger, a man, sitting on the opposite bench and clutching a worn backpack. He would be waiting for the bus that went the other way around on the same loop. It was unusual to see a stranger in the village, so small it might as well be called

Llados. The village's only saving grace was not being a total dead end — so the local buses drove round the route to Llareggub in both directions.

'Bit late, Williams,' said one of the older boys, 'Stop for a roll in the hay?'

The village kids always acted like we were some sort of hill-billy settlement up the lane, not just two people that grew up together. Sometimes I think they really believed we were actually related, not just neighbours. Maybe it was the shared skinny, tow-headed look that confused them.

The man across the road turned and looked at us. I mean *really* looked. There was something about the way he held his head that made me think of the working dogs on the farm. Nose to the wind and scenting. Very weird, because there's no way a man can catch a smell that way, I knew that even then, and what was he going to smell, anyway? Two teenagers just dragged out of bed.

'Well, I think it's nice they have each other,' the girl said as she turned her patronising gaze in our direction.

The man across the road, no word of a lie, looked at me like I was the most appetising thing in the world. Not a woman but a thing, prey, food. I shifted nervously and tried to get out of his line of sight by shuffling behind Dave. The man's gaze seemed to sharpen even more.

The older boy snorted. 'Nobody else would. Not even with bags over their heads.'

The kids laughed and jeered but, across the road, the man's hands tightened and then loosened on his bag, like he was a blissed-out cat kneading. I ignored the restless feeling that settled around my stomach and nudged Dave. He put his arm around my shoulder and tried to stare the man out.

'Bloody paedo,' Dave muttered as the man looked away.

I thumped Dave. It didn't bother me when the others called me ugly or said that I looked like a little kid but Dave was supposed to be my friend.

He glared. 'What was that for?'

'Oh, like you don't know.' I glared back.

'But I don't.'

He blinked. I decided he really was clueless and turned my back on him and the stranger.

All in all, not a big deal or particularly dramatic, and barely worth reporting.

It was May, so it was late spring running into early summer with nights drawing out, and we had plenty of time to run around the woodland by the farmhouse after chores and dinner that evening. When Dave and I were smaller, we used to run around being knights and slaying dragons, as well as assorted smaller animals that can be tackled with the catapults and air-guns Dave's dad let us use.

By fifteen, we were making staves with fire-hardened points that doubled as spears. For what it's worth, the fire-hardening was Dave's idea. He'd read it somewhere in passing then methodically researched it so that by this particular evening we were busy stabbing defenceless plants.

Consider this fair warning. People like Dave and I are what happens when you don't buy your kids a games console and you live in the middle of nowhere.

'We need to try the points on something harder,' Dave said, not happy with the plants' response. Or maybe that should be lack of response.

'Like what?'

Dave shrugged. 'Dunno. Maybe we should catch some rabbits.'

Rabbits, like most other biological forms, are disturbingly squishy when you get down to it. I'm often surprised how few people realise it but, like I said, middle of nowhere.

'Rabbits aren't exactly hard, Dave.'

He made a non-committal noise.

'Set a snare tonight and check them tomorrow morning?'

It was the best suggestion I could come up with because there was no way I was staying out looking for one of the furry little critters that evening.

'Could do.'

'Just as long as you don't leave it 'til tomorrow night,' I said with a shudder.

I remembered a snare that hadn't worked quite as intended and had left an animal in pain for too long. Of course, the use of snares is illegal but it hadn't been a law we paid much attention to until then. The animal had been left that long because Dave couldn't drag his arse out of bed in time to go check the snare before school. I would do my best to ensure that never happened again.

'Town — '

A twig snapped, interrupting Dave's habitual insult of 'townie' and the habitual response of 'am not' that had already opened my mouth.

We looked at each other. There was nothing in here of a size to snap twigs and unconcerned enough about our presence to do it. The kids from Llados might — but they would be tucked up in front of their computers or consoles by now, not wondering about a piece of woodland the size of a postage stamp.

' — ie,' Dave finished while moving his hand into the language we'd developed in our years of dragon hunting, indicating 'separate'.

'Am not!'

I didn't really need to pretend I found that insulting. I'd been living down this lane for ten years by that time and I was just good as him at what his dad called the 'father-son stuff'. I stepped back two paces as quietly as I could. That should put us far enough apart that any charge by the idiot stalking us could only hit one of us at a time.

I waggled my home-made spear slightly, meaning 'Scare them or run away?'

Dave cocked his head to one side, listening. I mimicked but couldn't hear anything else, just us breathing. Even the birds on the edge of the wood had stilled. Definitely not an animal that snapped the twig, then, if Nature was holding its breath.

'No snares tonight. I can't be bothered,' said Dave. He waggled his own spear a little, then turned it so the point was down on the floor, meaning what I took to be 'scare but be careful'.

I said, 'Okay,' and copied that move as well.

He grinned and I could almost read his mind. It made a change that we got to wind up the village kids. They treated us like an inbred leper colony or something.

'Let's go,' Dave called.

Another loud heartbeat and he spun, stepping towards the farmhouse. From where we stood, I could see it clearly between the trees and on the other side of a small arable field. A clear run to the house — once we'd scared whoever was trying to scare us. Maybe they were trying to catch us in our assumed affair.

I grinned as madly as Dave. The kids from the village were so useless outdoors, they were probably already lost in the postage stamp-sized woodland.

Then the undergrowth to the side of Dave exploded as something leapt —

'Oh, shit.'

Dave ducked, an instinctive move that left the attacker sailing over his head. Everything went slow-motion as I stared at something totally unexpected: something dog-like, but clearly not the right shape, attacking me with its off-white and very pointy teeth on display. All that went through my head was the thought that this wasn't a kid from the village. Consciously, anyway, as muscle memory took over.

I spun my spear so the sharp point was out, and grounded the blunt end between the woodland floor and my boots. I braced but fell over with the impact, snapping teeth barely held from my throat. I lay on the floor screaming.

'Get it off me!'

'Hang on! Hang on!' Dave screamed back as he stumbled over.

The snapping slowed then stopped. I realised that I couldn't feel the animal's breath on my neck. I felt hot, sticky liquid — blood, of course, but it took a while for the recognition to soak through my panic — all over me. In retrospect, I just wonder how I hadn't felt the blood gush as the animal knocked me over. I turned my head to look down at the head and saw —

The animal had looked like a misshapen grey dog when it charged me. Lying with it on top of me, it didn't look that way anymore. It was human. It was if the fur melted... dissolved... no, it was absorbed into the man's skin, the visual channel still stuck in action film like slow motion. His face, still caught in a predator's snarl, was the man from the bus stop, still staring at me like I was something good enough to eat.

'Get it off,' I whispered.

Dave grabbed and I pushed and we managed to get the man's body laid out on the floor beside me. I stood up on shaky legs.

'Oh God!' said Dave putting blood-stained hands over his face, 'Oh God! We've killed a man! We killed a man, Elkie!'

More aware of what might happen to people who used the Deity's name in vain than Dave, I settled for whispering 'Oh shit!' a few more times.

The spear was stuck into the man's chest, maybe only a hand-span or so in but right where our biology lessons told me the heart should be, angled oddly from sliding between ribs to get there. The spear was starting to sag from the wound and fall out under its own the weight. I reached out a shaky hand and pulled it from the body.

The whole thing was starting to seem very far away and unreal and I could hear a roaring of white noise.

'I killed him,' I whispered, 'Not you.'

I looked at the result, the first naked man I'd ever seen, which was slightly less traumatic than thinking of it as the first blood soaked corpse I'd ever seen.

'But I saw — I was — I'm an accessory to murder!' Dave said.

I stood the spear up and leant on it, my legs shaking too much to hold me without support. If I sat down, if I gave in to the white noise and the distancing, I knew I'd not get up again.

'It wasn't murder,' I said carefully, thinking of the muzzle, the teeth, the fur, 'It was self-defence.'

'What are we going to tell the police?' Dave's voice was getting higher.

I continued to consider the muzzle, the teeth, the fur — all that was no longer there. I thought about what the police would do to me for killing an obviously unarmed man in a small woodland in the back of beyond. The white noise receded and things didn't feel quite so far away anymore.

'We don't.'

Dave took his hands off of his face. 'What?!'

I looked at him. 'We hide the body, we find his clothes and bag and hide them, too, then we never talk of this again.'

'But — '

'Ever.'

'But — '

'What?' I yelled.

'Where are we going to put it?'

I slid down the makeshift spear, landing on my knees in blood. I was not the ideas person in our little team of two.

'I don't know.'

Dave paced. After a moment he stopped. He still looked pale, maybe even green around the edges, and his voice caught as he talked but he was the only person I could rely on to come up with something.

'Well, we're going to need the Land Rover to move it. Use an old tarp to put it on so I don't get blood all over the back.'

'But we don't drive,' was all I could say.

'Time to learn.'

'Where are we taking it?'

He didn't answer.

Method 2: Electrocution

A few weeks later, we had our second run-in with a werewolf. Not that we had a word for what the man had been, yet, that's a way off. Right at this time, we were quietly panicking about what the authorities would do if they ever found a particular body — male, naked, most definitely human and hidden with the clothes, bag and wallet we'd tracked down. The kind of time when local gossip is almost guaranteed to catch you up.

'I see Mister Lloyd's visitor is still here.'

Although when it does, you don't often realise it until the last possible minute, when you're already caught like a rabbit in headlights. Or one of Dave's snares.

'Been here two weeks, then,' said one of the elderly women of Llados.

I didn't turn to see her leant over the counter, all rapt attention for the village postmistress. I've seen it enough times to be able to picture it.

'Uh-huh. Just like that other one,' the postmistress said.

Anyway, I was busy turning jars of chocolate-hazelnut spread and working out how many I could buy with my weekly pay-out from mum, the remains of her wage and my pocket money. If I left it to her, and let her buy it out of the household budget, she'd come back with some crap supermarket rip-off. I'm after the real deal, the branded stuff. It's my drug of choice.

'What happened to the last one?' the old woman asked.

Dave leant forward and said, very close to my ear, 'Two.'

I turned. 'What?'

At the same time the postmistress finally answered, with salacious — get a dictionary if you don't understand it — joy, 'No idea.'

'Really?' the old woman was scandalised.

There was a suitable pause as the women digested this snippet of information although I couldn't understand the significance and didn't care to work it out.

'You can only afford two jars,' Dave said, 'As ever.'

I frowned. 'If I don't b — '

'Economics one-oh-one.' Dave grinned as he drew the syllables of the number out. 'Know your budget.'

I tried to defend myself, getting as far as 'bu — '

'And stick to it,' Dave said firmly.

I went back to turning jars round, rolling the numbers around in my head like I did every week. I started another protest as I tried to work out a way to squeeze one more jar into my weekly budget. What stopped me was the postmistress speaking to the little old woman again.

'The other one,' the postmistress said in a conspirator's mock whisper designed to be heard throughout the small shop and possibly the whole of Llados, 'Was last seen getting on the bus out weeks ago. Not been heard of since.'

It was if the jar leapt from the shelf without any help from me. I have no memory of touching it or of it slipping, just the sound as it hit the ground and looking at the coagulated mass at my feet. The spread held the glass together but it was broken, misshapen and unsafe to attempt a rescue of the contents. It only goes to show how bad the situation was that I barely mourned for the jar's suicide in my shock.

'I hope you're going to pay for that, Elkie Bernstein,' the postmistress said, all enjoyment — lecherous or otherwise — gone from her voice.

Dave's hand found its way to my shoulder and I shook my head at him. I took a deep breath, focussed on the fact that I could only afford one usable jar of spread that week and tried to sound as if there were many more important things in life.

'Yes, ma'am,' I replied.

For a moment, I almost believed it. I paid for the broken jar — which I left for the postmistress to clean up — and one, solitary whole jar to comfort me through the rest of the week. Both Dave and knew it would be eaten within minutes of getting back to our pretence of a wood, if only because I felt bad about killing the other one. I got halfway down the jar before Dave dared to interrupt me.

'Old Man Lloyd knows the... that man was here.'

Panic is white. It shows in the face, the fists, the eyes. Dave had gone white in the village shop and hadn't regained his colour at all. He'd at least managed to sound like he was breathing normally and I doubt anyone else would have been paying enough attention to us to have known.

'No,' I said as calmly as I could while inwardly praying for 'that man' to disappear, 'Old Man Lloyd just knows the first... that his visitor left on the morning bus. He left the village when he had the chance.'

I shuddered, thinking of the man on at the bus stop on the other side of the road and then, later, on the end of my spear. It could only have been Lloyd's visitor — whatever the man had been here for. No-one comes to Llados casually, with no reason. What I'm trying to say is, it's hardly a bustling thoroughfare even if it's not a dead-end road. Anyone passing through would be notable.

'This man, this visitor, has already passed through. Like everyone else,' I added, for good measure.

Everyone knew he had gone, except us — and possibly the bus driver, who would know where the man got off, but the next bus stop was miles from where we found the bag and clothes.

'But people know he's been here,' said Dave, almost whining, 'If someone comes asking questions.'

By 'someone' he meant police. By 'here' he meant Llados.

I closed my eyes again and drew in a deep breath. 'Let's go see the Lloyds, then. See who this new visitor is, and if there's a chance they're worried about the last one.'

It was not the most sensible suggestion I've ever come up with but Dave rocked where he sat as he considered it; one oscillation, two.

'*Iawn*,' he said. Fine.

With a sigh, I put the lid back on my jar of spread and cached it under a few stones so I'd be able to find it again the next time we came back. I gave the little pile of stones a pat and we left.

We took a route through the fields to the Lloyd's place like people aren't supposed to. One of the benefits to being not just a local but a local associated with one of the farms round here. If we'd been anyone else — and seen, of course — we'd have had an irate landowner after us, but Dave and I were known and tolerated. It helped that we stuck to the edge of the fields and didn't march through the middle scaring live-stock and trampling crops.

As ever, we skirted temporary grazing marked out for Ieuan Jones' prized White Parks. They lowed at me, their long horns sweeping impressively in the process.

'Later,' I told the affection-hungry idiots.

Not that I would be going near them. Despite the almost irresistible cuteness of a few early calves, the promised later would be sometime at the other end of eternity. I always wanted to make a fuss of one of them but never dared to even lean over the fence.

'Bet they're disappointed,' Dave said.

'They're too dumb to know what I'm saying.'

'So why bother?'

I shrugged.

'At least they're smart enough not to turn themselves into barbecue on the electric fence,' Dave said.

We both looked at the poly-wire fencing that held the beasts in as if they were murderers. It didn't click like normal battery-run fencing. There was a slight buzz but it could just as easily have been from the power line that ran through the fields, and that Jones connected his fence to.

'The man's bat-shit insane,' I said.

'The man's a cheap bastard,' Dave corrected. 'Like every-one else round here.'

At the Lloyds' place — too recently just Old Man Lloyd's place for the way we referred to it to have caught up with the facts — we found a sleek, expensive car the like of which the village had probably never seen. It's highly unlikely it will ever see that like again. Just saying.

Old Man Lloyd — not past forty-five but he was born a miserable sod — had been left on his own when his wife and kids did a moonlight flit. If the gossip in the Post Office was true, they'd come back from their Easter holiday and the wife had upped and left to be with some holiday romance. I don't know about Old Man Lloyd but I'd certainly suffered for it, my morning bus ride not quite as interesting without his son, Ben, to stare at.

So, the curtains were drawn and there was no answer when we knocked on the door. We knew the window that used to be Ben's but there was no point trying to attract his attention. Not that we wanted to, now or then. Ben might have been the school's golden boy but, outside of my dreams, he was just another school kid who liked to make us miserable. Dave more so than me, as I actually found Ben nice to look at and had never been on the receiving end of anything worse than the odd bit of verbal abuse.

'Not very lively,' I said to Dave.

He grunted.

'Not like we can find anything out,' I said.

But as Dave turned to frown at me, I saw a curtain twitch and Old Man Lloyd looked out at us. He did not look happy.

'Or do we ask him if he cares what happened to his last visitor?'

Dave shrugged unhappily.

'Doesn't look as if he's searching very hard,' I said with a nod at the window.

The curtain twitched shut.

'Guess not,' Dave finally said.

'Chocolate spread?'

He grinned and walked away, his hands in his pockets. I followed and nothing happened. The body remained undiscovered, the jar got finished and Dave and I returned to our former, lower level of panic. In other words, we weren't quite as white and twitchy.

Three days later, though, that sleek, expensive car we'd seen pulled up on our lane. An equally sleek, expensive business suit got out.

'Children,' the suit's wearer said with an insincere, wolfish smile, 'I understand you've been bothering Mr Lloyd.'

Dave and I looked at each other.

'Children?' mouthed Dave.

The man reached into the car and produced a briefcase. He laid it on the bonnet of the car with a reverence that implied something very special was about to happen. We were left wondering whether we should run away, call for the little men in white coats or bow in respect.

'It's not a good idea to trespass on Mr Lloyd's property.'

The briefcase catches were snapped open with a flourish.

Dave decided to play stupid male teenager. 'Yeah? So? What's it gotta do with you?'

The wolfish grin widened.

'I've decided to make it my business. A repayment to Mr Lloyd for services rendered,' the suit-wearer said smoothly, 'So I'm going to ask you nicely to leave him alone, and you're going to do as I ask.'

'Or what?' Dave bluffed.

'I won't ask again.'

Dave glowered. I blinked.

'I get the feeling you're not a particularly nice man,' I said.

'Very astute of you,' the suit-wearer replied.

He pulled what looked like a grey fake fur out of the brief-case and shook it with a flourish.

'In the court-room, they call me a shark,' he said, 'But I prefer to think of myself as a lone wolf.'

He smiled at some private joke and threw the fur over his shoulders, like it was a blanket or a cloak. He started to change as the edges of the fur touched. It took a moment or two but the human shape was replaced by a furry, not-dog shape almost identical to the one that had charged us two weeks before. He didn't say anything but his breathing got heavier as if the twisting of his body took effort.

'Does this mean we've just turned you down? I don't remember that,' I said. It came out garbled, squeaky and high pitched, though, so there's a fair chance it came across as a panicky nonsense. I had to assume that Dave's bravado counted as saying 'no'.

'Elkie!' Dave shouted, his voice catching and breaking, 'Run!'

So we ran.

We jumped the stone wall into the field and sprinted

across to our copse. At the first line of trees I risked a look back and saw our not-dog right behind us. He, it, ran on four legs like an animal but the shape of him was more human, the proportions not matching the way it moved.

I'd go so far as to say the not-dog was a misshapen monster, having something of canine speed in small movements but unable to maintain it for any length of time. It chased us in bursts, slowing down to a more normal speed as it panted before throwing itself forward in another desperate burst that almost caught us.

This did not stop my lungs burning as I ran and I can only be grateful that I was in better shape that most of the girls at my school.

'Keep going,' I gasped to Dave, who was running in front.

He nodded without looking back and we charged straight through to the next field. A stone turned under my foot and I tucked and rolled — my P.E. teacher would have been proud if she'd seen it.

An idea struck me as I regained my feet.

'Dave!'

'Yeah?' he threw back without stopping.

'Jones's!'

Dave turned his head just enough to show his confusion, which was quickly replaced by smiling comprehension. In hindsight, it's amazing how quickly the panic and guilt of killing someone disappears when being faced with a situation where it's necessary. Is this how murderers start?

So, we ran for the White Parks. We hurdled over the fence — with quick, mental prayers about not falling on the live wire — and ran straight through the middle of the herd. Luck being what it is, Dave managed to run straight between a cow and her calf. He maintained afterwards that he did it on purpose. But the slow to anger mother didn't get either of us because we kept running for the other side of the fenced area, jumping out of the loop as quickly as we could. We looked over our shoulders and what we saw slowed then stopped us.

The cow lowed and swung her great head, still responding to our run past, and caught our pursuer by accident. The not-wolf shape was thrown against another beast that jostled him off course. He hit the fence at a run, what was presumably the left arm connecting with the fence as the right leg made contact with the ground. I swear I heard a pop, like when static electricity grounds.

My physics teacher said that it's electric current that kills. I guess the current went straight across the man-beast's heart and stopped it. He fell to the ground, otherwise unharmed. As the fur seemed to vanish, slowly absorbed through the sharp suit, Dave and I looked at each other.

Dave was pale and breathing heavily but each breath took back ground from panic white, his eyes not rolling like an animal in terror. I suppose I went through the same change as the adrenaline started to leave my body.

I fell to my knees again and grunted with the impact. There was a half-caught whimper as I realised that at least this time I wasn't kneeling in blood. It was more the horror of realising that things weren't so... horrific the second time around that made the noise escape.

'How the hell are we going to get rid of his car without anyone noticing?' Dave asked.

I looked at him blankly. It took a while to realise that his fear was racing ahead, to hiding the traces and making sure no evidence remained, to what to do if people came around asking questions.

Method 3: A Train

So, like any other teenagers, we had a stash we seriously didn't want anyone else to find. Only ours was made of something a little larger than a tobacco tin or a few magazines.

We kept it as far away from where we lived as we could reasonably walk, run or borrow the farm Landie to get to without anyone thinking something was up. It sat in our minds more clearly than it sat in the rocky, muddy landscape.

Well, I guess Dave felt the same as I did. For me, it was like having a hulking great monster hanging over my shoulder. It called to me and I had to work not to go back to look at it. It was like trying not to look at a car crash when you drive past it.

One Saturday, I knocked on Dave's bedroom door. I even waited for a minute or so before I gave up hanging around for the expected 'come in'.

He hadn't heard me. He was sat on his bed with a pile of those slim, cheap romance books that I had assumed only lonely housewives read — up until then, anyway. At least there wasn't anything compromising about his position with said books.

'Umm,' I said, not at my most articulate. 'Hi, Dave.'

He looked up and flushed.

It wasn't a normal thing for me to be in Dave's room — ordinarily we'd be outside if we weren't at school — but even we drew the line at horizontal rain. And teenagers aren't exactly known for hanging around in the living room with their parents.

We'd already made plans to meet up and go into Sweet that Saturday. Sweet was not an impressive town although larger than Llareggub, it has a few more amenities including a football team, to be referred to as Sweet FA should it ever come up again.

'What are you doing?' I asked, wondering if I could get him to admit it aloud.

He blinked and looked down at the open book in his hand. I edged closer to the bed and picked one up. I wasn't convinced it was impossible to catch something from the book in question. I know what STDs — or is it STIs, these days? — are, it's the 'cooties' I'm unsure about.

Dave finally croaked out, 'Research.'

I gave him a sharp look and finally noticed the highlighter pens beside him along with the sticky notes used to book-mark various pages. The book I held had two or three of them sticking out and I turned to the page bookmarked by the first — a pink tab — and my eyebrows shot up of their own accord.

'You know,' I said as I tried to take my eyes away from page fifty-nine, 'There are more important things you could be researching.'

Dave was a crack researcher by nature, provided he was interested in the subject matter. He was fairly average at school — he couldn't stand to fail but he had no interest in most of the stuff we got taught — but what he hadn't learnt about survival, weaponry and wildlife... Well, actually, what he hadn't figured out how to do probably couldn't be done in the British climate and on a limited budget. Everything else had likely been forgotten as no use under our current conditions.

'This could be useful!' Dave protested.

I agreed but didn't admit it. Page fifty-nine was definitely more interesting than I expected. Especially the bits Dave had highlighted. My mind was already starting to make detours that only the harshest of reality checks would stop. I focussed on the other stash I shared with Dave and the surreal mon-sters that might still be in our future.

'More useful than why Old Man Lloyd has had two visi-tors who've changed into... somethings... that have wanted to kill us?' I asked.

Dave flinched.

I closed the book I held carefully and put it back down on the bed. The care was due to wondering what Dave's reaction to me mentioning the unmentionable would be. I didn't expect him to swoop in on the book, grabbing it away instantly along with the rest of the pile. He disappeared it under the bed. Only Dave could treat what was effectively a porn stash that seriously; and dead bodies were no longer the only secret we shared.

'That won't be happening again,' said Dave in the firm voice of denial.

'Hmm. If you say so,' I said.

I wasn't sure whether he meant the porn, me finding him with it, or the attacks.

'It won't.'

I stared out the window at a very grey, soggy Saturday. If I remember things properly, it was maybe three weeks since the lawyer had threatened us and five or six since the naked freak had charged us. And it was almost two months since Old Man Lloyd's wife and two kids — one of them being star athlete and all-round golden boy, Ben — had done a moonlight flit.

But, at that moment in time, I wondered what Ben was doing now and whether he'd ever consider doing things like page fifty-nine. In doing so, I missed any obvious connections between Old Man Lloyd and men who like fur.

'So,' Dave said, 'How about that film?'

He was already up and on his way out the door in the time it took me to clear my head.

Getting into a place big enough to have a regular cinema takes two buses and a train. There's a part-time cinema, a village hall that has a film night every two weeks, just a bus ride away in Llareggub, but this wasn't one of those days. And Dave and me rarely went in for the 'classics' and romantic comedies that were usually billed. So Dave and I did the four node trip we only managed about twice a year — bus from Llados to Llareggub, train to Sweet station and bus from there to the part of town that had the cinema. Our main reason not to was the difficulty raising the tenner each to make the trip.

I can't remember what we watched, although it was probably action or comedy. We didn't come out of the cinema discussing it, so it wasn't so bad we wanted a refund or so good it captivated us. It wasn't enough to distract me from my third werewolf. I spotted him at the railway station.

We'd arrived just in time, as usual, to miss one train home and had just shy of an hour until the next. We waited. We complained. 'This always bloody happens,' and so on.

Eventually, our train arrived, fifteen minutes before it was officially turned around and sent back as the one we would go home on. A rangy guy in jeans, hiking boots and rain slicker got off. There was something about his expression, eyes half-closed and nose in the air as if he were following scent instead of his sight. The way his head twitched as he passed Dave — in retrospect, perhaps I had just missed a compromising position when I walked in on the research or maybe Dave had taken longer in the cinema toilets than I'd realised — reminded me of the naked freak. The way he clutched at a backpack as if it held the crown jewels reminded me of the lawyer.

I nudged Dave.

'What?' he asked, intent on getting off the windy platform and onto the warm train without getting wet in between.

I made the mistake of pointing and the movement caught the man's eye.

'*Aderyn brith*,' I said, trying to keep things between us.

Dave's brow wrinkled, not quite understanding my use of 'cuckoo' — or 'dodgy character'. Something had displaced the thoughts of our stash, our little secret, I guess. At the time I was just disgusted that the person responsible for teaching me phrases like '*aderyn brith*' had no idea what I was talking about.

'There's another one!' I said, compounding my error.

'Another what?'

The man changed direction to shoulder past us and, in doing so, grabbed my wrist. I pulled back but he was stronger than me.

'Dave!' I said, not quite loud enough to attract the public attention I probably should have tried for.

My feet started to follow my wrist almost of their own accord and I threw a panicked look at Dave. I watched him blink and then resolution came over his face — reading about the overblown alpha males in romances had given him ideas. But he was being left behind as the man dragged me along behind at a hurried pace, not quite walk, not quite trot. Dave could only do his best to keep up through the train station.

It was never a crowded place but there were enough bodies that a straight pursuit wasn't possible — something my abductor was using to his advantage. I could also thank the lack of business for my not being under a train right then. If there had been one to throw me under, I wouldn't be alive now.

I know the man's decision to kill me makes no sense. He could have walked past and ignored us, like everyone else. We were just a couple of country teenagers and of no interest to anyone. But these guys seem to have a special kind of madness. Paranoia, maybe?

Like most urban places, there are less travelled, former industrial places within a stone's throw of the railway station. Even Llareggub has the remnants of a Victorian warehouse or something similar next to its two track station. Sweet railway station had the town centre in one direction and an industrial area — a mix of old abandoned factories and smaller modern boxes that probably didn't make things — in the other.

This man, my third werewolf, dragged me in that direction. He had the awareness not to get rid of me in public but it's debatable how smart it was being seen dragging me off to abandoned warehouses. This didn't stop me being scared. At least I managed not to beg for my life and freedom. Instead, I held on to my mind as best I could, trying to watch Dave chasing after me and keep my footing at the same time. If I fell, there would be no chance to get up, just the pain of being dragged along across the asphalt on my face.

No-one else followed us from the train station, perhaps thinking it was our own business and nothing to do with them. We passed no-one else on the street the man dragged me down. But Dave kept running and calling after me.

Each time Dave called, the man let out a growl and tugged at my wrist, running a little bit faster. I called a few times but it was difficult with burning lungs. A few spurts of speed, some almost bringing me to my knees, gave us a slightly longer lead. We'd still only have been maybe a few hundred metres from the train station. Far enough away not to be noticeable to the general public.

The man threw me against a wall. I guess he knew that the impact would daze me for while. At the time, I just watched him pull his skin out of his backpack with black spots dancing in front of my eyes. It was my fear that kept me still long enough for him to put the skin on, that and not being able to control my legs and get them under me.

'Elkie!'

Dave, my one chance of survival and right then more handsome than anyone else in the world. If you'd told me he was Prince Charming, I wouldn't have argued. The men in his 'research material' had nothing on him as he hurled himself against the werewolf. Mainly because romance heroes do not, as a rule, fight werewolves.

The impact of the tackle was enough to knock the man against the wall and Dave scrambled off, all alpha male dignity lost.

'Run!' he shouted as I blinked away the last of the black spots.

So we did, yet again.

'What's the time?' he yelled at me as we ran.

Without thinking, I checked the time on my watch and shouted it back. Our train would be leaving in less than five minutes but that didn't bother me quite as much as doing my best to get away from my attacker. I was still recovering from being dragged around and ready to stop running any time now, please.

Dave flicked a look back over his shoulder and then turned down a road, little more than an alley, that I didn't remember using on the way in. We'd run straight down the 'main' road and taken one turn, not through back roads.

'This way,' Dave said when I paused.

I followed him, if only because I could hear the panted breath of our pursuer. The strange man, running on all fours and hampered by human-forced-into-wolf-skin shape, seemed to be only a few paces away. Every time his breathing eased a little, he gave another burst of speed and I would hear his claws on the asphalt. He'd caught up with us too quickly.

Shock made the wrong thoughts circle through my brain, thoughts like 'running through town in a fur is not the way to go undiscovered'. At this stage, I still wasn't sure what my attacker was but I knew revealing his other than human qualities wasn't a good idea.

'Where are we going?' I gasped at Dave but he didn't answer.

We stopped at palisade fencing. Just in time as far as my legs were concerned. They wobbled, about to give up, right up until I heard the scrabble of claws on asphalt. Our pursuer really had caught up this time.

'The railway? But we've got no chance of catching our train!' I said.

Dave grinned at me and gave a quick nod. 'The railway. And we should be able to. Well, if the train's still running.'

He'd made a logical leap that I couldn't quite follow but I guessed the first step of his plan involved the train tracks.

'But the fence...'

Our pursuer's breathing was too laboured for him to have a burst of speed but I was almost hypnotised by the need to listen for the breathes easing out, for when he'd make the next rush.

Dave grabbed my arm and we ran along the fence, looking for a weak spot. We found a place where one of the palings had been removed. We got through it just a heartbeat before my attacker's hand — paw? — reached out. He missed me by a breath of air.

Our attempted run turned into a walk, forced by the upward slope of the low but steep embankment. I heard the panting breath of our pursuer as he forced himself through the palings and walked up the slope behind us. No point in hurrying when the prey is so weak and slow.

31

From the top, we moved as fast as we could down to the tracks. It made my knees ache and the fear of falling on to the tracks balanced out my fear of the steady panting I could hear just behind me. I heard a horn and turned my head in time to see a train bearing down on us.

'Ready?' asked Dave.

He grabbed my hand and squeezed it. I looked at him, his face white with panic again but resolved.

'Wha — ?'

Again I was dragged into a trot. The fastest I could manage as we crossed the train tracks for the other embankment, the other side. I heard the screech of metal brakes on metal wheels as my attacker wasn't so lucky. The size and mass that trains are, you know damned well they'll not slow down in time, even if they're already slowing down for the station.

The third werewolf was dead even before he was hit, as soon as that awful screeching started, he just didn't know it. The thud of impact was almost eaten by the noise of the brakes. The train itself came to a stop exactly where it was supposed to but Dave wouldn't let me stand and look at it.

'We've got to go.'

'The driver,' I said. 'He'll be traumatised. He's just killed someone.'

'I don't care. We don't want to be seen right here and identified.'

He hustled me along and we trotted off, a more relaxed pace but quick enough to get us away before we were noticed properly. The last thing we needed was police looking for us. Travel home by train was off the agenda, now, because the station would grind to a halt while the body was cleared up and the driver... Well, I guess he or she ended up in therapy, one way or another.

So Dave and I made our way back to the bus station instead, hoping to find one going in roughly the right direction.

I couldn't focus on what was going on, though, and ended up bawling my eyes out while we waited. Dave held me and rubbed my back. At the time I was grateful for his composure but I have no idea where it came from. Perhaps he decided he'd rather be the hero of his story, not the sidekick.

'We've just been to watch a film,' he said to a curious woman.

'A sad one?' she asked and he nodded in answer.

I buried my head in his shoulder so she couldn't see my face and, in doing so, realised he'd grown without me realising. We were the same height.

Method 4: A Spade

'You know they've got to be coming from Old Man Lloyd's, right?' Dave asked me.

Until that moment, we'd not come right out and voiced it. I wasn't entirely sure I wanted it said, because it tarnished the golden image of Ben by association.

'What makes you say that?'

We were halfway up the lane, between home and the village, and sitting on the stone wall. I was just about getting to that stage when the cold and hard stone was fighting back against my desire to sit down. It would soon be more comfortable to be on my feet.

Dave stared at me. 'Other than the first man we — '

'Defended ourselves against,' I hurriedly said over however he was going to put it.

He gave me a look and continued, 'Had been seen leaving the Lloyd's. The second man came around after we were seen by Old Man Lloyd — and referred to him as his client, for God's sake — and the third man got off our train. As in, he'd come from Llareggub.'

'So?' I tried for nonchalance.

I'm not dumb, by the way. I just like having everything laid out in front of me. Preferably with diagrams and proof of logic. Dave makes the mental leaps and researches possible answers. I deal with what's in front of me. I'm also not a big fan of getting it wrong. Sometimes I think Dave doesn't care about that — or he just assumes he's right all the time.

'So he came from here, from the Lloyd's. They all did. I bet the last one was another visitor.'

'You said it couldn't happen again,' I said, like it was Dave's fault, like blaming someone would make it all go away.

Dave fell silent, staring at the greenery along the lane. In our geekier moments, we would compete over who could name the most plants. There is a use to it. The more you know about your environment, the easier it is to tell if it's been disturbed. Or if it's a likely place for the animal you're after. We'd never hunted anything bigger than rabbit, though, and these men-with-fur were out of our league.

Huh. Makes us seem insane when I put it into words like that.

'So. What are they?' I asked. 'What kind of man puts on a fur?'

A shrug and a 'dunno'.

The cold stone beat my need to sit down and I started pacing circles on the dusty lane, careful not to stand on the plants on either side for no other reason than I felt like it.

'Bet Old Man Lloyd knows,' said Dave.

'Well, he'll be charging them for lodgings,' I said, 'But he probably doesn't know or care about the rest of it.'

Which lead to thoughts about what kind of person pays to rent a room in a remote Welsh farmhouse, apparently never goes out for two weeks — based on village gossip and when we ran in to our various attackers — and then goes home. Except that three of the visitors would never go home.

We had two dead bodies and various pieces of their former property stashed in a place we could never admit to. The third body had been scraped off the railway a week before. It was being dealt with by police who would, hopefully, never connect it with us. There was no fur-skin or anything else that would back up our stories if the police did haul us in, should they identify us as the teenagers seen playing around the tracks, as reported in the local paper. If we were lucky, should we be caught, we'd just be put in a secure mental hospital.

There were times I wondered if it would really be so bad if someone else found out. How hard would it be to take a parent to one side and say, 'Mum? You know how we hardly ever talk? Well, I have something I need to tell you.'

'Cue scene cut to the Lloyds' house,' I said instead, 'Where Nancy Drew and the Hardy Boys discover the bad man without the trek over muddy fields.'

He glared at me.

'I'm just saying,' I said.

If I'm honest, I just didn't want to know how men who could wear fur — who could become something other than men — could exist. Talking to someone who might know just made it... real.

Not to mention potentially more dangerous. What kind of idiot walks right in front of an angry wild animal on purpose? The kind of idiot who thought he needed to prove how strong and powerful he is, I guess — and the kind of idiot that thinks she can look after the first.

Eventually, I shrugged. 'Fine. It's not like we have anything better to do.'

And because it's not worth telling, here's the scene cut to the Lloyds' house where Nancy Drew and the Hardy Boys discover the bad man without the trek over muddy fields.

After walking around the outside of the house a couple of times, we approached the door. There were no animals, no vehicles but the farm Landie, and no sign that Old Man Lloyd had a visitor. With a bit of luck, this was all a wild goose chase. I began to hope.

Dave knocked on the weathered wooden door at the Lloyds' place.

'It's not like he's going to open the door to us, either,' I said.

Of course, I was wrong. Old Man Lloyd did open the door, just far enough for us to see a worn, tired face old before its time.

'Go 'way,' it snapped.

Dave ignored him, or at least his words, 'Mr Lloyd, we need to ask you some questions.'

'No,' Old Man Lloyd said, 'You don't. No more than I need to answer them. Go 'way and leave be.'

'Mr Lloyd — '

I cleared my throat. Dave stopped and looked at me.

'He doesn't care. Whatever it is he's doing, he doesn't care that his... boyfriends?' I paused as Old Man Lloyd flinched into disgust and I knew that reality had as little connection with the village gossip as ever. The postmistress would be disappointed. 'That his visitors have been trying to kill us.'

'None of my business,' he confirmed, shutting the door on us.

My heart sank. If he had nothing to do with the men, he would have denied they were anything to do with him, rather than just denying their actions. Only money could buy that kind of disinterest around here.

Dave protested, of course, 'Hey! You can't do that!'

'He just did,' I said.

'Maybe he's left a window open,' Dave said and he was off, circling the buildings again as he looked for another way in.

I stayed at the door and waited for a sign that Old Man Lloyd was either waiting to open it or had gone from it. I saw a nearby curtain twitch, displaying his middle-aged going on ancient face, and then hang straight and still again. He'd moved on.

I wanted to hammer on the door and call him out. I wanted to sit down and cry. I wanted to run and tell my mother, regress to the days when a *cwtsh* and a kiss really did cure everything. I wanted to live in a world where Old Man Lloyd hadn't pretty much admitted he was responsible for me being attacked not once but three times.

Meanwhile, Dave came back from his pacing with a heavy spade.

'What the — What do you think you're going to do with that?'

He looked at me and then at the Lloyds' door. His jaw worked for a moment and then set in that alpha male determination that was becoming more common.

'This,' he said.

The window where the curtain had twitched broke with a satisfying if clichéd crash when the edge of the spade hit it.

'Right, you old bastard,' Dave said through the hole he'd made, 'What's going on?'

He dropped the spade and pushed glass through the window so there were no sharp points where he wanted to be. We both ignored Old Man Lloyd's goldfish impression.

'Dave, stop it!' I said and I pulled at his arm.

'You can't do that!' the Old Man protested, when he managed to get words out.

Dave brushed me off his arm and pushed through the window. 'I just did.'

I held my hands out to Old Man Lloyd, to show they were empty. I intended to offer to pay for the window once we'd hashed this all out. It would take me the rest of my life to pay the debt off but, at this stage, it was still a debt.

I said, 'I just wanted to know why some very strange men have been trying to kill me.'

Dave was out of sight in the time it took me to say that, taking the opportunity to explore a building we would never otherwise have been in. My throat tightened and I felt a sob trying to come out.

'I — He — I think Dave's just a bit more serious about it than I am,' I whispered around the lump in my throat.

I could hear him opening and closing doors, and the way the sounds had Old Man Lloyd twitching made me wonder if that was a good idea.

'Dave?' I called out, my voice cracking, 'I don't think you should be doing that!'

'He might get more than he bargains for,' said Old Man Lloyd with a sickly grin.

There was something about the way he smiled, the way he watched me rather than Dave — the one who might be releasing more of those men-with-fur — that made me wonder if he was all there. Losing your whole family in a single night might just do that to a person.

'Dave! You seriously shouldn't be doing that!'

He didn't respond at all. Old Man Lloyd, on the other hand, laughed at me.

'Wait till he finds my dog,' he said.

I thought about that. I hadn't seen the familiar, pointy shape when Dave and I had walked around the building. A locally bred dog, Old Man Lloyd's working dog was a distinctive brown and white collie.

'What *did* happen to your dog?' I asked.

'Oh, it's upstairs. Young Williams'll find it soon enough.'

He laughed again and the sound jarred. It wasn't a happy

noise. It wasn't even the amusement-in-misfortune laugh that people will make. It was twisted — and I don't mean Evil Overlord twisted, I mean something really wrong twisted.

'I meant your *real* dog.'

Old Man Lloyd's face screwed up as if he were about to cry and he took a deep, shaky breath — he was one of those people that believe real men don't cry, I guess — and that's when I knew there was something more to his family's disappearance than a moonlight flit. I got through that window frame so fast, I have no idea how I actually managed it. I'm still a little surprised I didn't cut myself to shreds.

'Dave!' I screamed, running towards the noise of his movement, 'The Lloyds are dead! They killed them!'

And the dog, too. I have no doubts about that, even if it's never been said.

'And there's another visitor!' I added.

Dave was upstairs opening bedroom doors. There were two still closed when I found him and I'm not sure if he'd actually opened the others but he had definitely moved on from them.

'Don't,' I said, 'They're closed for a reason.'

And, again, Dave ignored me. The house isn't so big that he couldn't have heard me yelling from downstairs, after all. He was focussed and determined to take the lead like one of his romantic heroes. Have you ever noticed how they don't translate well into real life?

He reached out and my hands wrapped tighter around my current weapon of choice. Which is when I realised I'd picked up the spade before charging into the house. I was holding it like a weapon. The things you do when you're just reacting and not thinking, they reveal more about yourself than you realise and more than you'll be comfortable admitting.

The door opened. Nothing happened except for a smell that was something like a latrine. We looked at each other. It was fairly clear from what could be seen of the room — mess, posters, the usual — that this was a teenager's bedroom. This was Ben's bedroom. Ben, the missing son, star athlete and all round golden boy, who I now knew was dead.

'Ladies first,' said Dave.

'You what?' I squeaked, 'It might be dangerous in there!'

He laughed and said, 'If it hasn't run at us now, it's not coming at us at all. And you always did have a thing for Ben.'

'Like he ever noticed we existed.'

I stepped forward slowly, spade gripped tightly, as I considered Ben's taste in music — some of those posters were of seriously poor groups — and his lack of hygiene.

'You mean aside from the water-boarding,' Dave muttered.

He had a point. Like all the other kids in school, Ben was prone to choosing us as the butt of his jokes. More Dave than me, if I'm honest, because sexism is alive and well in the school-room. If you're going to flush someone's head down the toilet, it had better be a boy — unless you're a girl. If you see what I mean.

I stepped further into the room, avoiding the strewn clothing and gadgets with care. If I'd still thought that Ben had left the house alive, I would have known by then that he hadn't. He wouldn't have left so much of his stuff behind.

There was a whimper from over my left shoulder, behind the door and I spun to face it. I raised the spade as I turned and then it was falling out of hands gone slack with shock.

'Oh,' I said. Then after a pause, 'Shit.' Another pause, then, 'I guess you're the dog.'

Ben was strapped to the bed with the kind of kit people generally use for tying down trailer loads and some kind of muzzle or gag had been applied with the use of a leather belt. There was a distinct lack of clothing, just a towel to cover modesty.

'Oh-kay,' Dave said slowly from beside me, 'Now that's just kinky.'

Ben looked from me to Dave and back again, his eyes rolling with fear, whites clearly visible. Well, the human equivalent, seeing as we display more white than animals do in the first place. But Ben's look was slightly more pleading when he looked at me, straight fear when he looked at Dave. He also made twitches at the door that made it clear things would only get worse if Old Man Lloyd came in. Thankfully, he didn't, though I have no idea what he was doing while Dave and I were busy trespassing.

'You think he's one of them?' Dave asked.

The tone was rhetorical. Old Man Lloyd wouldn't have tied up his own son if Ben were 'normal'. I had a horrible feeling I knew who was responsible for the rest of the missing family — and the dog.

'It's okay, Ben,' I soothed, 'We'll let you out in a minute.'

Dave was horrified. 'Are you kidding? We ought to kill him before he gets us. While we still can.'

Ben's eyes rolled some more and I glared at Dave. 'Everyone deserves a chance.'

Well, a second chance, I guess. Anyway, Dave glared back and muttered something about 'chances to attack'.

'Go find something else to do, then,' I said, trying to stay calm.

I had a horrible feeling that the only reason Dave wasn't attacking Ben was because I was nearest the spade. There were a couple of heartbeats and then Dave stalked off.

I wrinkled my nose at the smell — it's not like Ben could walk himself to the toilet in current conditions — and knelt down by the bed. It didn't take long to remove the gag but the binding to the bed took a little more time. Ben lay there and shivered through most of it. He didn't speak. I'm glad he didn't. I didn't want my suspicions to be confirmed.

Ben rubbed his arms when they were freed and managed to get into a sitting position. He looked at me with wide eyes and I didn't know whether to run away or hug him. It's not like we'd ever been friends, so any comfort I offered wouldn't be welcome.

And my need to offer it came from some misguided, misplaced feeling of responsibility for my mental use and abuse of his body. With maybe a dash of my own need for a hug thrown in. Plus the desire to lift the towel and see what was underneath, even in his current state. I felt sick.

Ben worked his mouth. 'Where — '

But his question was cut off by Dave running into the bedroom.

'There's another one!'

Ben and I looked at him. There was a moment, I swear, when Ben cringed at the entrance, but it was quickly over-ridden by a sort of calm anger. Perhaps the anger was over-compensation for the moment of fear.

'Tied up. In the other room,' Dave gasped.

'Do we let it go?' I asked.

No matter that the others we'd met had tried to kill me, no-one deserves to be killed while they're trussed up and defenceless.

'Where — '

Ben started to ask questions again but was interrupted by Dave. 'Don't be bloody stupid. It'll kill us.'

'Ben hasn't,' I pointed out.

Dave glared at me and then Ben. 'Yet.'

It was unimportant, though, because that's when the other werewolf Dave had found came looking for us.

As soon as we heard the other man-in-fur coming, Dave moved. He dove over Ben's bed and landed in a heap on the other side. The thinking, if any thinking was done, was that he didn't have to get away so much as be the furthest from our attacker-to-be, like that joke about the lion and running shoes.

Ben managed to throw me after Dave. Probably more down to surprise making me unresisting than any particular strength on his part. In hindsight, I'm not sure whether that counts as an attempt at gentlemanly behaviour or protecting his food source. He then stood up on shaky legs, ready to meet the other man-in-fur. My attention was caught by the towel falling down.

'Elkie,' Dave hissed and smacked the back of my head.

'Ow.'

My focus moved northwards in time to see Ben sweep up the spade in the kind of move that should have been in an action film. He swung in the same move and it smacked the visitor straight in the face. I half expected the spade to deform and little birds to start circling the other man's head. But they didn't.

The dazed attacker wavered and took a step backwards, blood gushing from a misshapen nose. Ben struck again. And again. And again.

I don't care how strong or fast anyone is, getting battered

around the head like that with a spade is going to do the trick. Especially as Ben didn't stop until our attacker was a heap on the floor. The mess in Ben's room had just got messier.

'Maybe next time you should cut instead of swing,' suggested Dave as we stood up. He looked pale but he watched Ben as if ready to face off himself.

The best I could manage was 'I think I'm gonna be sick.' It didn't help that the heap's fur was doing that melting through clothing to disappear into human skin.

Ben turned his head and for a moment I froze, expecting to see anger and blood-lust. There wasn't any. He grinned.

'Hey, does this mean I've got some sort of achievement or faction for killing werewolves?'

'Werewolves?' I mouthed.

'Faction?' Dave mouthed back.

Method 5: Parvovirus

'Werewolves?' I mouthed.

'Faction?' Dave mouthed back.

Then things changed again.

'Leave,' growled Ben, 'Now.'

We looked back at him.

'We just untied you!' I said, 'We helped you!'

At the same time, Dave said, 'We're not going anywhere.'

'Not you,' Ben said, jerking his head at me. Then he said, 'You.'

He jerked his head at Dave on that, the movement spilling his greasy fringe across his forehead. I swallowed my fear, or did my best, and wondered what a teenage werewolf would want with a teenage girl. One that he'd never particularly liked at that.

'What? So you can eat her? Or, worse, rape her?' Dave snarled back, pulling my arm as he tried to make me stand just behind him.

Ben blinked to a stop, a moment where I really could see his brain ticking over, and then he gave a strange smile. 'You're an idiot, Williams. Leave.'

'I'm taking Elkie.'

I pulled my arm away. I didn't care for either of them talking about me like this. 'No-one's not taking me anywhere,' I spat out. If I was going, I was going because I chose to.

Ben shook his head. 'Da's not going to like it if he catches you here, Williams. Not with our source of money gone.'

Which sums up the world I grew up in nicely. We're way out in the wilds here in North Wales, or as far as you get in Britain, and it's often joked that there are two types of men. In this instance, there's the kind that would strike out at anything and the kind that wouldn't dream of hitting a lesser being — like an animal or a woman.

'Did you two make them... whatever you are?' I asked, 'Or were they like that before they got here?'

But Ben didn't answer my questions. All he said was, 'If the client was loose, Da let him out and Da'll be through here soon to see if it worked and you're gone.'

'Climb out the window. Quick.' Dave said to me, with enough growl in his voice to make me wonder if werewolves were all that bad.

So we climbed down from Ben's bedroom and we ran away.

No. I ran away and Dave walked. I imagine there was plenty of stopping and looking backwards on his part. I didn't even bother to wait for him. I just went straight home to the empty cottage. Mum was still working — she always worked hard keeping a roof over our heads and would work whatever hours necessary, at least since I was fourteen and old enough to be left on my own.

I went back the next day, but I only stayed long enough to make sure the two Lloyds definitely had a meal from the supplies I found in their cupboards. I didn't know what else to do and it meant I had something to do other than wait in an empty house. If I'd done that, I'd have felt responsible for leaving them uncared for. Then I went back the next day. And the next. And the next.

It was weird being at the Lloyd's place. As far as everyone else was concerned, Old Man Lloyd had been left on his own when his family had run away after the holiday. To tell anyone otherwise... Well, who was going to believe me? Only Dave, and I was trying to avoid him.

I had that horrible feeling you get when you look at something familiar and realise it has a side or a depth you don't like. In this case, Dave and his idea of being a man. I was also a little worried that if I spent time near his family that I'd find out where he got it from. I don't know what was worse: the idea that the boy I'd grown up slaying dragons with didn't think I was his equal, or that his father who had started us on our dragon-hunting would agree.

Rather than lash out, I walked away. But I couldn't keep

avoiding Dave and, the next weekend, I went looking for him. I found him in a corner of the farm no-one ever goes. Nothing spooky, mind, just that it's where the sick animals have been disposed of. The farm animals are tracked too much these days, so it's rare to dispose of them like that, but when a dog falls ill it's often buried out the way to make sure the others don't catch whatever killed it.

'Hi,' I said.

Dave jumped up like he was caught doing something he shouldn't. He had, I was just too dumb to realise what it was at the time. Like the rest of us, he never went there — bad memories combined with the chance of carrying animal diseases.

'Oh. Hi.'

We looked at each other and I wondered what to say. I wasn't sure how to start a deep, meaningful conversation. Our usual topics were fighting or all out fantasy, not serious emotions.

'I'm going to have to go soon,' I said.

Dave frowned.

I added 'sorry' without thinking.

'He doesn't even realise what you're doing for him,' Dave said.

His tone dripped with disgust and, although probably for slightly different reasons, I agreed with him. If I had ever even considered... Well, it doesn't matter. I guess I just owe Ben in a weird sort of way for rescuing me. Even if the werewolf he rescued me from may not have existed without Ben.

However, 'It's not what you think,' was all I could say to Dave. Like I said, we never did go in for deep and meaningful conversations.

'You mean Ben's little woman isn't allowed out to play, after all?' Dave asked.

The tone was carefully even but the words were dismissive. I couldn't quite make myself believe he meant the words anything less than the way he said them, that I was second class. I shifted my weight from foot to foot. I didn't want to be here. This wasn't the way things were supposed to go. This wasn't the way life was supposed to be. It needed more than a jar of chocolate spread to fix.

I should have been in my room doing revision, or maybe we should have been friends, equals, partners and out on a cleaner patch of ground than this. Instead, I was listening to this... crap that I couldn't see as anything other than dismissal.

'It's not like that,' I said, as if that would straighten life out.

Dave's face shifted into an expression that resembled a werewolf's snarl enough for me to wonder if he'd been bitten in our latest adventure.

'I don't give a shit what it's like, Elkie,' he said and turned his back on me. 'Just go help your new boyfriend.'

I watched him stalk away and wished I hadn't wasted time at the Lloyds' place. It really did feel like a waste. I was just starting to realise Ben's interest in his console was obsessive and that Old Man Lloyd was damaged beyond repair. I just couldn't *not* look after them to the best of my limited abilities. Life being what it is, the drain on my free time coincided nicely with GCSE exams that I fully expected to fail. I'd never be thanked and I'd never achieve much but what else was I going to do?

I ran most of the way to the Lloyds' place — instead of the cottage because Mum was out working, again — and found another car parked up in the yard. I pretended like the expensive, polished sleekness wasn't there and walked in the house.

I didn't bother to go looking for Ben. He would be in the living room in front of the TV. I wasn't prepared to go in there and stir him from his game. I wasn't ready to look at the mess he made not even standing up to go to the bathroom. Yes, he was that obsessive about the whole thing. Yes, I guess I should have called for help but who knows how to deal with a teenage werewolf with a computer game problem?

Old Man Lloyd, though, needed to be found. The car meant another visitor, maybe to be turned into a werewolf if he wasn't one already, and I needed to stop that. I started checking rooms.

They were all in the stinking living room. The visitor — male, expensive suit, hair slicked back — had his nose wrinkled in a disgust that matched Dave's from earlier.

'This is it?' he was asking in total disbelief.

I answered before Old Man Lloyd, 'No. This isn't. They're winding you up and you better go now.'

It was at times like that I would have wished for a mobile phone but, well, dirt poor, remember? And not quite as available at the time as they are now, either. Nothing would have got the (fake) point across like taking a photo and exclaiming over the visitor's stunned expression. I tried out something similar anyway.

'If you could only see your face.'

The visitor looked furious. 'You're making a fool of me! When I've finished with you...!'

But, despite the fighting talk, all he did was storm out. Have to say, the only person who made him look a fool was him.

'At least he didn't take his money back,' was all Old Man Lloyd said.

Ben didn't even look away from the TV screen.

I said gently to the former golden boy, 'Perhaps you could go and have a shower.'

He didn't pay any attention to that, either. I considered pulling the plug but didn't like the idea of betting killed just because I was suggesting some personal hygiene.

'I don't know what you think you're doing, girl,' said Old Man Lloyd, 'But if you ever interfere with our business again, I'll kill you.'

'You can find other lodgers,' I said. 'Ones that don't bite.'

He smirked. 'They don't bite until we're done with 'em.'

I looked at him, weirded out to the point of panic.

'Man's got to make money to keep a roof over his head and look after his kin,' he said.

'You're pimping your son's bite for money?'

He glared at me and left the room. I rustled up some dinner and washed up the pots from yesterday, then left without talking to either of them. I managed to keep it that way for a week and I only broke the silence because Ben started to look ill.

From what I could tell, it started with stomach pains — he actually bothered to talk to me, if only to complain — and a temperature. He didn't eat the food I put beside him but loss of appetite is difficult to call with someone who would rather starve than lose a few minutes of game time. His temperament shifted far enough to change the game from the violent beat-'em-up I'd seen him on the day before to a puzzle-based game that didn't demand fast reactions. I suppose that's a sign of listlessness or something.

'Ben's not well,' I said to Old Man Lloyd before I started making dinner and left it at that. They weren't really my responsibility. If anything occurred to me as odd, it was only that they hadn't really seen anyone else in a long time, so the bug had apparently come from nowhere.

The next day brought sickness and diarrhoea, with a side order of blood and a rotting smell. I guess that's what the stomach pains had meant. Anyway, I missed the actual start of them. I just arrived to cook dinner and found Old Man Lloyd elbow deep in cleaning up after a Ben so sick he couldn't even look at the TV screen. Which means it was bad. Very bad.

I helped muck the living room out. There were copious amounts of bleach involved, if only to cover the smell, and lots of water, which is the more important part. You clean up by shifting dirt, not covering it with bleach.

Like a lot of the local farms, the Lloyd's place was actually supplied from its own well. It's pumped and there's storage built in there these days — not like generations ago — but it's not metered and it doesn't really matter how much you use as long as you don't run it dry. I was starting to wonder if we were approaching dry getting Ben to 'relatively clean'. It didn't stop him being ill. That all kept going.

We forced liquids down him and I left for the day about there, scared out of the house by the smell of the sugar/salt drink Old Man Lloyd brewed up. I didn't try it.

Dave collared me the next day.

'Don't go back there, Elkie,' he said.

There was something about his tone that was pleading. Another sign I should have read more clearly, I guess. At the time, I only had one answer and it would have to do.

'Ben's ill.'

'Don't go back. Please.'

I shouldered Dave out of the way and ran for the Lloyds' again. Dave chased me all the way but I didn't care. I wasn't running to get away from him, I was running to get to them.

I found things pretty much the way they had been before. I helped Old Man Lloyd clean Ben's room — he'd apparently managed to shuffle back up there with help and currently had no interest in his games console — like we'd cleaned the living room the day before. We managed to get more liquid down Ben's throat. We managed to get Old Man Lloyd fed and watered, too. Even though Dave just watched the whole time.

'I didn't expect it to work,' he said as he watched.

Old Man Lloyd ignored him, probably too focussed on the task in hand to hear him. If Ben heard him, Ben was too sick to care. I heard him and I looked back, finally realising he was up to something.

'What did you do?' I demanded as we left.

Dave shrugged and didn't answer. I pushed him up against the wall of the farmhouse.

'What did you do?'

He shrugged me off and I realised there were more changes than him growing to the same height as me. He was starting to fill out and we weren't quite as evenly matched as we'd always seemed to be. It wasn't just his attitude that screamed 'unequal' at me.

'Don't go back, Elkie,' he said as he walked away, 'I don't want you catching it, too.'

'It?' I screamed after him, 'What 'it'?'

But he didn't tell me then. It took another couple of days and the bitter smile that Ben's return to health gave me. The idiot had plugged himself back into his console, so he must have been okay

'Ben's better,' Dave said.

He was sitting on the wall outside my house, scruffy and

still carrying his school bag. He must have been there since he walked home from the bus stop. I shifted the weight of my bag, the books a heavy reminder of the revision I should have been doing.

'He's been lucky. Had good care,' Dave added.

It had been Old Man Lloyd, killing himself to look after his son. I guess he'd shown the same devotion during Ben's change to werewolf.

'It's difficult to keep them hydrated,' said Dave, 'Most die just from lack of fluid.'

'What is it?' I asked.

'Parvo.'

'What?'

'Canine parvovirus,' Dave said with care.

'I know what it is! What I meant was 'What's a human being doing with parvo?''

Dave shrugged. 'Consider it an experiment.'

'An experiment?' I screeched.

'Sure. After all, who cares about someone everyone thinks has run away and left his dad on his own?'

I said the only thing I could think of. 'Humans can't get parvo.'

'Then he's not human.'

I stared at Dave.

'I thought I'd drop some of the soil from the...' he paused, looking for a word that fit but I already knew where he meant. Hadn't I seen him there a week or two ago? 'Pet cemetery. Put it in their well.'

'Dave, you can't just kill — '

'Experiment!'

I glared. 'Kill people.'

'He's not people. He's a bullying shit that thinks he's a wolf. I just wanted to see how much of a wolf he is.'

I stared at him. I couldn't figure this out. Ben had bullied Dave, sure, but this was extreme.

'You shouldn't go back,' said Dave.

'Why not? Humans don't get parvo,' I said.

'In case it's mutated while he's had it,' said Dave, 'It might jump species. Like he has.'

51

But I didn't catch anything.

'Got a temperature and stomach pains,' Old Man Lloyd said when he saw me next.

I swallowed down the bitter taste of the inevitable and said, 'Dave said it's parvo. He's poisoned your well.'

Old Man Lloyd's eyes sharpened, predatory like his visitors or Ben when I got too close to the console, but he sounded sensible. 'I guess Ben got it first because he drinks squash. Boiling water for tea would have killed the bugs. I'll have got it from his... cleaning up after him.'

'I told Dave that humans don't get parvo,' I whispered.

'Humans don't,' Old Man Lloyd whispered back, 'Unless you're showing any symptoms.'

'You're a werewolf?'

Old Man Lloyd clutched at his mug of tea, now his poison, and didn't answer. Ben was in another room, parked in front of a games console with squash instead of tea, just like always. Who had been turned first? Who had killed the rest of the family? Who had cared for whom?

'Why?' I asked, meaning 'Why all this? Why tie up Ben? Why sell his bite and not your own?'

Old Man Lloyd looked at me as if I were insane. 'It's not like we had a choice.'

I shrugged. They may not have been the best questions in the world but they had got a response, even if it didn't fit the questions I was asking. And, hey, I was only sixteen, so it's not like you can expect great eloquence.

'It happened on holiday,' he said, looking out of the window.

This is a world where grown men don't cry and don't talk about their problems. You have no idea how bad things have to be for a man like Mr Lloyd to talk to someone else about it. And talking to someone his son went to school with? We're in end-of-the-world-as-we-know-it territory.

'One of you got bitten,' I supplied.

It's the traditional method of spreading the werewolf thing, after all.

'Did it all happen abroad?' I asked, trying to remember where Ben had been boasting about going on holiday to.

'It was our first proper holiday,' Old Man Lloyd said, on a tangent, 'I'd always promised her one day and she insisted one day'd come.'

He put the mug down and started pacing. The way he rubbed at his face and his arms did not fill me with confidence. I always hated seeing adults that much on edge. They're supposed to know what they're doing and have life sorted out. Now I'm a little bit older, and maybe a little bit wiser, and know we're all winging it.

'The lad got bit first,' he said.

'Oh.'

He didn't even look at me. He wasn't really talking to me anymore. He was just talking — when the words made it out at all.

'Brought him back ill. Had to hide it from Customs in case they kept us out.'

I tried to imagine being kept out of the country just for being ill. Either the symptoms were horrific or Old Man Lloyd's paranoia extended to Her Majesty's Custom Officers.

'But I killed them,' Old Man Lloyd whispered.

His shoulders shook and I looked away, unable to watch.

'We didn't know what was happening. We didn't know...'

Intermission

Time passed and things moved on. Really that should be all I tell you. But there are things I feel I ought to say for the rest of my life to make sense to you.

I was the one who reported Old Man Lloyd's death. It was a shock to be doing something so... adult, and all I could think to do was call the emergency services. They sent out an ambulance and the police, both of whom arrived with all lights and sirens blazing, but it wasn't enough to rouse Ben from the games console for more than a few minutes. Even those few minutes were a rare gift.

'You'd respond better if this were a game and not real, wouldn't you?' I asked the back of his head. It was a rhetorical question and I hadn't expected an answer, but he shrugged a shoulder in acknowledgement.

So, I was the one who let the authorities in as if I lived there, not in my own home with my own, small family. In a way, I had more in common with Old Man Lloyd and Ben than I ever would have with my mother again. After all, the Lloyds and I knew about werewolves, my mum just knew about being dirt poor and working hard to scratch a living — something I knew I was doomed to learn myself but didn't negate the werewolves.

I was interviewed by the paramedics, who were interested in the symptoms so they could assign a disease to Old Man Lloyd, and the police, who wanted to be sure it really was a disease and I hadn't just found a cunning way to kill him myself. I tried not to bubble into hysterical laughter at every question that hit close to home.

'Did you have any disagreements with the deceased?'

'Do you know of any reason why anyone would want him dead?'

The sight of all that puke and bloody faeces is not something I'm ever going to be able to shrug off, never mind what the authorities thought. And that smell! But the symptoms of parvo are close enough to a number of human infections that Old Man Lloyd was diagnosed with a virus without an autopsy. This was a mixed blessing, as I wasn't sure what an autopsy would find with respect to Mr Lloyd's humanity. So it was best that way and I was relieved when the body was cremated. I wouldn't have to explain things I didn't understand, like werewolves and Dave's actions.

In all of this activity, no-one thought it odd that Ben was still around. The only explanation that came out — not from me — is the one I heard in the village Post Office: Ben had run away from his mother, after her own escape, when she'd met up with a man Ben didn't like. It's a logical explanation, as normal reality goes.

His sudden removal shortly after Old Man Lloyd's death was simply put down to his mother putting him in care, not wanting him to return or to stay on his own. He'd rejected her, so she rejected him. It was thought cold-hearted but understandable. There were a few questions about why he didn't just move in with friends but, the way it was said, everyone expected someone else to be the one to step forward.

I let the people in to take Ben away. When they distracted him from his games, he got upset. I talked to him in the same voice one uses to calm an animal and he watched me with wide eyes. I could see his anger at being disturbed.

'There'll be games at the hospital, son,' one of the men said.

Ben watched me and I nodded. But his anger had already got him an injection of something calming and a straitjacket as soon as they could hold him still.

The day after he went, I boarded up the windows and locked the door for the last time. I used the pneumatic nail gun I found in one of the sheds and the repetitive task was over that much quicker for it. I checked over the outbuildings and cared for the animals until someone came to take them away in lorries and relieved me of the keys.

I'm not sure whether I did all of this because Ben had watched me so on his way out, or because no-one else would.

Dave's dad has always said that the worst thing a person can do is leave animals without care. My mum has always told me that the worst act is not to do those things that need to be done, as if even chores are handed down from the Deity.

Back in real life, Dave passed his exams and went to the college in Sweet when the new academic year started. I failed mine and managed to get the finance to go through GCSEs again, but I chose to do it by redoing my final year at the Llareggub school rather than taking re-sits at college in half the time.

I didn't want to be anywhere near the boy who'd tried to murder Ben and got Old Man Lloyd instead. Being on separate buses in and out of the village, and on totally different timetables, made sure I didn't have to work at avoiding him.

Method 6: A Kitchen Knife

As you can imagine, it was a shock when I got an email from Ben about a year later.

We — mum and me, that is — didn't have Internet at home, so I read it in the library in Llareggub. Llados, the village I lived just outside, is way too small to have things like a library. We were lucky if we got a library van once a fortnight. For that matter, I hadn't even got an email address until that school year and having no friends to occupy me between class and home time, I spent lots of time in the library that year.

Anyway, the email from Ben.

'There are more men like me. Be careful. Ben'

That was it. No 'Hi, how're you?' No explanation. No hint of what had happened to him. And, I might add, it's not like I needed warning that there were other werewolves and that they were dangerous. I knew they existed but had no intention of going near one ever again. They were not part of my life and I didn't want them to be.

So, I stared at the message in disbelief for a while. Was it a threat? Or a warning because he was worried about my safety? What did Ben know that I didn't? What was he doing with *my* email address?

That last question made me look at the email address he'd used. It told me nothing other than he was still the golden boy from school, complete with total lack of brain. He'd taken the username 'WolfWarrior', for crying out loud. It was also from a webmail service — like my own — and gave me no clue to where he'd ended up. Did care homes give people access to the Internet that easily? Had they cured him off his games obsession?

'I've met one or two before,' I sent back with the closest text allows to dry humour, 'Where are you?'

Then I saved his message for another time. I thought about printing it off or writing the words down, to work out what Ben was getting at later, but didn't. It seemed too much like a schoolgirl crush thing to do, particularly as there were no more than eight words there. Nine if you include his name.

The next day, I had another email from Ben.

'There's one on his way.'

I looked at it for a moment before I could speak. It was a little while longer before I could say anything other than 'Oh, shit.' By the time I composed a response, I managed to string a few more words together to make 'What did you do?'

I got home as fast as I could. I even spent money I couldn't afford on the local bus instead of waiting for the school one, and a jar of chocolate-hazelnut spread.

'Mum!'

She didn't answer, of course. She was out at work again. This year it was only a part-time job but it covered the cost of the roof we rented from Dave's family. Which left me plenty of time to worry about what I would tell, if I could tell her, about being in danger.

The chocolate spread didn't survive the first half-hour. Then I felt queasy from all the sugar gumming up my mouth and drank too much water. Then I needed the toilet and then...

'Enough!' I said.

The house seemed to still around me as if it was the building that held its breath, not me. My brain wouldn't stop turning over, though, reminding me I didn't know what to expect. *Will he come in a car or on foot? Will he be in his fur-skin already? Can werewolves drive when they're, you know, dressed up?* Thing is, at least I was expecting him. I knew he was coming. Maybe not that minute, that hour, that day, but he would turn up.

I got so desperate for time to pass I gave in to Mum's instructions to clean the house. I heard a vehicle. I was so twitchy about the whole thing that I was actually listening over the sound of the vacuum cleaner. I didn't stop the vacuum but stood, holding my breath, waiting to hear where the vehicle went. There was only us and the Williams down here, so it was either going to stop at our cottage or drive on to the farm.

The vehicle stopped. The vacuum kept running but I wasn't pushing it around anymore. I was busy thinking something like 'What do I do?' Possibly with more swear words.

The vehicle door opened and closed. I still didn't know what it was. I hadn't been able to move my feet over to the window. I couldn't turn and see if it was in view.

There were footsteps crunching on the path. I took a breath, deep and calming. Whoever it was wore shoes. They weren't walking on paw pads. At the very least, I had the amount of time it took for a man to put on the fur-skin and become a werewolf. I guess experience shows. If I hadn't seen other werewolves change by putting on their fur-skins, I wouldn't know that I at least had an extra heartbeat or two of life before my attacker got me.

There was a knock. I looked around for something to carry as a weapon. I couldn't find anything and I was getting desperate when the knock came again, slightly more insistent.

'I'm coming!' I called.

An attacker intent on killing me probably wouldn't knock like that, I told myself but I still looked for something weapon-like in the living room.

I settled on a chunky wooden ornament and grabbed it with both hands, which became a bit of a problem when I got to the heavy old door. I couldn't open it while holding the ornament. I juggled for a minute and then put it down somewhere I could pick it up easily — allowing for the weight — while I opened the door. A better solution than trying to swing it clumsily with one hand, if I got as far as opening the door.

I looked through the letter flap and called, '*Helô?*'

The postmistress's husband looked back at me like I was cracked. For a moment, I agreed with him. There was no way he was much of a threat. His wife had emasculated him years before I'd arrived in the village.

I cleared my throat. 'Sorry. Getting a bit jumpy left on my own.'

I made the lock and handle clatter as noisily as possible to cover my embarrassment.

'Sensible,' the postmistress's husband said in a tone that disagreed. Once the door was open, he added, 'Parcel for your mam.'

He was holding a box wrapped in brown paper and clearly addressed to Mum. The return address was my unseen, unknown aunt in Oxford or, as she liked to put it, civilisation.

'Thanks.'

I took the parcel carefully and resisted the urge to shake it to hear what it might be inside. Last time I'd tried that it had turned out to have been some fragile crystal glass somethings. We couldn't work out what they had been from the shards and Mum was too embarrassed to write to her sister (who I'd never met and only communicated by occasional expensive gift) to say that we'd broken them. I maintain the glass had been badly packaged and was broken before I shook it. Probably.

'Don't need to sign, do I?'

'Nah,' my postman said, 'Just normal delivery.'

He turned and walked down the path to his van, the vehicle I'd heard, and I rested against the door jamb wondering how I was going to survive until Ben's werewolf turned up. My heart was going to give out long before he arrived.

I'm an idiot, I thought as I closed the door and put the parcel on the kitchen table.

I needed to be smarter, work out what I could carry around in public that could be used as a weapon if I was attacked. Or how to use the things around me better. It's a shame trains didn't run closer to the cottage.

I put the vacuum cleaner away and started preparing dinner. Something that would take some time and wouldn't spoil while I waited for Mum to come home. Something that meant I could hold a knife for as long as possible.

It was somewhere about the cutting up the carrots that I realised I wouldn't work out a way to go armed in public. I could probably get away with running around the fields and woods nearby with one of the sharpened staves that Dave and I had made but there was nothing I could actually carry around the village or into school or the library or anywhere else that was... Well, I guess 'civilised' is the closest word to what I'm trying to get at.

So I had to stay at or near home, out here in the back of beyond. If I was going to make that suggestion fly, I was going to have to put myself forward as the new housekeeper. Mum was all for me getting a job while we waited for my GCSE results to come through. Previous summers I'd helped out with Dave on the farm but I'd walked away from that last year. I'd taken a job alongside Mum that summer but the hours weren't as readily available this year. That might give me just about enough of an excuse to stay at home and take on the housework Mum had difficulty with. Maybe even try my hand at some of those DIY jobs that never got done.

It was difficult focussing on the house-work, of course, expecting the big, bad wolf at any minute, but I knew if I didn't make my work obvious Mum would have me job-hunting in less time than it takes to say 'but, Mum'.

In all, I spent three days moving around the house, the bread knife following me from bookshelf to table to other handy resting places, before the werewolf arrived.

He didn't arrive in a vehicle. There was no sound of a car door closing to alert me, no crunch or footsteps on the path, no knock at the door. Just the sound of glass breaking as he threw himself through a downstairs window.

I was in the bathroom, scrubbing the old, knackered bath. It was one of those roll-top, cast iron jobs that are currently all over the lifestyle magazines, only ours had cracked enamel and rust coming through. It was an original.

Anyway, I heard the glass break and pushed myself off the floor, knife coming to hand as I rose. I paused with my hand on the door handle. I wasn't exactly convinced I would succeed.

'Okay,' I said aloud, 'Time to find out.'

I came out of the bathroom with the knife pointed forwards and kept my body behind it. I walked slowly to the top of the stairs and listened for where he'd got to. I wondered if maybe I should stay at the top of the stairs. Higher ground was good in all the descriptions of historic battles I could remember, never mind the self defence stuff. People won wars by holding castles and hill forts, right? And they were always on higher ground.

But I wasn't entirely convinced it would make much difference with me against a werewolf. What was I going to be able to hit? The top of his head? Mainly I just didn't want to walk into whatever attack he had planned.

'Here, boy,' I whispered, hoping he would do the exact opposite. It hadn't even been my idea to say it. It was the thing inside of me that had picked up the knife so easily, without thought. The part that had swung the sharpened staff around without having to be told.

The shuffling noises from downstairs paused.

'Here, Fido,' I said slightly louder. *Shut up, you idiot*, I thought.

There were definite movement sounds, like someone confident they knew where they were going.

'Don't forget to open the door,' I said, as the me inside started to panic and run in mental circles, 'Not walk straight through it.'

There was a loud growl and the living room door opened.

'I'm right here,' I said. I tried to keep the squeak of fear out of my voice but I don't think I succeeded.

He growled again and stepped through. He didn't quite walk on all fours but he wasn't upright. I wondered, briefly, if standing on his back legs to open the door had been a strain. Werewolves don't look like they should be on all fours like a dog but they don't seem to like the two-legged way when they're furred up.

He stopped at the bottom of the stairs and sniffed the air, the distorted muzzle lifting to catch my scent.

'I'm up here, numb nuts.'

I looked down. My sports teacher always used to say that you needed to pick your target before you threw — or served, depending on the sport — and I figured this was much the same. But with more dangerous outcomes. I looked at the weird face and thought, *Eyes.*

I tightened my grip on the bread knife and crouched. I was as ready as I'd ever be.

'Here, boy,' I whispered again.

He charged. It felt like he was right in front of me in two strides. The hands, or front paws or whatever they are, reached out to me, nails twisted into strange, stubby claws. I stabbed out, focussing on one brown eye. The bread knife slid in, the movement disturbingly easy. The werewolf screamed and clutched at his eye, knife included. I yanked the knife out, ready to stab again.

That part of me that picked knives up easily had liked the idea of two serrated edges. It looked wicked. It looked like it could do significant damage on the way in and on the way out. It appeared to work and the way the werewolf rocked on his feet, the way he clutched at his face, it left an opening at his neck — to that sensitive spot between the collar bones. I took it, stabbing again.

The blood got everywhere. It was also the first body I'd had to dispose of my own, the fur-skin melting back into the human body to leave a scruffy but muscular twenty-something behind.

'Oh, bollocks.'

I sat and cried for the first half hour. Then I cleaned myself up as best as I could. Then I cried some more because there was a significantly-larger-than-me dead body on my stairs, with a side order of lots of blood.

I managed to get it onto one of those thick, grey woollen blankets and roll it up. The idea was that the blanket would stop me spreading more blood. It kind of worked but I still had some stains to get off the stair carpet — which did not make me any more eager to get to that stage of the clean up.

With the blanket, it was also a bit easier to get a grip on the body and drag it down the stairs. Probably a good job it was already dead the number of times it got its head hit, though. Down the stairs was easier than through to the kitchen and out of the back door. Gravity had been a co-conspirator down the stairs and somewhat less interested in helping the rest of the way.

Getting the body over the low stone wall at the bottom of the garden left me weepy, weak and ready to hand myself over to the authorities. I'd chosen there as the temporary hiding place because the grey blanket shouldn't show up too badly against a grey stone wall, surrounded by green weeds on the edge of a field in the middle of nowhere. At least not to the casual viewer. I'd have to work out how to get it somewhere less obvious later.

I leant against the wall for a while and took deep breaths. I had to close my eyes so I couldn't see the person I'd just killed.

'One day,' I whispered, 'I'm going to have to start praying for guidance about things like this.'

I opened my eyes and eyed the blanket trail critically. There was a faint slug trail of blood. Outside, the grass would right itself in time and the slight stains would be dealt with in the next downpour — forecast for that night, probably to coincide with part two of the disposal — but inside meant washing floors downstairs. Then scrubbing down the stairs with as much carpet cleaner, soap and polish as would disguise the smell as well as the stains.

I almost forgot the downstairs window until I walked past it. I could only manage the most basic of repair, so I removed the broken glass from the frame and the floor around it, and boarded up the hole. I tried to come up with some decent excuses for it being there.

By the time Mum came home, I was tired and ready to collapse in a heap. Which made my distress at having broken the window seem all the more real.

'It was an accident.'

'I knew you'd take it badly.'

That kind of thing.

I was grounded, although Mum never did tell me what that meant in real terms. It wasn't like I left the place, ordinarily, except for school. As soon as it was dark, I escaped from my room and spent almost all night dragging the corpse to the hiding place Dave and I had used. I couldn't risk borrowing Mum's car, she would have heard it, and there was no other way for me to move the ex-werewolf.

There was an email from Ben waiting for me when I next got in front of a computer.

'Sent him to you. So, did you complete the mission?'

Method 7: Stranglehold

'Sent him to you. So, did you complete the mission?'

I read Ben's words out loud and ignored the looks I got from the others in the library. I just stared at the computer screen. It's not like it would make that much sense to anyone who heard.

Mission? I thought, *How is having a madman set on me a mission?*

I didn't say that out loud as it was something that would be interpreted a little too close to the truth. If someone were to hear, and if they were paying attention, their first question would probably be, 'What happened to the madman?'

There was a bit more to the email, but my eyes just kept catching on what Ben must have thought was a throw-away question. It was too close to the kind of wording computer games used. It was too close to the kind of violent game Ben had enjoyed playing on his console. It did not bode well.

The bit more to the email, by the way, was 'I miss you'.

'You've never known me to miss me,' I typed out.

I stared at the words for a while, then deleted them. I stared at the blank email form for a little longer, thinking of when I would have melted just thinking of those three little words coming from Ben, before typing out a more flippant, 'I'd rather you sent me flowers.' I clicked on 'OK' and let my words into the wild.

I spent the rest of my allocated hour looking for a job in this abandoned corner of wilderness, wondering whether I dared leave my house, even if there was a job for me to go to. I had a horrible feeling that Ben was going to carry on playing whatever game he thought my life was. Flowers really would have been nicer.

My fear wasn't soothed away by the next email I received from Ben. 'Mission reboot.'

I walked away from the computer, and the library, without even pretending to look for a job. I didn't so much run home as wait patiently for the local bus timetable to catch up with my panic, which was trying so desperately to escape my throat. If someone had stopped and talked to me, the only answer I could have given them was a scream.

I wanted Dave to talk to. Not the Dave who I'd spent the last twelve months avoiding but the old Dave who'd played and fought and killed time with me. I wanted to be in this situation with someone else. I wanted to talk to someone who might have an idea what to do. The kind of someone you asked 'What do I do?' because they'll work on the solution, not someone who'll think you're insane for asking in the first place.

I couldn't have that, though, and I couldn't go to anyone else, like the authorities. What would they have done? It's not like they can actually do anything about a potential attacker until they've proven themselves dangerous.

Yes, I know what you're thinking. Like that's any worse than what would happen if that stash of bodies was ever found. What can I say? Fear doesn't help you think clearly and the possibility of putting off that kind of thing indefinitely — denial, I guess — is much easier than dealing with it today. Or something.

I guess it isn't that much different from any other teenage angst. We all tend to feel as if we're different, and misunderstood, and singled out for some kind of treatment — or even mistreatment. My werewolf issue, however, was a little more problematic than the usual fitting in with the local crowd.

It took a week but I talked myself round to going out into the big wide world — or, at least, Llareggub. I multi-tasked my online job search with staring at those two little words. I decided that I needed to sign up for martial arts lessons or something — every little helps, as the adverts go — and made a list of activities and classes. I hoped to persuade Mum out of her pacifist stance and an important ten pounds or so of our weekly budget.

I worked up the courage to send back, 'Isn't that a bit

repetitive? The same mission every time? And why would werewolves want to keep attacking me?'

I couldn't see what was in it for the werewolves, either. The werewolves before had come across us, me, as much by accident as by design. Why would grown men with better things to do think it was a good idea to hunt *me*?

'Forget the flowers,' I said aloud, 'I'd settle for a jar of chocolate spread.'

I sat and waited a few more minutes as if Ben would instantly, magically, respond. And then I realised it was idiotic to question his 'reboot'. Facing a werewolf is bad enough but saying something that might be mistaken for 'please make life harder' was asking for trouble.

I thought about it on the bus ride home and cursed myself as I stared at my scrawled list. My cursing got so bad that people pulled away from my seat and gave me a wide berth.

I stepped off the bus in Llados and knew I was doomed before my foot even touched the pavement.

There was a man at the bus stop in a light-weight cotton t-shirt and scuffed jeans. He clutched a backpack in one hand and didn't look like he was getting on the bus. When I stepped off the bus, he narrowed his eyes at me and the head cocked to one side, a gesture I associate with dogs but one that wasn't unusual in a normal human either. He lifted his other hand and unclenched the fingers, showing a smaller, scruffier piece of paper than my own. He read it and then looked at me.

'Elkie Bernstein,' he said.

The bus drove off. I shrugged and shifted my footing, ready to run. He wasn't furred up and I already knew that meant he wasn't as fast and strong as he could be.

'How did you know I'd be here?' I asked.

He let the tattered piece of paper go and it fluttered in my direction. I didn't need to catch it, let alone read it, to know that it had all the information he needed. For a moment, I had the weird feeling that I was dreaming some kind of action film sequence. Even down to that moment when the camera does that zoom in so that the background appears to move but the person in focus doesn't.

Actually, it felt more Western-like, as if we were two gunmen waiting to draw on each other. The werewolf had the clear advantage but I guess he didn't know he was the black hat in a movie, and that narrative demanded things didn't go all his way. Except this was real and I'd probably get killed.

Maybe this guy had come to prove himself. I'd been involved in six werewolf deaths to date. Maybe that was like having six notches on my gun belt. Did Ben tell these madmen I was some kind of prize? My mental picture shifted again, leaving me as a ten point stag being hunted.

Thanks, Ben, I thought.

'I'll be good,' he said with a smile that made me feel sick, 'I'll give you a head start.'

I looked around in the middle of the street. It's a small village, there's rarely anyone about but that doesn't mean I wouldn't be seen if I were dumb enough to give in to the urge to attack while he had something vaguely resembling a weakness. It didn't occur to me that it might also make me safe from attack. So I ran.

I led him to the Williams' farm, to Dave's place, and out to the copse where we used to hunt dragons. I suppose I can thank those days for being fast enough to get there ahead of my hunter. I could hear him running after me, his feet pounding over the summer-dry ground, as I tucked and rolled into the scrub on the outskirts of the tiny patch of woodland.

'You can't hide in that,' he laughed, a little breathless.

I'm not hiding, I thought but didn't say back.

'I'll get you anyway.'

He seemed to like being in human form — perhaps it was proving how good he was even without the skin — but then he paused to take his fur-skin out of his backpack. It gave me enough time roll to my feet and crouch, ready for my own attack now that we were out of everyone else's way. I didn't really expect to have that much of a chance in a straight fight but I was hoping to weight as many things to my advantage as possible.

I jumped on his back as soon as he entered the copse. I tried to arrange my arms in the way I'd seen on TV in those action films that Dave and I had watched at the cinema, into what I've since learnt is called a stranglehold, around the not-quite-human, not-quite-dog shape.

The werewolf did not take this well. He reared up on his hind legs and threw himself backwards against a tree trunk. Thankfully, I hadn't had my mouth open properly, otherwise I probably would have bitten myself with the impact.

'Bastard!' I hissed as the air was pushed out of my lungs.

I tightened my hold around his neck. He grunted and tried again, which made me swear again.

I'd always kind of assumed I'd be doing something much more fun if I tried to get this close to another person; my breath in their ear, my arms round their neck, and my legs tight around their waist. I felt sick — and I'm still not sure if it was because the second tree trunk had hit my head or because I was starting to realise that nothing in life is particularly clean and pleasant.

The werewolf's breathing got a bit more ragged. It didn't stop him from throwing himself backwards against another tree.

'You fucking bastard!'

This time it was a scream because it hurt so much. A painful stab in the ribs — not broken, though I couldn't tell at the time — followed by a dull ache that wouldn't stop.

He scraped at my arm with his claws and that distracted from the dull ache. Canine claws may not be sharp but they can cut through skin if the canine tries hard enough — or persistently enough. It was like having eight small, blunt knives running across my forearms.

I tightened my grip as much to make my arms inaccessible as to strengthen my hold. It didn't really work. He kept scraping, and breathing although it was a bit more laboured.

He threw himself back against a fourth tree and I was winded. There was dampness at the corner of my eyes and I blinked but it only made the black spots on my vision dance. I felt weak and wondered if my grip was failing. I thought *tighten* at my arm muscles but they didn't seem to do anything.

'Just bloody well die and leave me alone,' I whispered but I was still winded so it made no sound.

The werewolf fell to his knees — almost on all-fours — and my feet found the ground of their own accord. At the same time, there was a choking gasp and we both froze. It was a moment before I realised it had been me getting my wind back. Then, as I sucked in air like it had just been invented, the werewolf dropped.

'No!' I whispered and then half-sobbed, half-screamed in his ear as his heavier mass rolled over me. Once. Twice. The world span, a mixture of his movement and the pain, and I couldn't breathe because his weight wouldn't let me.

He stopped moving on the fifth or sixth roll. I didn't let go, though. I couldn't hear anything but my own sobbing gasps for air, nor see anything but those dancing black spots, and I daren't let go. I was crying so hard that all I could hear was my own sobs. So I held on until I stopped.

When I'd hiccupped and gasped my way to the other side of my storm, I tried to let go. I'd held the same position so long everything below the elbow had gone to sleep. I stretched them out slowly, through pins and needles. It took me a long time and some more tears before I untangled myself from the ex-werewolf.

I realised I'd got to hold him, crying and oblivious all the time, while the fur disappeared back into his skin through his clothes. I held the man not the monster.

I spent the next however long alternating between more crying and throwing up. It was then I realised that he'd clawed my arms to shreds. I'd broken the scabs when I rubbed at my arms — and I spent the next three weeks wearing long sleeve t-shirts to hide the bandages and later the healing scabs.

When I had no more tears or stomach contents left to lose, I looked at the body again.

'I'm going to have to leave you here,' I whispered, 'I'll come back and put you somewhere safer later.'

I hid him with leaf-mould, the remains of previous years' growth, as best I could and left him. The only person likely to come this way was Dave and, regardless of our lack of relationship, he knew better than to do anything about the corpse. Not unless he'd worked out a way to pin the other bodies solely on me, as well.

I went home and I cleaned myself up before I sought out Mum's company.

'Bad news?' she called up the stairs after me.

I guess she came to talk to me but had just missed me as I ran straight upstairs to the bathroom.

'The usual,' I called back, 'No work.'

Let her think I was in a teenage sulk about not having a decent job handed to me on a plate.

'You took a long time getting back. You should have been home before me.'

'By, what? Ten minutes?'

'You're grounded, Elkie. You know that. The only exception is work or looking for it.'

'I looked for work,' I protested.

I was busy wincing over the soap that got into the cuts and grazes on my arms, disinfecting, wrapping up. Cleaning any traces of werewolf from my skin. I considered a bath and knew I wouldn't get away with it. These things eat into Mum's schedules, what she expects me to do and when. Not to mention the cost of heating the water was an extravagance she probably couldn't afford. I wasn't feeling bad enough for a cold bath and I wasn't ready to be turned into the village wastrel.

In terms of the werewolf, I waited for night-time and what passes for cover in June. I snuck out and walked up the lane to the Williams' farm. The dogs barked but only a couple of times — they knew me, after all — as I borrowed a wheelbarrow that had been left in an accessible place and not locked up.

'Sorry,' I whispered, as if Dave's dad could hear me, 'I'll bring it back.'

Dave's light was on and his curtains were still not drawn. I wondered if he'd noticed me or the attack. I checked for footprints in the copse but didn't see any. I didn't dare turn on my torch, though, in case he was watching now. There's a difference between possibly being seen and confirming your presence. Then I put it all to one side and wheeled the ex-werewolf off to the hiding place.

'Shit,' was all I could say when I finally got there.

Things were a little different and I'd stepped on something that really didn't feel like slate or mud. I took my torch out and ran the beam over everything, then I put it away and moved the body into a better spot and left. I tried to pretend that Dave hadn't left one of those cheap romance books where I was bound to step on it.

'Well?' Ben's next email read.

'I'm not doing this anymore,' I sent back, 'This isn't a game.'

Method 8: Chocolate Spread

Of course I knew my refusal to play would mean nothing to Ben. I wasn't quite sure whether he was backing me or the werewolves but he was treating it like some kind of computer game where completing a mission builds experience and allows the player to level his character. I probably should have seen it coming when he asked about factions after he killed another werewolf. His obsession with games extended to treating my life like one.

Which would have been marginally healthier than spending all his time in front of a computer if he'd actually made the leap completely. For him, anyway.

For me? It was time to get on with life. I landed a part-time job in a tiny supermarket in Sweet — which meant a bus and train journey every morning and afternoon that used up almost all the money it earned for me — and wondered what to carry around in case of werewolf emergency. I had no-one to talk it over with and didn't really know enough about, well, being sociable to know what would be acceptable or barely noticeable. If we could have afforded a TV, the licence for it and a DVD player, I would have rented out every season of 'Buffy the Vampire Slayer' for ideas.

In other words, my mood at the time can be described as 'teenage angst'. Not very interesting to anyone but the person caught in it. Like any other teen, it was because I didn't think there was anyone I could talk to, which left me with a mind that constantly ran in circles. How do you raise the possibility of being hunted by werewolves in casual conversation? You don't. Better to curl up in a ball and hope it goes away.

So, the job. A typical paid by the hour job. I'd seen the advert in Llareggub library when I email Ben that I was finished. I wasn't convinced Ben would leave me alone, I just couldn't afford to sit around waiting. Caught up in my moment of — Rebellion? Activity? Energy? Whatever. I applied for the job before I considered things like transport costs, part of proving to myself that I had control of my life.

Anyway, by the following weekend I'd been interviewed and given a start time. Following a couple of hours of 'induction', which means being told about the company policies and how to lift a box — seriously — I was sent out into the big, wide world to be a responsible employee.

Well. I say 'big, wide world' but I'm not sure it was actually that much bigger than the Llados post office.

The only thing that got me through the working day was being able to stare at the stock of chocolate spread in the back. That and imagining how that stock pile must look in a larger supermarket. Small town, see, so there were only actually a couple of boxes.

'Not much,' said one of the two other people on the floor with me. I think he meant the store in general because he continued, 'I've been in places they call small in London with storerooms bigger than the whole bloody shop.'

I stared at the boxes and imagined. I may have had to wipe away a small amount of drool. Not that I'm greedy. I would have settled for our own storeroom — at best ten by twenty metres — full of chocolate spread. That would have been enough of my favourite drug to get me through teenager-hood.

'I know that look,' the other colleague said when she passed me.

She leant against another stack of boxes, filing her nails and ignoring the no smoking at work policy. Our assistant manager was nowhere to be seen, as usual. My eyes caught on the movement of the metal nail-file and something ticked over in my brain. I knew I was missing something important but couldn't quite grasp it.

'Don't be taking any of that home with you, you little shit,' she said.

I heard her add something to the effect of being an inbred peasant. I ignored her. I'm the daughter of a lapsed Jewish woman and I have no idea who my father was. To cap it all, I lived in the middle of nowhere. I suppose I should be more precise and say nowhere near my mum's family — who I also don't know. 'Inbred' is definitely not the adjective I'd use. I laughed as I walked away, enjoying her ignorance more than is healthy or right.

I never really had the opportunity to make a better impression because Ben's next play-thing arrived only a couple of days later. A man who looked grey and ragged like a half-starved wolf-hound even without furring up. He sat by the doorway and watched us all walk past as we filed in at the start of the morning shift.

'Mornin',' he said to me, singling me out from the less than a handful of others I was starting the shift with.

I'd known what he was before he spoke, before he looked at me. It was in the way he scented the air as we all approached, the way his fingers clutched at the bag beside him on the floor. I was starting to wonder about the mind-set of a man who becomes a werewolf, never mind the ones who came looking for me.

Did I have some awesome reputation among them for killing several of their kind? How did they know? It's not like any of them had been telling tales on me. Except Ben, who seemed to be responsible for making me so attractive. But what logic is there in following a teenager's instructions to hunt down another teenager?

'Get you anything?' I asked, trying to stay casual.

The colleague who had warned me a couple of days before spat out, 'No thieving for your brother-father-husband-whatever.'

I shrugged and ignored her some more as I walked into the supermarket. There was no point protesting anything with that one. The werewolf, though, he curled his lips back in what might have been a laugh or possibly a snarl. The normal day settled around me like fog and I was almost eager for the excitement of being chased. Anything to break what was already becoming monotonous. Perhaps the werewolf thought it was fear he was leaving me to simmer in while he waited for a good time to attack.

He came into the building at some point, although I don't know when, and made his way into the back, into the employees only area. He must have waited and watched with more patience than I've known in a hunting werewolf before or since — not counting either Ben or his dad. Ben waits for others to do his work for him and Old Man Lloyd had no interest in killing, just supporting his family the best way he knew how. Unfortunately, Old Man Lloyd's way of making money turned out to be creating killers, but that's another issue altogether.

When I was on my own, when the werewolf *knew* I was on my own, he struck. But I'd been expecting an attack since I'd seen him. I'd prepared.

For a start, I lifted a metal nail-file from the stores. The idea that had niggled at me a couple of days before had hatched properly. No-one ever questions women carrying those handy, if delicate, little daggers with them. While it would be an exceptional attack to be deadly, landing the point in a sensitive area was bound to buy me some time. The book on self-defence I'd borrowed from the library suggested eyes, throat and just under the nose as sensitive areas for jab-bing attacks. I thought I'd do a little more than poke with my fingers when I tried it out. If I had to be that close.

I also had another, still half-formed idea about the crates, boxes and pallets. I wasn't quite up to setting traps, bearing in mind I had colleagues to keep in one piece, but I was keeping an eye on how things were balanced. I paced the three aisles and checked how the stacks of goods filled the space.

So, the rangy werewolf — now furred up — attacked. I heard the scratch of blunt dog's nails on the concrete floor and, primed for a rush, ducked to one side instead of turning to see what a dog was doing in a supermarket storeroom. The grey shape sailed past me, twisting and snapping in mid-air.

I didn't stand still long enough to see where and how he landed. I just ran. Better that than to stand gawping and get killed by a creature that's both faster and stronger than any human has a right to be. It didn't take long to hear his claws on the concrete behind me again or feel — or imagine, anyway — his hot breath at my heels. There was already that half-remembered pattern of bursts of speed, and heavy breathing that eased just before another burst.

I brushed against a stack of boxes on purpose, knowing this one was a little wobbly, and ran on. I heard the boxes crash. It wasn't anything heavy but I figured the obstruction might buy me some time. I couldn't afford to waste it by turning around to see just how much damage I'd done. I needed to be on the other side of the room and at the furthest point away before I could afford to stop. There was a growl and a little scrabbling. I guess he couldn't jump over.

I ran on and around while I looked for a way to push something really heavy over. I'd sort of had a half-baked plan to that effect but the adrenaline was definitely pushing it from my brain. All I could really think of was running.

I fell before I made the halfway round the room point. I hadn't quite made it as far away from the werewolf — or, at least, the start of our chase — as I could in the storeroom.

There was a noise that vaguely resembled a triumphant bark from my hunter but it was soon lost in a rumbling. It was so loud, I wasn't sure if it was a noise or vibration. Okay, I know noise is vibration, but you know what I mean. Something that you feel through your bones, not your ears.

I'd fallen against a set of shelves and it was enough to weaken the whole structure of that aisle — shelves, pallets, boxes, crates. Nothing fell but there was a moment when the whole storeroom just seemed to shift.

I struggled to my feet and back into a run and stumbled again. I hit a ladder but kept going. The ladder fell away from the bank of shelves I had fallen into. Nothing appeared to happen but again there was that noise-but-not-noise that indicated a shift.

I heard a male colleague call out from the doorway into the store, 'Everything okay?'

Perhaps he'd heard, felt or sensed whatever the shift was, too. I didn't bother to reply, though. I was too busy trying to run the werewolf in the small circle the three aisles of our storeroom permitted.

'Elkie?' my colleague called again.

It sounded nearer and without thinking I changed direction towards him. I can perhaps reason it away as trying to protect them from any damage the werewolf might do if he also instinctively responded to their shouts. I'd be lying. The excitement was definitely just fear, now.

I rounded the corner and stopped as I saw him — tall, a little overweight, staring at me with ruddy cheeks and dislike.

'What the hell do you think you're doing?'

I really wish people wouldn't bring religion into their swearing. My mum may be lapsed but that doesn't mean she forgot to instil me with a healthy respect of what happens to you if you upset the Deity. After all, just because I don't believe in Them doesn't mean They don't believe in me — and want to take it out on me. Blasphemy might just attract Their attention and I don't want to know what happens in that case.

'Nothing.'

I even managed to sound sullen in my panted response.

'So I see,' he snapped back and then gasped as the werewolf caught up with me.

I turned to face it, knowing what it was even though my colleague's face hadn't yet gone beyond surprise into the inevitable fear. I guess my reactions were getting faster. I fumbled the stolen nail-file from my pocket and got ready to face off against my hunter.

I heard 'What?' from behind me and then stumbling noises. The stumbling sound moved in the direction of a stack of boxes and I was already wincing at the expected sound of collapse. I knew where these things were, I'd mapped them out in my mind. The colleague who'd been here years longer than me apparently hadn't. The expected sound of collapse — boxes falling over, the 'thunk' indicating there were tins inside — and then... there were more, unexpected sounds of collapse. I mean *real* collapse. A tonne of crates and boxes off the top shelves kind of collapse.

'Oh,' I said as I watched them fall on my hunter, 'Shit.'

Then I pocketed the nail-file and started screaming for help, even though I wasn't sure whether it was a good thing or a bad thing that I never got to fight. I'd been preparing myself for it for the best part of my working day, after all.

Another colleague, the assistant manager and then the emergency services gave a staggered response. But they all found me kneeling over my fallen colleague. He'd suffered a heart attack and I was trying my best to keep him calm and comfortable — without knowledge of emergency first aid. Oddly enough, the first thing each wave of help did was bollock me.

The storeroom was a shambles with a significant amount of stock damaged and some destroyed. Among the lost and mourned for was the store's supply of chocolate spread. In places, the glass from the jars had torn through the wrapping. Underneath, they found the remains of a man who might have looked like someone my colleagues had seen me talking to before our shift started.

My heart attack colleague was forced to retire due to ill-health. I was suspended, without pay, pending a Health and Safety Executive investigation. The investigation was due to the dead body on the work's premises — who I might have known and therefore put me under some minor suspicion. It took the HSE about three days to decide the actual accident was caused by the heart attack. It took them a further six months, which isn't long in their terms, to pin down an underlying, shop-wide failure on best practice when it came to storing goods. And first aid training.

I was never invited back to work. I believe my former employers suspect me of being up to no good with a man I never met before but they think was some kind of relative and/or lover. I wouldn't be surprised if they're saying the heart-attack was caused by my colleague catching us at, well, whatever their filthy minds can come up with.

All in all, as death by chocolate goes, it's not my first choice. And it was a shameful waste of all that spread.

Method 9: Fire

'I'm not playing,' I sent to Ben on the day I was told to leave my short-lived job at the supermarket.

When I came in to Llareggub — the place with the school and the library — several days later to collect my GCSE re-sit results and check my email, I found Ben's response. Repeating my lack of enthusiasm for his game didn't make a difference.

'You won, then. More on the way.'

'I'm not playing,' I sent again.

I thought maybe it would work on the third attempt. I would have been better thinking that maybe I should learn to keep my mouth shut, or fingers still.

After a moment, I sent another one liner: 'Where the fuck are you, anyway?'

I wanted to ask him whether my continued survival meant he had won or lost but didn't really want to read the answer, just in case he wanted me dead. I took my paperwork and went home to think about it.

'How did you do?' Mum asked me.

I put the paperwork on the table in front of her. She'd wanted to come with me but I'd persuaded her to stay behind. She thought I was embarrassed of her, like any normal teenage girl, but I just didn't know when and where the next attack would be. I guess I wasn't sure how to adjust my new role of werewolf bait.

'Straight As.'

I should have been proud and tearfully happy, like one of my classmates would have been, like they were. As they like to point out, though, I'm not. I managed a strained grin when she picked up the papers.

'That's good,' Mum said.

I shrugged, 'Not the best. There's stars and two stars above that.'

'They're good results,' she said firmly, 'And we ought to talk about where you're going to go with them.'

I thought about all the things I ought to learn to give me a better chance against a physically superior enemy: better tracking skills, better combat skills, even weaponry. That's not the sort of education you get at college.

I shrugged. 'I dunno.'

Dave and I had always talked about the things and places we didn't want to go when we talked about what came after school. I had no idea what subjects Dave had settled on for college but I would have bet he had picked things that involved research. Reading up on things — and enacting them, where possible — was his thing. The outdoors play was merely the chance of having been born in a very rural family, without the money for lots of books and TVs and computers to entertain at home.

'What do you like?' Mum asked.

I looked out of the window and thought about it. I missed the trouble Dave and I used to get into. I missed having him to talk to. I hadn't exactly broken in to a sparkling social life re-sitting my last year of secondary school. The kids still thought me some weird peasant who barely knew how to wipe her shoes. I kind of enjoyed their assumption.

'Outdoors,' I said, 'And activities.'

'Like...?' she asked.

I looked at her and smiled, trying to hide the embarrassment. 'Plants, animals,' I said, mentally continuing with *Weapons, hunting, survival skills...*

I worked through my list of all the things I thought I needed to learn to run away from werewolves and found that I liked the idea of all of them. I couldn't find the words to tell her all of it without mentioning the Lloyds and what happened to them but I did manage to tell her that I'd like to learn martial arts.

'Fighting?' she said, her eyes widening.

Mum's a strict pacifist. If she'd known what Dave and I got up to in the woods with rabbits or fire hardened wooden spears — well, let's just say she would be very disappointed. I'm not entirely sure she'd be happy about my killing werewolves in self-defence, either, and not just because it meant I was being attacked.

'Martial arts are so you don't have to fight,' I said, trying to remember the words from the book I'd borrowed from the library.

Mum looked at me like I'd gone insane. I can't say I blame her. I didn't exactly understand most of the philosophical statements the book had made.

'So,' Mum said, 'How about ecology? The closest courses in A-levels r — '

'AS-levels,' I said, interrupting, 'Then A-levels.'

She nodded, 'Anyway, the closest subject in the local college is probably Biology but if you get good A-levels, you can go on to read Ecology at university.'

'No-one says they read a subject at university anymore, Mum.'

Mum's turn to shrug. 'I wouldn't know. I didn't go.'

I had a horrible feeling like I was re-enacting some scene from her life. Except that at about this age, give or take a year or two, she must have stood in front of her mother and admitted to being pregnant.

'I'm sorry,' I said.

Mum looked me straight in the eye and I flinched. 'Don't be. I chose.'

'Maybe I should do something more... vocational,' I said as if we hadn't detoured.

'I doubt the local college offers anything close enough to what you want to do.'

'I could go to the agricultural college,' I whispered, knowing she wouldn't be happy with it.

I wasn't entirely sure I was, either. As much as I liked being outdoors and the idea of working there, committing to agricultural college had that crack of doom feeling to it. Particularly when success is measured by making it into the mainstream and having an office job.

'You don't think that's... wasting your qualifications?'

It's not that she was dead set against me doing what I wanted, just that there's a typical route for people to go through education — particularly those of us who do reasonably well at it. But, amongst other things, going to agricultural college would keep me out of the way of people and werewolves.

'It's not like I don't need GCSEs to get in,' I said.

She nodded slowly. 'Well, seeing as you don't have a job anymore — '

'But I didn't *do* anything,' I protested.

Mum raised her eyebrows at me and I didn't bother to expand on my automatic defence.

'You have plenty of time on your hands to do some research and work out where to go from here.'

'Did you have any particular direction in mind?' I asked.

Despite how I made it sound, Mum didn't tell me what to do all the time, otherwise I'd never have been roaming the countryside with Dave. I just wanted to be told instead of thinking for myself. I wanted someone else to blame if it was a bad idea.

'If you want to go to agricultural college,' she said, 'You're going to have to give me a better argument than that.'

'Maybe I should just do an NVQ or apprenticeship. They do engineering courses.'

Which would also be cool. As much as I liked being outdoors, it didn't have to be my job if I could afford to get out in my spare time. And the werewolves didn't get me.

'Work it out for yourself,' Mum said.

'But what if I don't work it out in time to enrol?'

'Get a job until enrolment comes around again.'

I picked up my pieces of paper and went in search of a folder to put them in.

'One that doesn't involve industrial accidents that kill people,' Mum shouted after me.

'Well, there goes the plan for joining the army,' I shouted back.

Not that I'd ever really intended to. As much as they could probably teach me some important survival skills, I think my methods are a bit too freestyle for barracks life. And maybe I've seen too many bad films but I could see that all ending up with me having to capture live werewolves for someone else to prod with scalpels. Not going to happen.

I'll say that again: It's never going to happen.

'Is it okay if I get dinner before I start taking on the world?' I came back to ask after re-homing my brand new qualifications.

Mum laughed. 'Pretty much already done. You just need to turn up the heat on the stove for the last burst.'

So I did, encouraging the old electric cooker to change setting to something warmer. When dinner was ready, I wrestled it back to 'off'. Or thought I had. What actually happened is that, after I served up two plates of dinner, I left the pan on the ring to boil dry and then burn the food to the pan. Sometime early the next morning, the burnt food turned into burning food. The only good thing about it was the timing.

Like any of my run-ins with werewolves, it's the timing that's important. Or sheer luck, depending on how you want to put it. It's possible to make that luck or that good timing more likely by carrying weapons and being prepared but, when it comes down to it, survival is about chance.

Ben's next minion — or maybe he's a missionary as he was sent to fulfil a mission — broke in around midnight. I guess he hung around and watched us sleep before attacking. Maybe he smelt something from the kitchen and kept back until he had an idea of how things were playing out. While the burning smell might have meant the eventual arrival of police and fire services, it was unlikely they would turn up before the evidence burnt to the ground, given our location in the middle nowhere.

That's my best guess, anyway. I'm not privy to what goes on inside the mind of a madman, so I don't know why he accepted Ben's mission or why he didn't just kill us both straight away. Maybe he just started getting the side effects of smoke inhalation and that slowed him down or gave him a reason to pause. Is the average werewolf, or human, really smart enough to take full advantage of this kind of situation?

Smoke can cause coughing and nausea but the real silent killer part of it is the sleepiness and confusion caused by carbon monoxide and lack of oxygen. From what I remember of my GCSEs, the carbon monoxide binds more strongly with the red blood cells than oxygen does. After that, I'm not entirely sure what it does to the system to make you sleepy.

We had a single, solitary smoke alarm, fitted by a fireman who'd come over and flirted with Mum. Good old Fido presumably knocked it out when it first went off so we wouldn't be woken up. We were only to be roused when he was ready to kill us.

'Whuh?'

I woke pretty fast, as soon as I'd heard — still unconscious — someone walk into my bedroom uninvited. It still wasn't fast enough to avoid the furred hand — paw? — that clutched over my mouth. I wanted to cough more than I wanted to cry out but that not-human, not-dog thing made it impossible to do either. And I didn't have anything to fight back with but my bare hands. At least I had some pyjamas on.

The werewolf wuffled against my ear, sniffing like a dog checking out a scent. How did he know me by scent? Did Ben have something of mine that smelt of me? Did he give them a location to go to that meant they would definitely pick up my scent? Or was there some other reason he was checking me out?

Fido licked my ear.

With his paw over my mouth, I couldn't give proper voice to the disgust that ended up rumbling in my throat like a growl. I swear he laughed at me then, a breathy, dog-smelling laugh that whispered in my ear. I bit his paw as hard as I could.

The werewolf flinched, taking his paw from my mouth, with a quiet whimper. He didn't mean to react like that and his anger brought payback with it. He backhanded me across the bed and into the bedroom wall.

I screamed, 'You bastard!'

The werewolf growled out something that might have been 'You bitch!' if there had been mobile, human lips to shape it properly.

I moved as fast as I could, still feeling the need to stop and cough but fighting it. I didn't have myself together enough to notice that the air was tasting thick and heavy or that Mum hadn't reacted to my swearing. It might be an old, stone building but the cottage I grew up in was far from sound-proof. She should have been disturbed by my shout and the sounds of fighting.

It took me a couple of rushes to get past the werewolf. I have to be honest, he didn't seem to be trying too hard. I think he was simply trying to intimidate me and he hadn't got frustrated enough with me to forget whatever his original plan was. So I got passed him and shut him in, leaning against the shaky wood of my less than solid bedroom door.

When I opened my eyes, I was fully awake and together. I saw the smoke in the air.

'Mum!'

The werewolf was effectively forgotten. Mum and I had to get out of the building. If we got to the Williams' farm, Dave's house, we might be able to get the fire service down here in time to rescue the structure and maybe even some of the contents.

'Mum,' I yelled again, not quite willing to walk into her room uninvited, 'You've got to wake up! The house is on fire!'

She didn't answer and the tentative scrabbles on the other side of my bedroom door became a growl of frustration. His plan had just been jettisoned, at least while I was leaning on the door and keeping it shut.

I couldn't hold it for long, though, and I ran into Mum's room, slamming the door behind me again. I considered moving furniture to keep the werewolf out for longer and promptly forgot it. It wasn't due to thinking, either. Mum's room was right over the kitchen and the smoke was thicker in her room. I shook her but her response was weak and sleepy, an unconscious cough, so I dragged her out of her bed.

'Please wake up,' I begged, 'I can't throw you out the window.'

Nothing.

'Better air, then. Need to get away from the smoke. Towards my room.'

I half carried, half dragged her to the door and then remembered the werewolf on the other side. He hadn't broken the door down or even tried the door handle. Maybe he knew all he had to do was wait.

'Weapon. Need a weapon.'

I turned, holding Mum upright as I scanned the smoke-filled room as best I could. I needed something nice and heavy and blunt. Something big enough to cause some trauma and stop Fido chasing me. Unfortunately, there were no spades in the house.

'Vase. Vase'll do.'

I propped Mum against the wall, sitting her down so she had the air that seemed a little clearer, and opened the door.

I tried to swing the vase at the same time as swinging the door open, making it as much one controlled movement as I could. I was lucky. The werewolf leapt forward in time for the vase to smash him in the face. He dropped to the floor and I didn't stop to check if he was alive. But I did stop long enough to do the half drag, half carry thing with the most important person all the way out the house using the door. There was no way I was dropping my still unconscious mother out of a window.

We stood in the cold night air — not too bad as it was August — for a moment because I hoped it would wake her up and save me having to carry her all the way to Dave's. She wasn't capable of a run but I managed to get her there faster than a slow walk. Then we knocked on the door and screamed until Dave's dad opened up.

'Fire,' Mum said, 'There's a fire at the cottage.'

I cleared my throat and added, 'Better call the police as well, someone attacked me when I tried to get Mum out.'

Over Mr Williams' shoulder I saw Dave mouth, 'Someone?'

After that, I passed out.

Method 10: Dog Fight

'You could just try talking to me,' Dave said.

He had his hands raised as if walking unarmed into a gunfight in some old western film. I just glared at him wishing my fingers had something to twitch over. Or around. Preferably something I could cause him physical damage with.

'Don't fight in the kitchen,' his mum said as if she'd read my mind, 'Take it outside.'

'Don't fight at all,' said my mum, determined to make me keep her values even if we were no longer in our own home. Even if we no longer had our own home.

I stomped outside. Dave followed me.

'Talking?' he prodded.

I didn't answer but kept stomping across the farmyard. Once I got out of sight and ear-shot of the kitchen, the heavy walk turned into a charging run for as far away as possible. Again, Dave followed me.

When I stopped for breath in the copse we used to hunt dragons in, he spoke again — between loud pants to haul air back into his lungs. I guess he hadn't been outside as much without me to keep him company but, then, neither had I. My fitness levels came from running away from werewolves.

'Tell me what Ben's doing to you.'

I screamed at him, 'I'm not talking to the man who tried to kill him.'

I had to stop there and I watched Dave while I tried to catch more breath, ready for the next sentence I needed to shout. There was something about the way he puffed up at the use of the word 'man' that made me feel sick. While killing wasn't something I associated with boys, whether outright child or teenager, his attitude wasn't really mature enough to call him a man. He didn't really look like one, either, though he was taller, and broader across the shoulders, than he'd been the last time we talked about werewolves.

'What's Ben doing?' Dave demanded, trying to take control like a real man.

I folded my arms and glared at him.

'I dunno,' I lied, 'I would guess it's a little hard to do anything from a nut house.'

Dave shrugged. 'If the parvo'd worked like it was supposed to, he wouldn't be in a nut house.'

'No. He'd be dead.'

'He's a werewolf. The only good werewolf is a dead werewolf.'

I rolled my eyes at Dave's appropriation of a clichéd saying. I wanted to ask if he'd met every werewolf in the world so he could be sure it was true. 'And?' I asked instead, 'So was Old Man Lloyd and he never did anyone any harm.'

'Oh?'

'Not directly,' I tacked on belatedly and with a flush.

'Ben's a killer,' said Dave, 'Even if he's not tearing out people's throats with his bare hands.'

I glared.

'Or his teeth,' Dave added pointedly.

'You can't just kill people,' I said, ignoring my somewhat increased body count since the last time we'd talked.

Dave growled, 'He's a killer. It's him or us.'

'He's not attacking anybody.'

'No?'

'No,' I said.

'So what is he doing?'

I shrugged. I had no answer. Sending other werewolves after me was... what? How was he telling them who and where I was?

'What makes you think he's doing anything?' I bluffed.

'You mean other than a half-baked corpse turning up in the cottage?'

He didn't mention the newer body he must have seen in the stash — or leaving a book behind to show he'd visited. I waited to see if he would before bluffing some more.

'Could just be an intruder.'

Almost believable. After all, the werewolf *had* intruded.

Dave laughed. 'Like you told the police, eh?'

'Yes.'

'Don't believe it.'

'You don't have to believe the truth,' I said, 'It exists independently of whatever you believe.'

I walked back to the crowded, collapsing farmhouse without mentioning that the truth wasn't what I'd told the police. At least I was confident that the truth continued to exist regardless of what went on in other people's heads.

So, if you haven't realised, there wasn't enough left of the cottage to live in it. The stone shell remained but everything else had been destroyed by the time the fire service had got there. Well, enough remained to say, find pieces of former werewolf and severely charred beams. The Williams' had been kind enough to make room for us, giving us a mildewed bedroom that been given up on long before the fire due to lack of funds.

Mum had managed to wrangle Dave's dad into letting me work on the farm for the cost of room rental, which meant she was able to save some of her wages, but nobody was happy about the new arrangement. The Williams' needed our money and we needed to be in separate rooms. Unfortunately, it was unlikely that the cost of restoring the cottage could be met and it looked like the Bernsteins would be moving as soon as we could work out how to afford it. We'd had no insurance — couldn't afford that, either — and no other landlord would take us without it.

The good thing about working on the farm was that I got plenty of outdoors. The bad thing was that I couldn't avoid Dave, who was on his summer holidays and also doing odd jobs at the farm. I tried to walk through him a couple of times but he'd started to, as they say, grow into himself since the last time I'd done that. The extra height and breadth meant we were no longer physical equals, at least not in terms of brute strength. So this time I just kept walking away from him.

'You're going to have to tell me about the werewolves eventually,' he said — well away from anyone else, thankfully.

'What makes you sure werewolves have anything to do with it?' I bluffed and stepped around him.

'What else could it be?'

I crammed my hands into the pockets of my work jeans and hunched up. 'Just some man that broke into the cottage looking for a place to sleep.'

'How likely is that? Most people are townies.'

I stopped and stared at him. 'Townies?'

'You know. Live in an urban environment. Expect the weather to suit their clothes. Sleep in doorways if they can't find a building. That kind of thing.'

'What are you getting at?'

'It's highly unlikely that anyone would be nuts enough to be wandering around in the middle of rural North Wales in the middle of the night looking for a place to sleep.'

I shrugged. 'He broke in.'

'Not only does everyone know there's nothing worth stealing down this lane,' Dave said with a snort, 'It looks like it, too.'

I said nothing and stared away from Dave.

'So. Werewolves. What's Ben doing?'

I just managed not to protest his innocence in an outright lie, 'What makes you think Ben's doing anything?'

'He's the only live werewolf we know.'

'Maybe I know another,' I snapped back.

'I doubt it,' said Dave, 'You seem to be bad for their health.'

I waited for him to mention that extra corpse but still he said nothing.

'Nothing's going on with werewolves. Ben or anyone else,' I said. Then I turned and strode off back towards the farmyard.

Dave called out, 'I've done a body count.'

I stopped. Here it came. The part where he told me about leaving the book behind, about how he was so clever leaving me that secret, coded message.

'There's five of them, Elkie.'

He'd been back and seen the second extra body. He'd probably seen my footprint on his bloody book. I swallowed a ball of fear that caught in my throat. The fear was irrational. Hadn't I always known it was a shared secret? It's not as if the hiding place is safe because you can't see the bodies. It's safe because they're in a place no-one will look. Dave had chosen it and I'd agreed, so he knew where it was and what to see when he got there. He'd seen the evidence of the new 'missions', and he'd left me a message to show he knew.

'Is that all?' I forced out, 'Seems like more.'

He grabbed my elbow and turned me around to face the hills.

'Let's walk and talk.'

I didn't say anything but we definitely walked, across the lush green of the limited farmland and on to the stony slopes of the North Welsh mountains. Not, actually, that far from the bodies if we'd taken a right instead of a left.

We were gone an hour before I started to feel guilty about leaving work behind. I stood and did a panoramic view, turning on the spot to see what was around me. About a mile away — twenty minutes walk, give or take — a woman was walking a white dog. Neither really looked like they belonged out in the back of beyond; if only because dogs out in the middle of nowhere are usually collies, labradors, spaniels or terriers. You get used to being able to tell the difference quickly and from a distance.

'Dog walker,' I said.

Dave squinted. 'It's a bull terrier.'

English Bull Terriers really aren't associated with the rural idyll. The walker and her dog must either be on holiday or have driven out from some town or other for the day.

'Hmm. Least the weather's good for them.'

And thankfully no sign of it changing soon. No-one needs to be caught out on the hills, even in the middle of summer, and it's a bloody stupid reason to have to call out the mountain rescue team.

'So. Ben?' Dave asked.

I turned to face him and said nothing. Why should I explain what I thought Ben was up to, especially to someone who'd wanted to kill him in cold blood? Not that I'm saying what Ben was doing was right, but —

'He's not right, Elkie,' Dave said as if he'd caught my thoughts, 'And he shouldn't exist. Werewolves shouldn't exist.'

'So he should be killed? By us?'

Dave shrugged. 'Who else is going to do it?'

'What gives you the right to judge,' I shot back, 'He's a person. He doesn't deserve to be murdered.'

'So he needs to attack you with his teeth bared before you'll sully your honour with his blood?'

'I'd rather not kill anyone,' I said.

'He's going to kill a lot of people and cause a lot of trouble. He's better off dead.'

'No,' I corrected, 'You think your life will be better with him dead.'

Which was probably more true for me than for Dave, who laughed as if he already knew it.

'He's not bothering me from wherever he's holed up.'

I tried my best to laugh back. 'So what makes you think he's bo — '

I never did get to finish the question. I was interrupted by Ben's next mission. I'm still not sure whether it's me or them that were the targets, or for that matter whether it was them or me that was completing the tasks Ben set. Anyway, I was pinned to the uneven ground — my face shoved into the stones and patchy grass I'd just been thinking pretty — by a furred-up werewolf who was either too aggressive or too confident to care that I wasn't on my own.

The way I landed on the grass meant I couldn't get at the pen-knife I carried all the time, now that I was doing farm work and could get away with it. I couldn't strike out in any meaningful way and, as I'd been winded, I couldn't even give voice to my anger. Or scream in pain when I felt those teeth break through the clothes and skin on my shoulder. All I could do was shift slightly so that my neck didn't become a more reachable or attractive point of contact.

'Get off her, you bastard.'

Dave did his best to haul the werewolf off but the furred freak was holding on pretty well. I know that Dave struck at my attacker a few times because some of them landed on me. When my lungs worked again, I started screaming. And not that long after, I heard another growl join the werewolf's.

'What?' Dave said.

He stopped, no screams at the werewolf and no blows that missed and hit me instead. Then he said something it took me a while to grasp.

'Good dog! *Da iawn*! You go for it. Good lad!'

The bull terrier had reached us and thrown itself into the fight. My attacker's hold on me shifted and there was a whimper from my new saviour. It was enough for me to be able to throw my own weight around a little bit and I managed to get my hand into my pocket for my pen knife.

'Bad furball!' said Dave and, from the way the weight shifted, I guess he got a swift kick into the werewolf's ribs.

The bull terrier threw itself back into the fight, clawing over my bad shoulder in an effort to get to the enemy's throat. Although it hurt I was grateful because the attack got the werewolf off my back. The two furballs, one furred up human that wanted to be a wolf and one whose ancestors used to be wolves until humans decided they wanted it to be something else, rolled around on the grass and I managed to crawl away from them. It was only then that I started feeling the new bruises from landing on the stones. A few were on my face and I just knew I was going to have fun explaining this later.

'Dave,' I whispered.

He paused with a stick raised and looked at me.

'Leave them to it. She's bred for it and you'll only cause her problems.'

The woman, the bull terrier's owner, came stumbling up the hill calling for 'Gwennie', all designer walking gear and boots too good for muddy puddles. Then she saw the dog fight.

'Oh my God!'

'I really wish people would stop taking the Deity's name in vain around me,' I whispered.

'Get your fucking dog off of Gwennie!' the woman screamed and glared at us as if we'd hauled the dog, who looked to be only a quarter of the size of the werewolf, into the disagreement against its wishes.

'It's not ours,' said Dave, 'It's a stray.'

'I don't care! Get it off her!'

Gwennie looked like she was doing okay, holding on to the werewolf's neck like her life depended on it. Which it did. The werewolf wasn't doing so well, probably never having tried actual fighting, particularly with a dog, in its life. It had probably assumed that size and strength accounted for everything and would suffer for it. It already had a shredded throat and the terrier's stranglehold would be cutting off air and blood supplies.

'Technically, your dog attacked first,' said Dave.

'Shut up,' I told him.

I watched the fight fade from the werewolf before I dared intervene. I didn't want to dislodge Gwennie to find the werewolf trying to eat me again.

'She saw the stray attack me,' I said, cutting over whatever Gwennie's owner had opened her mouth to say, 'And decided to intervene.'

'They're not exactly the most dog-friendly breed,' Dave added.

'Shut up,' I said again.

The owner glared. 'Gwennie's a total sweetie.'

'To humans, yeah,' muttered Dave.

I glared at him, too.

When the werewolf collapsed, his rib cage barely moving, I stepped forward to Gwennie and stroked her back.

'Good girl. You can let go now.'

Gwennie growled but rolled her head and eyes so that she could look at me and, beyond me, her owner.

'Let go, there's a good girl,' I said.

'Gwennie, come here,' her owner demanded.

The terrier growled again but let go of the werewolf's throat. After a sniff and a scratch on the ground nearby to mark her territory, she trotted over to her owner.

'I'll be telling the police about this!'

'Would you like the number of the local station?' I asked as I clutched at my torn shoulder.

Method 11: Live Burial

So we — me, Dave and Gwennie's owner — were staring at a werewolf with a torn throat. It was still in its fur, so it couldn't be dead but it was only a matter of time before Fido's body caught on to the situation and left us with a human. I had was no doubt it was going to die.

Gwennie the English Bull Terrier was now yipping around her owner but it had been her stranglehold that knocked the werewolf unconscious and had, as I already said, torn its throat. Fido just apparently hadn't admitted defeat yet.

I was nursing my torn shoulder, wondering if I was going to end up like my attacker and if we'd stayed around too long. The longer we hung around Gwennie and her owner, the more identifiable we became — and the more identified with the soon to be deceased.

'What do we do?' Dave whispered.

I looked at him. Traditionally the ideas man out of the two of us, I was a little surprised — to say the least — that it was *me* who had to come up with a big plan. Or that I was the only one who'd realised a big plan wasn't necessary.

'What do we do?' he whispered again, the words holding a hint of hysteria, 'She's ringing the police!'

I looked over at the dog and owner and saw that Gwennie's human was holding her mobile to her ear and pacing.

'Hope she's not wasting the call handlers' time with a 999 over a dead stray,' I answered Dave loudly.

I got a glare from the strange woman for my troubles. I don't think she was convinced the grey furred thing wasn't our pet dog. As she was also dumb enough not to notice the shape wasn't canine, either, I wasn't exactly bothered by it. We just needed to make sure she saw no reason to come back to it, when it would be rediscovered as a human corpse. People tend to see what they want to see — and change what they remember to fit what they already know.

'Well, I don't suppose we can do much,' I said in a more normal volume, 'We might as well go.'

'We can't just leave it here!'

'Why not?' I asked.

If I'm honest, I already knew the answer. When the body realised it was dead it would absorb its fur and the werewolf would be a man again. A man with his throat ripped by a dog. But we hadn't touched him. We hadn't been seen touching him. There was nothing here to connect us with the death. Except the slim possibility that this woman might end up in a position to connect a dead 'dog' with a human corpse that had the same injuries. She didn't seem that smart.

'We've been seen,' Dave hissed.

I shrugged as if it were a mere detail. She didn't know us and wouldn't be able to trace us. She connected us with a dog, not a man. As long as we weren't around when the change happened.

'And you're not taking that... that monster off this hillside,' Gwennie's owner said.

I jumped because she was nearer than I'd thought. She must have seen Dave acting suspiciously and come closer to listen in. I guess we'd said enough to prove ourselves connected to the body.

'That dog is staying here, so I can bring the police to see it.'

It was Dave's turn to jump like he was guilty of something. I just looked her straight in the eye.

'Does this mean they've asked you to go to the local station to report the incident?'

'That body doesn't move from here,' she ground out.

Thankfully, Gwennie had better manners and leant against Dave's leg until he scratched behind her ear. Despite our run-ins with werewolves that don't like his look, I've never known a real canine take offence at Dave.

'Fine,' I said, 'It's not like it's anything to do with us, anyway.'

The woman seemed to make a mental adjustment. Perhaps

it was starting to sink in that it wasn't our dog. Perhaps this was all defensiveness, and she scared that we would report Gwennie as a dangerous dog. The then current public mind-set about dogs being what it was, the police were more likely to believe that Gwennie was more dangerous than just about anything short of a man-eating tiger simply because she was a bull terrier.

'What do we do?' Dave asked again.

I looked around at the hillside, noting the stones that lay about, and smiled. The thing about hills — real hills that are too steep for arable crops, not the gently rolling of, say, the English Home Counties — is that there's usually plenty of rocks and stones around. I suspect it's our most productive crop.

'A cairn.'

Gwennie's owner did not react well. 'A what?'

I raised my eyebrows. Much as I was coming to terms with the fact that she was an idiot — after all, it made the real secret easier to keep — I would have preferred it if she could have met me, say, halfway.

'Cairn. A cache. We pile rocks on it,' I said slowly.

I don't think she liked the idea any better for knowing what I meant. I don't think she liked the fact that it came from either me or Dave. Watching her precious little terrier fight another animal had upset her deeply. That her dog had made the first move and had won probably only put her more on edge.

I knelt by the body — wishing I had gloves on so I wouldn't leave any traces behind — and straightened it into an approximation of a dog lying on its side. If I lay it flat on its back so that the weight of the stones was directly on its chest, and forced all air out of the lungs, I might make the less canine features more obvious and I couldn't risk that. If she reacted this badly over a dog fight, imagine how she'd feel about Gwennie being put down for killing a man.

'Weird looking stray,' I said in passing.

I was trying to make it clear I'd never seen this beast before but I dreaded calling too much attention to it at the same time. If she noticed too much, well, then she'd say something that showed her brain wasn't glossing over the facts.

The woman sniffed, indicating a background that included more than just a penchant for expensively labelled outdoor clothing. 'Damned mongrel.'

She was still seeing what she expected to see. Nothing else. In her experience, werewolves didn't exist, dogs did.

Dave was starting to show a little more white around the eyes than is normal but I couldn't tell him I was banking on the police shrugging off this woman's worries in present company. Even out in rural North Wales, they have better things to do than go chasing off after a stray dog that's already dead. With the investigations of the death at work and the death in the fire still part of my life, this little nothing was of very low importance.

The key thing was to get the word 'stray' out of her before we all parted company. It would show she'd accepted we were nothing to do with it. In that vein, the use of 'mongrel' might be a good sign.

I looked around for the biggest, flattest stone I thought I could pick up on my own. I didn't so much carry it over as wobble behind it, trying not to drop it on my feet. For the sake of social niceties, I put it down as gently as I could.

'If you're still conscious,' I whispered to the corpse-to-be, 'Sorry but this is going to hurt.'

Then I got the next stone and the next as Dave, Gwennie and her owner watched me. Gwennie, of course, couldn't help. Her owner, well I guess she just wouldn't. Dave did eventually but it took him a while before he could bring himself to get his hands dirty. Odd, really, because his last murder had involved him digging up contaminated soils.

We kept piling stones until it was impossible to see the body and there was no chance of it getting out again. If the woman wanted the police to exhume it, well, that was her problem, not mine. I hoped.

'I think that should do it,' I said when the top of the pile was up to my hip. I turned and looked the woman straight in the eye. 'We're off.'

'I need names,' the woman said, 'If you're going. I'll need to pass them along to the police.'

I shrugged. 'We've got nothing to do with the stray. It attacked us and Gwennie defended me. That's it. We've got no complaints against you or Gwennie.'

She sniffed again, but didn't make another demand for our names. I made the effort to say goodbye to Gwennie and call her a good girl for holding her own against the big, bad stray. I turned my back on her.

About the same time Dave caught up, the woman's voice strained to get to me. 'I'll report it as a stray, then.'

I hid my inner smile. It was too early to declare victory and I wouldn't until I was sure the police did nothing about it. The woman's call, and the uncertainty in it, meant she didn't have much confidence in what she'd intended to say so it was unlikely the police would have much confidence, either.

'I'll bet she thinks all dogs are micro chipped,' I muttered, 'Bet she thinks she'll catch us that way.'

It was all the distraction I needed, and I found myself comparing the good condition of the other woman's clothes to my own.

'How come they know where to find you?' Dave asked.

'What?' I stopped, still caught in my envious thoughts on money and small, neat, feminine shapes, 'What do you mean? The police won't know anything let alone where to find me. That's the point.'

'Werewolves apparently do,' he snapped.

I opened my mouth and shut it again. I really didn't want to get into this. Dave, being an intelligent person, could probably work it out on his own. Which he did. It was exactly what he'd been badgering me about all the time we'd been talking.

'It's definitely Ben, isn't it?'

I shrugged and started walking again. More specifically, I was trying to walk away from Dave, even though I knew he was unlikely to allow it.

'Where the hell is he? Why is he doing this?'

'He has some kind of game going on,' I said.

It had always seemed wrong — totally cracked, even —

when I'd thought about it but actually saying it aloud just made it that little bit more insane. Insane, sinister, hugely unappealing. Shame I had no way to stop it.

'Where is he?'

'No idea. Some insane asylum or whatever they call them these days. I get the feeling 'insane asylum' is a very politically incorrect phrase. He sends me emails. I guess he has some way of getting in touch with other werewolves. He sends them after me.'

'Why? Is there a reason? Why don't you tell him to stop?'

'Last question first,' I said, 'And what makes you think I haven't? Second question: 'reason' has nothing to do with it. He's in a nut-house, for crying out loud. First question: He's treating it like some kind of game.'

He had got way too attached to games long before he'd been taken away, to the point of sitting in his own refuse just to carry on at a computer console.

'What's his email address?' Dave demanded.

I frowned. 'What? You've turned into a world-class hacker in the last year? You don't even have a computer!'

'I'm just trying to help!'

I said nothing. I really wanted help. Telling me what I already knew, or making me go over old ground again, wasn't help.

'Look, I know someone who might be able to trace it.'

'It's an online account,' I said.

Dave shrugged at me. 'Still might be able to find something.'

So I reeled off Ben's email address. No harm in trying, after all. I was never going to be able to stop him but, if we could find out where he was, his keepers might.

Method 12: Harvester

That bite drove me to distraction. With having to hide the injury and worrying about whether it would turn me into a werewolf, it turned me into a real bitch. It didn't help that Dave followed me everywhere — or that I couldn't afford all the jars of chocolate spread my stress levels were craving.

'Dave, just sod off, will you?'

He got everywhere. More precisely, he kept getting in my way while I worked. It didn't matter who else was around, he was at my shoulder. Within a few days, it got to the point where my second word of the morning was 'off'.

'Elkie!' my mother gasped.

Dave's dad just laughed and walked out of the farm kitchen. 'Come on, kids. Elkie has work to do and Dave has some getting in the way to do.'

I guess Dave's parents just put it down to unrequited love or lust. Me, I was just wondering what he expected to do to me if and when I furred up.

'I'm just watching your back,' he said when I asked.

I glared at him. 'Waiting to stab me in it, you mean.'

He shuffled.

'Believe me, Dave, the way you're acting, you'll be the first person I come after if I turn wolf.'

The scabs itched. I prodded at them every day, looking at the bite marks in the bathroom mirror. Was it healing faster than usual? Slower? I could practically hear Dave thinking the same thing on the other side of the wall, in his bedroom. If I concentrated, I could probably hear his breathing — or maybe I was just imagining it. But at the time I thought I could and I thought it was a sign of the change coming on because Old Man Lloyd and Ben had never told me what it was like.

All I knew was that it made people sick because Old Man

Lloyd had talked of looking after Ben. I thought about that, wondered how bad it had been. It hadn't been Ben who'd killed the family while he was ill but Old Man Lloyd. I guess Ben was too obsessed with games to look after Old Man Lloyd as well as Old Man Lloyd looked after Ben, so it had been his father who had been out of control just as it had been his father that died from parvo and lack of care. If I changed, what would I do with only Dave aware of what was going on?

When the scabs finally fell off, I walked up to the cairn.

'It didn't happen,' I said to the stones.

The cairn hadn't been disturbed since Dave and I had piled it up, so my words covered both the change and the discovery of a human corpse.

I'll never know, I thought, *whether Dave can stop a werewolf.*

'The question is 'why not?'' said Dave.

I spun round. 'What? Can't I have five bloody minutes to myself?'

He stepped back, hands up in symbolic surrender. I didn't care.

'Get your own life and leave me alone.'

I wanted to run away but stood my ground. Dave would only follow me until he got whatever result he was after. He was that kind of person. Maybe not becoming a werewolf was enough to let me off the hook, though.

'I'm trying to take care of you,' Dave said.

He looked away in that half-embarrassed way kids have when they've been caught doing something they know isn't quite wrong — or when they're caught telling a big truth they don't want to say. Although he'd topped me in height and broadened out, he looked too boyish to ever be better at looking after me than I already was.

'Then you're asking the wrong question,' I said.

He blinked and looked squarely at me. 'What?'

'The question that matters for my survival isn't 'why didn't I become a werewolf?', it's 'when and where is the next threat going to turn up?'.'

I kind of knew that answer. Based on previous experience, I had at least another week before Ben could raise another minion to attack me. And, if I'm honest, not even that was the real question. I should have been asking 'Why is Ben doing this?' Beyond knowing he thought it was some kind of game — and he was obsessed with games — I hadn't thought about it. I didn't want to because somewhere in there, he was still the golden boy from school.

'Do you always come back to... the scene of the crime?' Dave asked.

I looked back at the cairn and remembered how it felt piling on each one of the stones I'd held. I didn't like the use of the word 'crime'. It implied I could be punished for my part in this insanity.

'Don't you?' I fired back.

I knew the other cache of bodies was undisturbed, even if it's mostly hidden in plain sight, but that doesn't mean he hadn't been back, too. We'd chosen that place because it was rocky, with no way of leaving traceable footprints.

Dave didn't answer, though, he just did what I hadn't been able to bring myself to do. He turned and walked away. Which was as good as a 'yes' to me.

So, why? Why go and do something stupid like return to the scene of the crime or to resting place of your victim?

'You're an itch,' I told the cairn and what lay underneath, 'A scab I have to scratch at.'

While I'm geographically near a corpse I've hidden, I have an urge to check up on it. The urge doesn't disappear with distance, it's just harder to justify the time and money it would cost to go and look. It's like an itch that needs to be scratched and sometimes you just can't scratch it and you have to live with it. Then, sometimes, I guess you just can't live with it. Which is how people get found out.

'No more standing and talking to you,' I said, 'In case people see it and think there's something interesting underneath.'

I walked away, thinking about bodies that didn't need to be hidden. There are bodies I'll never have this problem with. The werewolf crushed in the supermarket and the werewolf burnt to death in the cottage were disposed of through official channels. I suppose the guy who got hit by the train, however many parts he ended up in, was similarly sent on his way by the authorities. Old Man Lloyd got a cremation, which I was happy with because it ensured the parvovirus was destroyed. Both Dave and I went to the ceremony though we weren't speaking at the time.

By the time I got back to the farm, I thought I had a plan to make sure I never had to hide another body. I just had to wait for a chance to send an email.

While hill-country farms tend to be pastoral and animal-orientated, we still have some harvesting to do. Most farms try to produce their own hay, haylage or silage, depending on how long they can wait to make the cut and what their storage is like. The day after I walked up to the cairn was the day I set out on the machine you would barely recognise as a tractor with a harvester that probably dated from the fifties.

'Text me if anything happens,' Dave said but he didn't follow me.

Mr Williams looked up. 'What did you do, Elkie? Beat my son up?'

I grinned. 'It wasn't necessary, sir.'

But Williams senior had already made it clear that Dave had other jobs to do — that presumably wouldn't get in the way of me driving up and down, up and down.

While the skies are clear and the days long, grass has to be cut, turned over to dry and bailed. The Williams didn't own many fields that were for fodder only but then they didn't own new gear, either. It would take the best part of a week to cut it all, another week to turn it so that it dried thoroughly and another week to bail and bring it back to the farmyard. I suppose I should be glad I didn't get sent out with just a scythe and a pitchfork, although a scythe — if I knew how to use one — might be a decent weapon.

I was hoping to get a rain break in the cutting period to disappear off into Llareggub and use the library's Internet connection. It would make the whole job longer but would mean I would have solved my own problem without having another body to hide.

This being North Wales, I got the rain break I was looking for and got to send my email:

'What do you think you're doing? Why do you keep doing this to me? You're ruining my life! How do you expect me to get on with my life if you keep contacting me? Why don't you just get on with your own life and leave me alone? Whatever you're trying to do, it won't work, you know. You're sick. You're pathetic. Game over.'

Ben's response came through almost instantly. It was just the one line. 'The game isn't over until you're dead.'

I smiled my triumph. See, I'd not mentioned exactly what Ben did to me in the email I'd sent. Neither Ben nor I have mentioned werewolves or killing in previous emails. He talks of 'men like me' and 'missions' and 'winning'. I swear and call him 'sick' and obviously get upset. It's fairly clear he's making me do something I don't want to — from a distance. People being people, it would probably be assumed there was a sexual dimension to it all without me having to tell an outright lie.

I printed everything out and prepared my best 'woe is me' look for the police. Let Dave try and find out Ben's location from a webmail address, I now had a death threat that should see Ben's internet access revoked.

It took me a while to be seen, of course, but I managed to get hold of a policeman involved in the supermarket investigation before it was handed over to the HSE as a purely industrial incident. His first words on seeing me were 'Oh. You.'

He subscribed to the inbred yokel theory and so was someone who had a low enough opinion of my morals to assume that my contact with Ben, and just about every other male I ever met, was sexual.

'Please, sir. I didn't know who to talk to,' I said with wide eyes. If I could have managed to make them water, I would have done.

I handed over the clutched, slightly folded paperwork. I was happy that I looked distressed and that the printed out emails showed they'd borne the brunt of my nervousness while waiting. He gave the top printout a cursory read through, read it again with more interest then looked at me with his brows pulled together.

I crossed my legs as if I were in desperate need of the toilet and wriggled slightly in my seat. I didn't have to pretend enough embarrassment to look away. I knew he would assume that Ben was pimping me out over the Internet to men who liked it rough. It wasn't much of a logical leap as he'd already assumed I was up to something naughty in the supermarket store-room with the man who got squashed.

'Well,' he said slowly, 'Boys will be boys.'

I tried not to grind my teeth. I had hoped for this, after all.

'I'll contact Mr Lloyd's guardians and have a word.'

The policeman put the printouts to one side. He didn't ask if I wanted to pursue the matter or for any further details. On the plus side, he didn't ask for any further details and end up discovering that Ben kept sending me men to kill. So, I won. I think equality and fairness — not to mention official procedure — took a major hit, though.

The real problem, of course, wasn't so much that my local police station still operated to standards as old as the harvester I should have been using. This was arguably a good thing, particularly if you go for all the nostalgia trips on TV. The real problem was that I didn't like being treated like some country bumpkin from the Welsh equivalent of Deliverance and I was starting to realise I'd never be treated as anything else. There was no escape.

It was a worse feeling than knowing there was someone out there trying to kill me. Even if the policeman put the wheels in motion, even if the next attacking werewolf was stopped, there was still Ben — who had never seemed to single me out as a target before he'd changed — thinking I was a worthwhile target.

Of course, the policeman didn't get to Ben in time to stop one last werewolf. I found that out when an expensive car pulled up on the road alongside one of my hay fields. I just knew, looking at that car, that it couldn't be anything else. Why else would that kind of quality vehicle come to, let alone stop in, this area?

Anyway, he parked up on the road and got out to watch me drive up and down the field I was cutting. I watched back.

When I got near enough, I raised a hand and called '*Helô*'. He waved back.

Nearer, at the end of my row and about to turn round, I gave in to naivety and asked, 'Why?'

He shrugged. 'I hear you're hard to kill.'

Stood there with slicked back hair, with his suit, with a briefcase near to hand, the words 'it's nothing personal' were implied. It didn't make the whole thing any more palatable.

In case you think I killed a complete stranger, I'd like to point out that I didn't do anything to him, then. I fired off a text to Dave and just kept on doing my job, driving up and down with the contours of the field. And watched the were-wolf, of course.

He put the briefcase on the car bonnet but I was going in the other direction when he must have taken the fur-skin out and put it on. Fido was charging down the field at me by the time I was coming back up. See? He wasn't just an innocent stranger, after all.

There wasn't much I could do but play chicken. Tractors are slow at the best of times and if I wanted a decent cut I could only keep to jogging speed, say seven or eight miles an hour tops. In other words, I was playing chicken when it was easier for the other man to win because he was smaller, faster and more manoeuvrable than the antique I was sat on. Not to mention I could be knocked off.

The werewolf leapt to come over the top of the engine and I ducked, swinging to one side. I ended up in a position you only see on horseback, in cowboy films, being held up by one foot on a foot rest with one leg over the seat and the rest of my body trying not to fall off the side. Something about the way I flailed around trying to keep my balance meant I ended up kicking the werewolf, though I doubt it had that much affect on his route over the tractor. He just hadn't thought I'd duck and had judged his leap with the assumption that someone would be in between him and the business end of the harvester I hauled behind me.

Well, what can I say? I expect removal of a limb usually involves severing an artery — leading to bleeding to death — would work quite well. Beheading is an old favourite of various mythologies and no doubt works if you have something sharp to try it with. As it took a few cuts to behead people with their head on a block, I don't recommend trying it with a moving target. But, all in all, I'd say throwing someone into a harvester is just overkill.

Dave and I barely found enough of Fido to make hiding the remains worthwhile. The damage to the delicate old harvester's internal mechanisms added an extra couple of days to my work and I spent an uncomfortable winter giving the sheep and cattle sideways glances as I fed them, wondering if they could develop a taste for human blood with what was mixed in with the hay.

His fancy car joined the lawyer's. One day maybe I'd figure out a way to put them back on the road and make some money out of them. As things were, they had to stay in the hiding place, away from farms and people and the DVLA.

The whole thing was nothing more than an aside, of no interest in itself. The main event was the stunning lack of communication from Ben. There was no email after this twelfth embodiment of guilt and when I sent a blank email to his account it was bounced, the 'WolfWarrior' address no longer recognised. Ben had been shut down. Score one for old-fashioned policing.

'He's gone,' I told Dave.

Dave, caught up in whatever other subject he had developed interest in, had no idea what I was talking about. 'Who?'

'Ben. He's offline.'

Dave looked around, making sure there was no-one around to overhear words that might imply guilt or responsibility. 'Dead?'

'Don't know. Don't care. Did your friend find him, yet?'

Dave, I might add, hadn't had to work full-time on the farm like me this year. In the past, we'd both given time over to his dad during the holidays but only for a few hours a day as children do. Now I was his dad's employee and Dave didn't have to put any time into the farm unless he wanted to.

'I haven't heard,' he answered.

He didn't seem too upset that his big plan had been cut-out so effectively. I never bothered to tell him it was because I'd seen an opportunity to get around it.

'Might as well call them off,' I said.

Dave frowned. 'No.'

'We don't need to find Ben,' I said, 'He's been called off.'

'He's still a werewolf.'

'He's not a threat.'

Dave was unimpressed with my apparent pacifism. 'He's still a monster!'

He stormed off before I could summon a response and that was the end of that conversation.

Intermission

I was right in my earlier assumption. Dave had given up on the wildlife and weaponry in our year of avoidance. Arguably, he'd given up on the idea of survival if his response to the last couple of deaths was anything to go by. I guess it's a stage all boys and tom-boys go through and most of them have an opportunity to leave it behind. I now knew my combat days were over but I couldn't quite bring myself to relax into it like Dave. Still, I did my best once we realised the bite had healed and wasn't going to affect me anymore.

We made up, in a fashion. Dave has always been a researcher at heart and I got to be his partner in reading up about law and psychology and biology, his three A-Level courses. I was starting to realise it was the only way I'd ever learn anything beyond GCSE level.

Occasionally, we had a change of subject matter to Dave's collection of romance novels, discovering that page fifty-nine was as interesting to perform as to read. Dave's parents turned a blind eye, and the occasional deaf ear, but Mum wasn't very happy.

'Do you want to end up trapped here?' she hissed at me repeatedly.

She didn't see that I already was. Once I was over eighteen, I'd not be able to finance further education. The opportunity to leave this life behind probably wouldn't come up until Dave's dad was ready to retire. This was assuming he managed to persuade his extended family of cousins that they all wanted to sell, or at least buy him out. Then I'd just be out of a job because I wouldn't be able to buy in.

So eventually I snapped back, 'If you feel like that, you can always leave.'

I was a bit surprised when she took the advice I hadn't meant to give, and ran with it. It took her a fortnight and several hushed conversations with Dave's parents but she got another full-time job in Sweet. She found a small one bed-room place there, too.

'Why are you leaving me?' I asked as I helped her pack her bags.

She paused and looked at me. There was more than the annoyance at my apparent choice, the pit of despair I was digging for myself. She was sad and struggling out of her own pit of despair that I'd never noticed before.

'I'm not,' she said simply. 'You don't need me anymore and I can't stay here.'

It wasn't that she was overtly angry with me. There was no 'and never darken my door again', no arguments and very few uncomfortable silences. She just got on with her life and let me get on with mine. But I knew come the next September, the start of the next academic year, that Dave would also be leaving the house and that would effectively be me on my own.

At least I didn't have to face off against werewolves any-more but, if I'm honest, I missed the sense of purpose it gave me. I also resented the way it had left me without choices. If I hadn't been distracted by the Lloyds, I'd have got my GCSEs the first time around and I'd have been at college with Dave. I'd have looked at university prospectuses with a view to going myself, not watching Dave leave me behind.

So, June comes along and I'm snappish and scared, not sure where things are going for me but knowing that every-one else's life — at least everyone I cared about — is, or will be, carrying on fine without me. And then comes a particu-lar evening when I'm lying in bed, trying to hold on to the post-coital glow as we spooned.

'We found him,' he whispered in my ear.

It was probably some weird sense of self-preservation, or just self-serving, that had made him keep it to himself until we were lying in a single bed and I hadn't enough leverage to hit out. Of course I knew what he was talking about without asking. My life was so small with so few people in it that I couldn't *not* know.

'Where?'

I also whispered. I even managed not to grip Dave's hands although he felt me stiffen. It was enough to get him out of bed and flouncing. I probably should have seen a big exit coming on when we'd ended up in my room, not his.

'You could at least pretend you don't care so much about him.'

'Care?'

I threw one of the pillows at the door and grabbed the second ready to aim for Dave. He had stopped, knowing the next shot would be for him — and that it would land squarely where I wanted it to.

'I don't *care* about the person who tried to kill me,' I said, 'I just want to make sure he can't try again.'

'So you want to kill him?'

'I never said that.'

I think I'll cut the conversation there before I bore you completely. We managed to repeat variations of those two sentences — which were really 'So I'm right?' and 'No', if you didn't work it out — for a couple of days. After those two days, Dave didn't so much cave in as return to the original subject when he took me to the hospital that held Ben.

I say 'hospital'. The sign on the outside of the building actually said 'long-term care facility'. I'm not entirely sure what the difference is. All I know is that was one of those places that used to be someone's home in the days when the household included maybe an army of servants. The old estate wasn't what it used to be but there was plenty of uncut lawn around. Guess the health trust couldn't afford the upkeep.

'Here?' I asked.

The longer I stood and looked at the former stately pile, the more cracks I could see in the render. It looked as if some of the more ornate carving had either worn away or been broken off at some point, too.

Dave shrugged at me. 'This is the address I was given.'

'I'll go ask about Ben.'

'Where?'

I think he was just busy taking in the building in front of us and the other, smaller buildings across the lawns. He didn't mean to sound like an idiot.

'The reception.'

There were the usual NHS signs pointing the way and I followed. Dave didn't move and I left him behind without even a backward glance.

'Excuse me?'

Of course, it wasn't really any better inside. It didn't help that I turned up in my grubby work jeans and t-shirt but with equally grubby, worn trainers instead of my rigger boots.

'Yes?' The receptionist managed to lose her joy at life with the sight of me. She'd been smiling right up until she started speaking to me. 'How can I help you?'

She made it sound like I was beyond help. So much for originality.

'I'm looking for a friend of mine. He — He was taken into custody a couple of years ago.'

Her eyebrows rose. 'It takes you a couple of years to find your friends?'

I wanted to say 'When we're both legally minors, he has no surviving family in the area and I'm busy working so I can keep a roof over my head? Yes.' I settled for, 'We weren't that close. But I have some news for him.'

'So who is the lucky young man?'

'Ben Lloyd.' She looked at me as if I'd grown an extra head and I corrected myself, 'Benjamin Lloyd.'

She didn't even twitch. She just kept looking at me. It was that carefully schooled, smug superiority look, otherwise I might have worked out whether this was a good silence or a bad silence.

'Could I leave a message for him or something if I'm not allowed to see him?'

'I'm not a messenger service,' she said, her voice becoming clipped with outrage not just disapproval.

'That wasn't exactly what I meant.'

The eyebrows lowered into a frown, a scowl that would have put the fear of the Deity into anyone who hadn't already faced down something scarier than a receptionist. 'That's what you said.'

'Not exactly,' I said trying to stay as mild and toneless as possible. Unlike a werewolf, I wasn't allowed to kill this one if she attacked me. At the very least I'd have problems dragging the body to a hiding place from somewhere so public.

She seemed a little disconcerted that I didn't apologise, her superior look starting to show a sliver of something else. Let's call it uncertainty.

'Please,' I said, pushing the possible advantage, 'I just need to let him know about something that happened. If I could see him, or write him a note, or something.'

The receptionist smiled. She'd found a solution to her problem and I had a feeling I wasn't going to like it. When she realised I'd seen her moment of realisation, she hid it by fiddling for a moment with the computer in front of her. The expression flickered as she looked at whatever she pulled up on the screen.

'Please,' I tried again, 'It's important.'

'I'm not allowed to give unauthorised visitors access to patients,' she said crisply.

'Please,' I said for the third and last time.

She smiled again at the computer screen and then raised her eyes to look at me. 'There is no Benjamin Lloyd here.'

'But he used to be?'

'I'm not allowed to give out patient information to — '

'Unauthorised visitors. I get the idea.'

I put my hands in my pockets and walked out of the reception. Somehow, a single beam of sunlight on this grey day had broken out to shine on the hospital in total opposition to the way I felt. Mum had left me to get on with her own life, Dave would soon be following, and somewhere out there was a werewolf called Ben. But at least the attacks were over.

Great.

Method 13: Broken Nose

About four years later, long after I thought the werewolves were gone from my life and I'd accepted that I was stuck here in the middle of Welsh nowhere, Dave invited me along with his parents to his graduation. He'd even given me a ticket to the graduation ball. *Ah*, I thought when I tore open the neatly written envelope and hold the little strips of paper in my hand, *maybe he's not leaving me behind. Maybe he wants me to come with him.*

Except there was a girlfriend. Or should I say 'another girlfriend'?

It was supposed to be just me. That's all we knew about. I say 'we' because I was living with Dave's family. They can't have not heard me and Dave, any more than I don't hear them. We're very good at giving each other privacy by ignoring things we aren't supposed to see and hear but it doesn't mean we're actually blind, or deaf, or stupid.

So, Dave's parents and I were sitting in the crowd watching the line of undergraduates snake up to the university's Chancellor, gravely shake his hand and become graduates. There were two in the line that are now important to us. The still skinny but not quite as fit as he used to be Dave and his petite, fair and hyper-feminine girlfriend. I smiled and clapped at the appropriate moments. I wasn't sure that the girlfriend didn't know that I, the tall, muscular farm-hand in the second-hand dress, was the 'other woman'.

'I can't believe,' Dave's mum whispered to me, in Welsh so we were less likely to be understood by the others around us. She couldn't actually finish off what she didn't believe, though. It wasn't necessary.

'Well,' I said, inanely and also in Welsh, 'We were always friends first.'

She gave me an unconvinced look as she brushed my fringe out of my eyes. It wasn't the first time she'd ever made the gesture but it was at Dave's graduation that it made me realise just how strange it was, as if I had been exchanged for Dave. He didn't come back to the farm often in those days. It was no longer his home. He'd escaped. I'd been caught in the poverty trap and lived with parents that weren't my own, taking on family commitments that should have been his.

'It's my own fault,' I added.

I should have asked about girlfriends any of the handful of times Dave had made it back from London. I should have asked if he'd met anyone else but I didn't want to know the answer. Sometimes I'd imagined I could even smell other girls on him, like a werewolf might have done.

Dave's dad growled, though he'd seemed happy enough with her when we'd been introduced. He'd shook her hand as if it was a delicate flower. 'He shouldn't need to be asked.'

We now knew Dave'd been with this girl for the last two years. He'd never brought her home. I guess that puts him firmly in the 'bastard' camp. It definitely put me in the 'desperate to hold on to the man in my life' camp. At least, the person I'd been before meeting his chosen partner.

'He's an idiot,' his mum said.

'He's about to graduate,' I said and nodded towards the stage.

Then I saw the werewolf. He was in a suit, sat nearer the front and clutching a briefcase. If he'd been an actual wolf I could have said 'his ears pricked up' when he heard Dave's name without it being a clichéd analogy. It was the movement as he leant forward in his seat to catch a glimpse of Dave that caught my eye. It was the tight grasp on his briefcase that screamed 'werewolf' at me. It was the way he then cast a look around the hall that made me realise he wasn't here for Dave.

'Ben.'

A hissed whisper from the other side of me. 'Pardon?'

It was the mother sat on the other side of me that looked at me. I'd growled the name without meaning to.

'Sorry,' I whispered back, in English, 'Thought I saw someone else I recognised.'

She turned away from me, satisfied I wasn't going to ruin her precious child's graduation after all. This didn't stop all the thoughts whirling around in my brain.

The werewolf was hunting someone specific, someone he'd never met if he was perking up at the mention of names at a graduation ceremony. If the name was Dave's — and it was — but he wasn't focussed on Dave as a person, then he was after someone here for Dave's graduation. That could only be me.

Ben had to have done it again. It had taken four years but he'd got Internet access again. He'd traced Dave — not hard when his name and face was splattered all over the university's website as a soon-to-be-graduate — and assumed I'd be nearby. At least the werewolf had more brains than to attack in the middle of a crowded ceremony.

I watched Dave shake hands with the Chancellor and receive his certificate. Actually, the Chancellor handed him a piece of white plastic pipe with a ribbon for photographic purposes. The certificate was in an envelope back in Dave's place and therefore staying pristine. I'd already seen it during the brief introductions with the girlfriend. I'd also seen hers.

Then Dave, totally unaware of the hunter in the crowd, walked down the steps, posed for the official photograph and exchanged hugs with his waiting, equally proud girlfriend. He was a Williams and she was something beginning with K that now escapes me. They'd studied the same subject, psychology, so she'd been through the process about fifteen minutes before him. They held hands as they walked down the aisle of the great hall and through the doors. The audience wasn't allowed out until the current line had finished.

I considered telling Dave there was another werewolf after us but didn't. It was a lie because the werewolves Ben sent were never really after Dave. I was never sure why as it was Dave that tried to kill Ben, not me. Also, I haven't worked out a reliable hand signal for 'werewolf' or a way of discussing them in front of several hundred or so people without making me seem insane. Much better, I decided, to not be associated at all with this man-in-suit-with-briefcase so that when they find his body they can't trace his death back to me.

It doesn't help that the possibility of telling Dave didn't really happen. There wasn't much time outside, and it was only marginally less crowded than being indoors. So it was only freedom relative to being inside, and was given over pretty quickly to get into the next building. We were herded in to a foyer where we were handed drinks and were expected to congratulate the newly minted graduates. I'm not entirely sure how townies cope and I don't suppose I make much sense.

Anyway, while making all the right noises in the direction of the happy couple and keeping a smile plastered on my face, I kept an eye on where the new werewolf went to. He was focussed on us in just as discreet a manner. He didn't so much watch us as hover in line of sight, careful not to be associated with the group. He talked to a few people — he looked like he was asking after someone but as no-one ever pointed him in our direction, I guess it was a fictional 'friend'. A good cover story.

'Dave,' I said, 'How about you introduce me to some of your other university friends. I'm sure...'

I searched for the girlfriend's name and failed to come up with it. I looked at her, trying to telegraph for some help. She let her smile slip just enough for me to know that all she wanted to do was get rid of me.

'Actually, that's a good idea. Run along and see some of the boys, babe. I'll entertain the rents.'

"Rents'?' I echoed as Dave hauled me away.

'She means 'parents'.'

I laughed. 'I know what she means. I just think it sounds bloody stupid.'

Dave glowered at me.

'And she knows, Dave, so you better get used to her hating my guts. And maybe never come home again.'

'It's not that bad,' he protested.

He was about to lead me off in another direction but I pushed back. *No, I want that direction*, I all but said to him.

'Not for you if she'd rather hate me than you for your

being a cheating arse, no. And as you don't really like coming home, either, it's probably all win-win for you.'

'It wasn't like that,' he protested and then stopped in front of a small group of boys.

Young men would be stretching the truth as I seriously doubt any of them even knew how to fend for themselves in a kitchen, let alone the rest of life.

'Not like what, Dave?' one of them had the good sense to ask.

'Hi,' I said as enthusiastically and loudly as I could manage without sounding deranged, 'I'm Elkie Bernstein. I grew up with Dave.'

I projected to the werewolf but it was the curious boy's hand that I grabbed and shook to complete the introduction. It was soft and smooth, in total contrast to my own work-roughened paw. The boy recoiled from me, as did his friends, as if I had 'plague victim' tattooed across my forehead.

'Nice to meet you, Elkie.'

That was pretty much all the others said to me and it left me wondering just how much of the world I was going to be cut off from in the life I'd ended up in. It's not like I didn't try to keep up or didn't have a cupboard full of cosmetics and such. The longer I was here, the more obvious it became why *I* was the other woman and not the girlfriend.

On the positive side, the werewolf had again tensed, recognising my name, and the boys' lack of interest in my company meant I'd be able to disappear soon. I managed about a minute of standing around in the awkward silence before I left. I was happier going to face my hunter than staying to face Dave and company for any longer. I excused myself for 'the call of nature' and followed the signs down a side corridor.

As it was the wrong call and fairly unnatural — there's nothing normal about werewolves — I walked straight past the toilets and carried on exploring corridors until I was well away from the graduation bun-fight. It was important to avoid being disturbed or being associated with the man who would surely be following me through the building. The fact that he could do it by smell was an advantage as I didn't have to keep in charging range to lead him around and no-one would see us together. I even checked for CCTV cameras and was happy that there was nothing to link me to the werewolf following me.

When I was confident I was well out of the way, I turned and waited. That's when I realised just how crap my plan was. I had no weapons, nowhere to hide and I was about to face off with an attacker that had probably had time to fur up by now. I didn't even have a nail file.

'Oh, sh — '

But then there wasn't time for thought or even much fear. The werewolf came round the corner and launched at me. I ducked, spun as fast as I could and turned to face it yet again. I may not be as strong or as fast as one but there's no way I'll willingly turn my back and accept the inevitable.

'Why the fuck do you people keep doing this to me?'

Fido said nothing, although I think I got a grin for my stupidity. Furred up werewolves can't speak from what I've seen, which is a shame because I could have done with a few bits of information like: Where is Ben? How does he get so many werewolves to come after me? Are you all so convinced that killing me will give you some kind of status? How come there seem to be so many of you? Why are you stupid enough to think that being a werewolf is a good thing? The usual questions, really.

I ducked the next attack and spun to face it again. Only I put my foot wrong — I was wearing heels rather than the flat rigger boots I'm used to — and face-planted instead. It ended up in an undignified scramble to my feet but at least I hadn't been in the way of the werewolf's leap.

I lashed out without really thinking, just putting all of my weight behind it, and made contact. With its nose.

'Ow! Dammit!'

The pain of actually making contact, and badly, had me shaking out my hand and hoping my fingers weren't broken. On the receiving end, the werewolf was clutching its nose in both hands — paws? — and whimpering. See, contrary to popular belief, you can't die of a broken nose. However,

122

it's painful and a good distraction technique. So, technically, it was the distraction that caused the death. That and the repeated blows to the head that followed.

He whimpered and clutched and never got the chance to fight back because of that first shock. I backhanded with the same hand, making him spin into the wall, then I punched him in the stomach. He slid slowly down to the ground, still whimpering, and there was a slug trail of snot, spit and blood on the wall. I kicked repeatedly, scuffing the leather of my new-to-me shoes and spattering blood spots all over them and the corridor.

When he changed back into a badly beaten, badly dressed man, I ran to the nearest toilets to clean myself up. I hadn't got any obvious blood on my clothes but my shoes were pretty messed up. My hands were sore but nothing that was obvious. I could feel the grazes on my knuckles from the first punch but no-one else would be able to see them. I could have done with a jar of chocolate spread but settled for a sip or two of cold water.

Then, having pulled myself together, I found my way back to the party to hear Dave and the girlfriend extolling their map of the future to their parents. She was going into the family business as a trainee manager while he was going to stay and do more psychology schooling.

'You've chosen a specialisation, of course,' the smug father of the girlfriend said.

Dave nodded. 'Clinical lycanthropy.'

I found myself smiling into a drink. I guess Ben and the werewolves left a large and obvious mark on Dave after all. Even if the werewolves came after me and not him.

'That's people who think they're werewolves, right?' I asked.

Dave glared but his girlfriend's smile was condescending. 'I didn't expect a... lay person... to have such a good understanding of psychological terms.'

'I've read the term somewhere, and some things stay in the brain more easily than others.'

'Oh,' the girlfriend said, 'You read paranormal romance, then?'

She asked in a tone that suggested that being able to read wasn't a skill she expected me to have — and, if I did, it was bound to be something low brow like tabloid newspapers and pulp fiction.

'I think you're thinking of urban fantasy, and not really. It doesn't really make its way to our library. I actually picked it up from a computer game,' I lied. I savoured the look on Dave's face. I guess he remembered Ben and his obsession with playing games on his console. 'Anyway, we're discussing Dave's career.'

'So, Elkie. What do you want do?' the girlfriend's mum asked me.

Dammit.

'I work on the Williams' farm. I've just finished my first year of part-time study in agriculture. I also volunteer with the local mountain rescue. I don't really need any more.'

Look at me, I thought, *I do real things that matter. I have a barely paying job that produces someone else's lamb and beef while rescuing idiots who don't know not to go up hills in t-shirts and shorts in my spare time. I am definitely not sitting around waiting for my sort-of friend, sort-of lover to come home to somewhere he wants to escape from. And I don't have time to chase him.*

'Oh,' said the girlfriend's mum, unimpressed but too polite to say so.

Method 14: Fall From Height

I managed to stand around and make small talk until the body was discovered. I managed to look the police officers in the eye and say, with total honesty, that I had no idea who the man they found was. Then the 'rents' left so the younger generation could go to the graduation ball with clear consciences.

I drank too much, danced like an idiot and pulled someone I'd never met before, and hope to never meet again. I'm not sure I'd recognise him even if I did. His only notable feature, as far as I'm concerned, was that he wasn't Dave.

Twenty-four hours after meeting Dave's real girlfriend, I finally made it back to North Wales. It had been a train trip, so I didn't have to go hugely out of my way to call in on Mum, in Sweet, but the way I was feeling I would have driven across the whole UK just to see her. Partly because I felt the need to apologise to her for being so close to Dave's family.

'Hey, Mum.'

She smiled but didn't seem to notice my stress the way I was hoping. Two words in and the conversation was already well off my plan.

'Hello, Elkie. How was Dave's graduation.'

'OK.' I should have told the truth: bloody awful.

She stepped aside so I could step into the minuscule flat. 'Good. Cup of tea?'

And that was as close to comfort as I got that day. She didn't even brush my fringe out of my eyes.

It was several days before I allowed myself time in Llareggub to check my email. I didn't want to read the message I knew would be waiting.

'The game's back on. So how did my best girl do on her latest mission?'

It was another webmail address, a 'WolfPrince' that told me nothing. I forwarded it to Dave — one of the few reasons I would bother to contact him after the farce at his graduation — with an added 'Still know people who can track down email locations?'

Then I emailed Ben back.

'Where are you? Why are you doing this? What do you think you're doing?'

Not that I expected an answer to my questions, or even sense. After that... Well, after that I got on with my life and waited for the next attack. It's important to stay as calm as you can force yourself to. Practice denial of reality, if necessary. Things aren't always as bad as you fear.

As Ben had sent the last werewolf to Dave's graduation, I inferred he wasn't sure what had happened to me or Dave and had tracked us down on the Internet. Dave's name and photo were splashed all over his university's website with the graduation and I don't suppose it took a genius to track him down using a search engine. There was nothing to say that the werewolf would come here. Right at that moment in time, I wasn't especially bothered if the next werewolf chased Dave and ate him, either.

Not that it would. They all seemed obsessively focussed, and unfortunately on me. I still wonder what line Ben fed them to make them so determined to get me specifically. If you're going to go on a killing spree, it isn't necessary to hunt down one particular woman.

'I've changed my mind,' I sent to Ben about two days later — a lot sooner than I would ordinarily have been back in Llareggub — 'I just want to know where you keep finding all these strays.'

I sent the email before checking whether he'd replied to the last one, although it had taken a huge amount of control not to. It turned out he hadn't, though, and my urge to constantly refresh the inbox didn't make a response appear any faster.

There was an email from Dave. A short sharp 'come stay' that I doubt his girlfriend knew about.

'No,' I said to the screen and didn't bother typing.

I was at home in the hills. I could hide bodies where no-one else would find them. In London, I was more likely to have to explain my mounting body count. How many deaths does it take before you're officially a serial killer?

It took another four days for Ben to send me an email back — while I didn't check my inbox as often as that, I could read the time-stamp.

'You still out in the wilds, Elkie? Where do I send the next one to? Oh, and they were on a two for one offer.'

'Two for one?' I screeched, 'Don't send two. Don't send two!'

I got a look that's best described as 'funny' from everyone in the building. I ignored them and a second 'come stay' from Dave.

I did strongly hint at Dave's parents that we should maybe get an Internet connection when I got back in. Well, I yelled something about having to do a thirty mile round trip just to read one-liners from their good for nothing son.

'We'd still be missing a computer,' Dave's dad said, probably just as his son would have done, and put me on the receiving end of another 'funny' look.

'A minor point.'

'He's taken.'

'He was taken before he went to university. I'm not the one who's done anything wrong.'

Dave's dad shrugged and I got on with my work.

For what it's worth, that's as in-depth as Dave's family and I ever got on the matter. I hadn't done anything wrong. I knew, we all probably knew, that with him staying away so long between visits that it was unlikely there weren't other women. It's just that he never said, never made it clear that the other people — or, rather, that the other person was the important one. While I wasn't too bothered about him not being mine, it kind of stung my pride that I wasn't his.

Stung pride got me through working and living while I waited to see if Ben sent two werewolves at the same time.

That and reminding myself he still didn't know where I was. Receiving 'Answer me! Where the hell are you?' underscored that fact nicely and gave me my first real smile in a fortnight. I didn't reply, of course. I considered deleting the email account — starting again under a new username and letting Ben's messages bounce around in the ether without me. I didn't do that, either.

What I did do was go to the training session for the rescue team. In order to be able to scramble around the hills and all the other things we do, we have to practice and practice as a team. Oddly enough, we get to do things that office-bound people pay a fortune for, either to unwind with or as team-building exercises. Far as I'm concerned the team building is what we do in the pub afterwards but the climbing and such are skills we need if we're going to help others.

It had occurred to me that being stuck in a climbing harness halfway up a rock face with my fellow volunteers was a bad place to meet a werewolf, if only because I'd have difficulty explaining myself. Well, assuming I survived and so did my colleagues. I was grateful that it didn't happen.

Instead, I gave in to a different kind of wolf who goes by the name of Mike and agreed to go climbing with him, one of those casual not-dates that could end up being so much more entertaining. As long as I didn't take him back to the farm or end up making explanations to Dave's outraged parents. Even given the circumstances, they wouldn't have appreciated me replacing their son quite so easily. Obviously, they also didn't know about the boy at the graduation ball.

It wasn't the first time Mike had asked and I'd turned him down more because I didn't fancy explaining Dave, should it have been necessary, than any particular lack of interest on my part. I still shouldn't have because, despite his cooler-than-thou attitude, he was nothing more than cannon fodder should a bigger wolf turn up.

And yes, it was actually while I was half-way up a rock face with a harness with my big, bad wannabe wolf scrambling somewhere below me that the almost real thing turned up. It was just as I'd pictured it during the training session. It didn't bode well, if only because it meant Ben had decided to try the old address anyway.

So, before the attack, on my rock climbing date, alone with Mike.

'You're doing pretty good for someone who only started rock-climbing this year,' he called up.

We weren't doing the belaying bit, so he was on the same climb maybe a couple of metres below and to the side of me. It's a regular climb, so there are rings embedded in the rock face and you hook your harness to them as you progress. I was a little disturbed that he seemed to be enjoying the view of my bum. Other than that, things were going quite well.

'It isn't exactly rocket science,' I said, brushing off his compliment.

'You're certainly fit enough for it.' Mike laughed from below and I tried not to grind my teeth. He might as well have patted me on the head and that did not bode well on the dating front.

It only took a glance to see I was properly attached and I had the rope to get away with it. I dropped the couple of metres to look Mike in the eye. He clung to the rock face with wide open eyes and wide open mouth. What can I say? Facing off against werewolves has made me pretty confident about my physical skill provided I know the odds are stacked in my favour.

'Please,' I said into his goldfish impression, 'Tell me that line doesn't work. Restore my faith in womankind.'

He blinked.

'What? Not used to being out-cooled?' I prodded.

The dazed look cleared into an impish grin. 'It's not a line.'

I shrugged and climbed steadily back to the point I'd dropped from.

'And it works!' he called after me.

'Bollocks!' I called back.

I got to the top of the rock face and looked down at Mike before hauling myself up on to the ground level. It might not be the hardest climb in the world but when you do things like this, you need to have your full focus on what you're doing. One mistake can forcibly remind you that gravity is king. So

I tapped a harness hook against one of the embedded loops to make a noise that would attract Mike's attention. He stopped when he had four points of contact with the rock face and looked up at me with a grin.

'I'm going over the top.'

'Watch out for the enemy,' he quipped. Then, 'I'll be right with you.'

He might have been joking but the unease his words triggered was enough for me to take my time getting up to ground-level. I looked over the edge and checked out the terrain first. I probably would have done that anyway, old habits are hard to get over, I'd just not have taken quite so long about it if I hadn't heard from Ben or if Mike hadn't unintentionally remind me I was a sitting duck.

Because I took my time, I saw the nose poking out from behind some rocks, the glint of eyes just behind. If I squinted, I could make out paws in the grass. If I squinted, I could pretend it was an odd looking husky.

'Yeah,' I muttered, 'The enemy.'

I made a show out of pulling myself up on to the ground, aware that Mike would be wondering what was up if he had the concentration left over to notice what I was doing. I left the rope securely attached, though, and only crouched on the ground, otherwise the harness would have been pulling against me uncomfortably. I turned my back to the grey fur, doing my best to look like an inviting target — which I would have thought near impossible when crouching over a long drop.

Whatever else it was, the werewolf tackled like a rugby player. It shoulder charged me and I, having expected an attack if not exactly what happened, let gravity take me. It took me as far as my rope had play.

'Elkie!'

I bounced off the rock face — thinking *please don't scream, please don't scream* at the werewolf — then looked up at Mike and waved.

'Fine.' I pushed the words out with a diaphragm that didn't want to work. 'I'm fine.'

He was beside me in the time it took to get the words all out.

'What happened?'

Thankfully, he didn't look down to see what had pushed me off the cliff. I hadn't checked what condition the werewolf was in but I consciously put 'remove corpse' on the top of my to-do list. Just as soon as I'd got Mike somewhere else. I avoided looking down in case it made Mike follow my gaze and see the evidence.

'Dunno,' I said, 'What did it look like?'

I carefully restored my four points of contact — two hands, two feet, each one accompanied by a relieved sigh. I might be bruised but I could get to the top of the rock face and get on with life. Everything had happened pretty much as I expected from the second I'd seen grey fur in the grass.

'Like you played some damned stupid trick pretending to fall off the cliff-top,' Mike said.

I looked at him and raised my eyebrows. He hadn't seen a man-sized blur of grey? I wasn't sure if his continued ignorance was a good thing, or if he was just an idiot with no awareness of his surroundings and no ability for self-preservation at all. At least there were no other climbers about to point out what he'd missed.

'Did you?' he demanded.

I grinned to keep the doubt there. If I'd been clumsy up top, he'd want to know why. 'No. I slipped.'

'People who pull tricks like you did earlier don't slip,' he said, reading the grin rather than hearing the words.

I countered with 'People who are clumsy but like to do extreme sports have all the safety gear so sorted, it doesn't matter if they slip or they jump.'

I let the grin fade, so he'd know I was upset about not being believed. I wasn't sure if I was or I wasn't, though.

'That almost made sense, Bernstein,' he said as if he was receiving my own confusion.

I bit back on a bubble of laughter as I started climbing for the top again. Mike followed me.

'But it's bollocks,' he added.

I had to stop climbing because I was laughing too hard to

control my movement. He would have been a fun time but he wouldn't have been able to keep up with my games, let alone Ben's. I was just going to have to stick with chocolate spread, and maybe a new toy if I dared visit the right shop in Sweet.

Mike said, 'And we're never doing this again.'

I was surprised to find the idea hurt. It stopped me laughing. 'Oh?'

'That was the stupidest thing I've ever seen.'

My eyebrows rose again, although the expression was wasted with us not looking at each other. He was young, male and still convinced he was the coolest thing on the planet. He had to have done worse things.

'I can't do with people who take stupid risks,' he said, as if repeating the word 'stupid' somehow clarified his position.

Method 15: Drowning

Of course, Ben had sent me an email, time stamped for about the same time I was putting on the climbing harness for the original training session.

'I'm going to assume you're still living down the lane as the last guy didn't get back to me. He must have found you. New mission started.'

That was when I realised that Ben hadn't received any information from his strays; and he hadn't actually been getting anything back from me but textual whimpering.

He had no idea the cottage had been gutted in a fire or that I was living with Dave's family. He might have taken an educated guess that Dave and I had ended up sleeping with each other but he had no idea if there was a relationship beyond our original friendship and what tense could be applied to it. Ben wouldn't know anything about how life had continued, with or without his interference.

The upside was, I now knew where I was most likely to be seen by the next werewolf. Ben would send them to the lane and my attacker would scope out — or perhaps that should be scent out — the target, me. After that, it would be up to the individual werewolf whether they took me there or decided on trailing me to another, possibly better situation. If the werewolf in question engaged brain, attacking me right on the lane was highly unlikely but I'd be able to scout the lane and the fields next to it for signs of their passage regardless. I could be more prepared for the next one.

'I figured,' I sent back, 'Mission completed.'

So, when are you going to send the next? I thought but didn't type out.

When Old Man Lloyd had been using Ben to make more werewolves, they'd come about every two weeks — which I'd later realised was the period of time it takes for a man to become a werewolf following a bite. That meant Old Man Lloyd had been looking after the men he'd sold Ben's bite to. I'll bet his prices reflected the two weeks care.

When Ben was in the nearer hospital, they'd arrived with roughly the same regularity. I'm not sure whether that was because he was somehow getting away with making them in the hospital — presumably out of members of staff allowed to leave the premises, if he was — or whether he had contacted them through the Internet. The idea of there being an online community of these idiots chilled my blood as much as the possibility that Ben was so poorly housed he could go round creating more.

Anyway, I went back to the farm. I carried on with my life, with allowance for checking the lane and the land around it. I checked maybe three times a day but varied the times as much as I could so it didn't become a routine and therefore a weakness to be exploited.

Most days, I didn't find anything of interest. I certainly didn't see anything that screamed 'unknown human', let alone 'werewolf', although I saw more of the local wildlife than I had since Dave and I used to run around stalking it. As it was a whole four weeks between the climbing incident and the next attack, I guess Ben didn't have an endless supply of mission fodder, after all.

I found a couple of footprints and a cigarette butt near the cottage. The easiest interpretation was that someone had been down the lane in a vehicle and had got out to look at the ruin that used to be my home. No-one local would do that and I wasn't expecting a visit from someone else. Seeing as I worked for and lived with the people who owned the shell, I could discount it being a legitimate visitor I hadn't been told about.

I hadn't seen or heard a car but then I hadn't been working near the lane. I just knew the footprints — huge marks that promised a large attacker — and the cigarette remains hadn't been there when I checked the area a few hours ago. I wandered away, trying to look as if I hadn't seen anything in case the werewolf had come back and watched from a different location.

I didn't get jumped on. I went unmolested long enough to check my emails again on my usual day in the library.

'What happened to the cottage? Where are you staying now?' Ben had sent.

This one had reported back to Ben, then. I wasn't sure what to take from that. Did this mean it was incapable of making decisions? Or that it was more organised and more likely to get the job done?

'It burnt down over four years ago,' I sent back.

I ignored Ben's second question. He would already know I lived near to the cottage if the werewolves he sent after me could actually find me. Scent barely lingers for four days, let alone four years, and that's based on more sensitive canine noses, not my own. I have no idea how much a werewolf can actually make out.

I left the library with an itch between my shoulder blades. I was being watched, even if I had no idea where from, and it made me vulnerable. I had no control over the situation and Ben didn't exactly have a say in the matter, either, as he was... somewhere else. This werewolf could attack at any moment and now I knew it.

I have no doubt the werewolf knew it, too. The real question was whether my attacker-to-be cared if I knew. It got a little close to the 'he knows she knows he knows she knows' joke for me to bother thinking too hard but the main issue for me was whether a) Fido would feel a need to reveal he was stalking me — the pleasure of an intimidated prey — or b) whether he would take me on as quickly as he could, now his initial report to Ben was complete. The answer was 'a', although I get the impression that the timing didn't go to his plan, either.

He followed me, in human form, to another training session with the rescue team. He walked past innocently enough, looking every inch the rambler, except for two things. First, he made eye contact with me and held it all the way. Secondly, he walked straight through Mike — or tried to, anyway.

Mike was the same with me as he had been every other training, too much of a irredeemable flirt to ever actually give it up. While we both knew he had no intention of following through, he was still happy to touch when he possibly shouldn't. For whatever reason, either having seen Mike touch me or smelt Mike's scent on my clothes, the werewolf tried to dominate Mike.

'What the hell was that for?' Mike demanded.

The man, the werewolf, was big and powerful. He looked gym fit with that extra edge that says the muscle can actually do more than lift weights. The dark skin just made him stand out in pasty white North Wales and emphasised the muscle. I was tempted to growl or, possibly, howl after him myself. My motivation was somewhat different to Mike's, though.

Mike, an extreme sports junky, was lithe and slim. In comparison with the man who'd just jostled him, he looked like he could be broken in one bite — an idea reinforced by just how much ground he'd given up when the werewolf had shouldered him aside.

'It's not important, Mike,' I said as calmly as I could.

I watched the broad shoulders of my attacker-to-be rather than the team. I would lay money on this werewolf liking phrases such as 'You have to break a few eggs to make an omelette'. The point being that he would be willing, and probably capable of, taking down the whole team just to get me. I, on the other hand, preferred to keep them alive and ignorant of the existence of werewolves.

'What do you mean 'it's not important'?' Mike demanded, grand-standing in front of everyone.

'He's just a tourist,' I said, 'He'll be gone soon.'

Mike growled. 'He tried to walk straight through me!'

'Then he's an idiot.'

I walked away and the werewolf walked on, as if Mike's outburst had never happened. I could feel my attacker-to-be watching us and I could have pointed out where he was, but I didn't.

I think, but I can't be sure, that the werewolf was following the team with the intention of attacking during the next training session. The information he was gathering was about how we interacted together, who was weakest, who was the best target to take first. A sensible option, I guess. It would put him in a remote area where he was unlikely to be witnessed by anyone but his victims, and it would get him a pretty high body-count. Something about the muscle-bound menace said 'over-achiever' to me, in a strictly physical aggressive way.

Whatever the plan, it didn't work out that way. My team doesn't get called out all that often. We meet up to go through mocked up rescues and or a particular skill set, like the climbing last time, once a month. We maybe come out in full summer, basically during the school holidays, about once a fortnight when we have a large number of people wandering the footpaths. In winter, there are fewer call outs but they're usually more involved, due to lower temperatures and harsher weather. We don't all necessarily get out on a call, as we're volunteers. Our own lives can get in the way, no matter how willing we are. Try covering ten miles of country roads in ten minutes in a safe and legal manner, for example.

Anyway, the mobile went off while I was tending to animals with Dave's dad, which actually meant I was in a position to drop what I was doing and run.

The volunteer manning the phones said, 'Kids in a quarry lagoon.'

I had a moment of freezing cold — what if they saw? — then reminded myself it might not be the same quarry.

'I'll meet you at the quarry instead of headquarters,' I replied, 'It's faster.'

Whichever quarry they meant, I could guarantee I was as close as they already were. The volunteer confirmed the address and I almost sighed with relief. I drove as fast as I dared in what, for me if not the rescue, was not quite the right direction. My relief didn't last long. A black pick-up to appeared in my rear-view mirror and stayed there.

As it happened, my stalker and I got there before the team. I parked the farm Landie — Dave's dad insisted I use it for work in case I was called to a rescue — next to the police car and ran for the bottom of the disused hole in the landscape.

'Mountain rescue,' I said to the two police officers who were already dealing with three tearful teenagers, 'Ahead of the team and the equipment, though. What's happened?'

The tearful teenagers struggled to get out the words, while talking over each other, that made it clear there was a fourth in the copper-blue water of the lagoon. I resisted the urge to pace over to see if I could spot them. Without equipment, I could easily end up in as much trouble as the missing teen, if not more.

'I would've thought they'd send a chopper out,' said one of the police.

I shrugged. 'Maybe they will but we're quite a ways from the base it flies from so it'll be a while.'

'He's stranded on an island toward the deep end,' the other police officer said, indicating with a nod of his head.

I squinted and realised that one of the boulder like shapes was moving a little.

'Well, he can obviously swim if he got out there in the first place,' I said, wondering at the rather surreal excuse for a call out.

'He can't, though!' said one of the teens.

The first police officer nodded. 'Drifted out on a blow up something — '

'Whale,' another teen supplied.

'And it brushed up against the rocks, deflated and left him stranded?' I asked, eager to keep the conversation short.

I could see why no-one here had swum out after him. It had been a large quarry in its time and the lagoon was deep and wide, filling a significant chunk of the quarry bottom. I rang the call-centre.

'Elkie. Out on site,' I said to the operator, 'They've got the small boat with them, right?'

'Yes. Don't try swimming over.'

'I won't.'

Deep water in the bottom of quarries didn't get a lot of sunshine and rarely warmed up. Jumping in was a good way to give yourself a shock that might end up in getting you drowned. Which is why these kind of places have warning signs all over the bloody place. But the cool was also why teenagers routinely ignore those same signs on boiling hot summer days. We were just lucky there was a chance for the rescue team today, that the teenager hadn't just disappeared

138

in that deep water and now needed the police divers to find him.

'The full rescue team will be here soon with a boat,' I said to the teenagers, 'How about we go nearer the lagoon and let your friend know?'

We called out and the scared, wet not-a-boulder seemed to understand. The poor kid was probably shivering like mad but we weren't close enough, and couldn't get close enough under these conditions, for those kinds of small movements to be seen. We were doing our best to explain what was going on when the team arrived towing a boat trailer, holding a fibreglass hull and a small outboard motor.

I joined the team as they decanted from the vehicle and noted who was there and who wasn't (like Mike). The police moved the three safe teenagers out of the way while the team prepared our equipment. I tried to work out where the werewolf must be. Now would be a good time to attack with multiple kills available and no chance of being caught, unless the police managed to radio out our distress. I'd go for them first, if I were an insane, furry killer.

'I'll go out,' the most experienced of us on the call, the team-leader, said. Then he picked another team-member to go with him, leaving the rest of us to stand and watch.

I tried to keep away from the other groups. If we were spread out, we were harder targets or, at least, couldn't be taken all at once. I kept an eye on the little fibreglass boat's progress but was looking out for the werewolf at the same time. I didn't see him. Instead, I located him by the sudden impact to my back.

I hit the surface of the lagoon with no air in my lungs, already gasping for breath because of how he'd struck me. I tried desperately not to inhale any of the bright blue-green water — a legacy from the lagoon's more industrial past — and to grab hold of my attacker. I guess I'm grateful that the lagoon was so deep, otherwise the attack would have ended in a face-plant into shallow water and a rather ignominious death.

We rolled over in the water a few times, gasping breaths when our heads broke the water — the kind of thing that's exciting to watch and more like terrifying to take part in but unfortunately fairly boring to verbalise. I couldn't get away from him but he couldn't pin me down with a couple of metres of water beneath us. Fido was heavier than me but also didn't seem to have a natural buoyancy, or maybe his muscles just meant his floating level was lower than mine.

What actually won me the fight was finding that where I'd been stood was a ledge over the lagoon, not a bank that dropped steeply into the water. It wasn't really much of a ledge, not even jutting out half a metre. But it was enough. When we were struggling to come up for air, I pushed the werewolf towards the ledge. Desperate for air, it panicked and the great paws clawed at me but it couldn't work out that it was rock holding it beneath the water's surface.

I managed to pull away and grab a breath but I came back, just in case I had to push Fido back under the water again. I did my best to make things look as if I were searching for whatever had knocked me into the lagoon. I don't really know how long it took. It felt like an eternity but people can't go without air for that long. When the furred werewolf became a fatigues-clad man again, I hauled myself out of the lagoon.

The team, police and teenagers were looking at me, some open mouthed, but not one had moved closer. Not one had intended to help me. I gritted my chattering teeth.

'What was that?' one of the police demanded.

'What happened?' one of my fellow volunteers asked.

I shrugged wearily and sat down on the ledge. 'Dunno. Couldn't find it. Thanks for jumping in and helping.'

The volunteer had the grace to flush. 'We know you can look after yourself.'

I managed a chuckle, although it was unlikely they would grasp the same point of humour as me. I can handle myself in a fight against a werewolf. They only think my capabilities extend to swimming, climbing and walking.

'Whatever happened, something attacked me and now it's lost in the lagoon.'

I rubbed the scratches on my arms. They were more like welts than cuts as the claws that had made them were blunt like a dog's.

'It looked like a dog,' the other police officer said as if he read my mind.

'Left the right kind of marks behind,' said the first. From his tone, I inferred that this would not be making it into the incident report.

'Well, it's down there somewhere if you want to have a look,' I said, thinking of the well-muscled human body that floated just below me.

'No point in pulling out a dog corpse,' the first police officer dismissed.

I shrugged again. If he wasn't anxious about identifying a corpse, I wasn't anxious to point it out. I appreciate such lazy policing.

'Wonder why it didn't like you,' was the last that was said on the matter.

Method 16: Allergies

Ben sent, 'As the ex-soldier stopped reporting for duty, I guess you got him. Well done. You've got another week then I'll start the next mission.'

I stared at the computer monitor, a little surprised that Ben already knew and only a day after I'd been dunked. It didn't take much for me to picture the last werewolf in his human shape, the way he'd looked when he'd tried to walk through Mike and the way he'd looked underwater. It was fairly easy to see him as military. Probably a squaddie, and one that resented those with authority as much as he wanted their authority. It fitted with the bullish pick-up truck that had followed me to the quarry, even if the army are more known for driving Landies, not black, anonymous pick-ups.

'What else did you learn?' I asked aloud, wondering if the ex-squaddie had told Ben more than my current address.

No-one else in the library appeared to pay attention. Maybe they'd gotten used to the crazy girl who had an emotional relationship with her email.

I didn't send a reply to Ben. There was no point. He knew I was alive and there was nothing more for me to say. He wasn't interested in conversation, just continuing this weird game he had going. The werewolf being dead — and me being alive — meant everything had been reset. Another would be on the way as soon as Ben found out. I left the computer and the library behind me and turned the situation over in my mind as I walked to the car park.

'Maybe we should take up chess.'

That time I did get some strange looks. So now I knew talking to myself in front of a computer was more socially acceptable than talking to myself in the street. I grinned, making things worse on purpose, and hopped into the Landie.

I'd borrowed it for a reason. My excuse was getting the shopping, which I did next, but what I wanted it for was to drive back to the quarry. The pick-up was still there. This was not surprising as I knew where the driver was. I'd thought about disposing of the vehicle, driving it straight into the lagoon and leaving it. I'd decided against it but it gave me ideas about the other two vehicles I had hidden away.

'Hello? My name's Elkie Bernstein. I'm a member of the local rescue team and I attended the incident at the quarry yesterday.'

The police officer at the other end of the phone made the appropriate noises and put me through to one of the two officers that had also attended.

'Hi. Do you remember that pick-up? The one that was parked next to my Landie?'

I patted the battered old farm vehicle affectionately. It was practically a classic and, while it wasn't mine, I'd already spent enough time working on it to feel proprietorial. As I was taking on more of the workload that required driving, I was spending more time with it than the actual owner.

'Well, it's still here,' I said.

On the way out yesterday, we'd already established that the pick-up had arrived between me and the rest of the team. The police had assumed that the dog that attacked me had belonged to the pick-up owner and that the human had fled rather than face possible charges for owning a dangerous dog. I admit to encouraging this view point.

'Yeah, I just thought I'd check it out, seeing as none of us saw them actually leave the vehicle,' I said to the officer, who assumed I'd only wanted to make sure the human was safe. This is what rescue teams are for, and it could be safely assumed I felt some kind of calling for it. 'I guess I've had to rescue too many unprepared people. Do you want me to wait until one of yours gets out here?'

Thankfully, there were just enough people based in the nearest police station that I never had to deal with the one who'd been involved with the supermarket issue and Ben's email again. He never thought well of me and I wouldn't have been able to get away with even thinking about leaving the scene.

'Okay,' I said, 'Let me know if there's anything I can do.'

I drove off. If things went as I expected, the police would come out and look over the vehicle. They wouldn't get that much out of it and so they would look for signs of the man. They'd probably have to get the sniffer dogs out and, maybe, that would lead to the lagoon.

I do know they dredged the lagoon within a few days and found the ex-Fido. No-one seemed to notice there was no dog. There were short formal interviews to confirm everything the team had said on the day about when the vehicle had arrived and not knowing the corpse.

'Elkie Bernstein, eh?' One of my interviewers asked. Well, said, really. There was no questioning intonation, despite the wording.

'Yes, sir,' I said.

'Your name's come up a few times, I see.'

I blinked. 'Oh?'

'In connection with dead bodies, he means,' said the other, possibly the only woman in the local police force.

I looked at my hands. 'Just bad luck, I guess.'

'Of course,' the policewoman said with a taut smile.

'How about we examine your luck with respect to the latest incident?' her work partner said a little more smoothly.

They led me through my statement from the actual day and my phone call about the vehicle. I mentioned having seen the black pick-up in my rear-view mirror.

'Really? Did you recognise it?'

'Other than that they pretty much followed me to the quarry, no,' I answered.

The connection was shrugged off. Although few people drove our country lanes, he was an off-comer, not a local, and there was no obvious connection between the two of us.

'And the others said something about a dog attacking you? You mentioned it in the phone call, I believe...' The policeman ran his finger down the pages in front of him, looking for my comment. His finger stopped when he found it but he didn't read out my words. He just looked at me.

'Yes, sir.' I said. 'Well, I assume it was a dog. I didn't see it, it just went for me. Pushed me into the lagoon. The others got a better look at it.'

'Hmm,' said the policeman.

'Did you find a dog's body?' I asked, knowing the answer but also knowing I was supposed to ask.

'No,' said the policewoman.

I opened and closed my mouth a few times before daring 'You don't think that he...?'

'No,' the policewoman repeated, although I have no idea what she thought I was going to ask. Only an insane person would make the illogical leap of asking about a dog to asking whether the dog and the man were the same creature.

They asked a few other nonsense questions about the statement, ending with, 'Well, Miss Bernstein. You're certainly lucky. And you're free to go.'

The policeman watched me with a tight smile. The policewoman had gone back to disapproval under a bad poker face.

'Please don't find your way back into the police station again too soon,' the policeman added.

As soon as I left the building, I had to find somewhere to throw up and get rid of the nervous knot in my stomach. I broke into a cold sweat. I couldn't believe I'd managed to hold it all in while they'd talked to me, no matter how harmless the interview had turned out. A guilty conscience eats away at your insides so that even an innocent question can make you ill.

We were back into hay cutting season again, a good excuse to avoid looks and questions following the interview. Well, there was some rain that delayed it by a couple of days until it cleared and then another couple until the grass dried out. So my escape wasn't quite as easy as I'd hoped.

By the time I was out on the archaic tractor, an Indian summer had begun and the air was thick with the dust the harvester raised along with the pollen from the late pollen producers. In case you're interested, that particular list includes nettles, mugwort, docks and, unfortunately, ragweed. Aside from the ragweed issue, they're all fairly well-known, at least out where I lived, as hay fever fodder.

The better thing about having an Indian summer is, of course, that I don't have to worry about rain putting me off during the whole proceedings. Otherwise, it's a rare year when I don't end up cursing the weather at some point. It's so normal that I tend not to remember it. Only special occasions like a straight run through actually stick in my brain. That or another werewolf attack.

The down side is that these Indian summers are something of an anticlimax. They're heavy and dusty and slow, though not necessarily as hot as the full-on summer that went before. Getting the energy together to do anything is a chore and, even without being a hay fever sufferer, it feels like you're breathing nothing but solids. So there are no words to describe my disgust when I saw the grey ears pricked in the uncut grass. The last thing I wanted to be dealing with was another werewolf.

'Just go away and leave me the fuck alone.'

The ears twitched but I doubt it heard my actual words. I'd barely managed to growl them, let alone put the volume behind them to reach over the noises of the tractor and harvester. Cutting hay in a mellow late summer is like that.

It seemed like my attacker-to-be felt the same laziness. It stayed put while I drove backwards and forwards in the field, the line of cut grass creeping a little closer to where it lay. Then the ears were gone. I half-heartedly scanned the field and found the whole animal, sitting in the cut grass and panting like the family dog. Well, someone's family dog. The kind that sit in photos and grin winningly for the camera.

'Good move,' I said just loud enough to hear myself over the machinery, 'I'd hate to cut you up like the last one that tried this.'

I listened to the mechanism for a while, thinking about how really it hadn't been right since the last time. We still hadn't got together the cost of a replacement as the only way to do that was to get a more modern harvester rig. Not something that attached to a tractor but something that drove around on its own. We didn't have enough meadow to justify the cost of buying such specialised equipment that would simply sit and devalue, from almost zero to absolute zero, for eleven months of the year.

After another couple of up-and-downs, I stopped the tractor.

'Let's get this thing over with, shall we?'

I jumped down and walked slowly to the werewolf. I stopped maybe three metres from it, hoping I was out of the distance it could leap from standing. I eyed it and wondered if I could move in closer, although there was nothing obviously wrong with it. There is no indication of age in a werewolf's fur. They're all grey.

The panting, well all dogs pant in hot weather, and I guess werewolves have to react to heat like dogs do. The volume and frequency had actually improved since the dash across my path, and I put that down to having been laid still for the best part of ten minutes since.

'This is where you leap at me,' I prompted.

It got to its feet and gave a bark although there was an edge of dusty cough to the sound. With the air of age and Indian summer weariness, I wouldn't have been surprised if I heard its joints creak.

'No offence, but how old are you?'

The werewolf glared at me.

'Are you older or younger than my tractor?' I asked, waving a hand at the machinery in question. 'You look ready to keel over already.'

I wanted to scream at it but didn't. I don't murder. I don't kill unprovoked. I only kill in self-defence. If this old, creaky hound would just see sense, it would live to see the remains of its old age. There was nothing I could say to make it stop, even if it appeared slow to catch its breath or start with the attacking, nothing but kill it when the attack came. I didn't want to. I walked away with all the energy I could summon.

'Seriously. I'm not worth it.'

There was a sound approximating a howl of fury and I heard the werewolf start to charge, to chase me, so I picked up speed. I made it into a run, although it felt like I was swimming through the air. The dust and pollen were so heavy it felt like I had to drag in two breaths to achieve the same result I usually just needed one for but it didn't make me panic. I could hear deep, rasping breaths behind me and I reckoned I could outstrip an elderly werewolf. I was almost wrong.

As I jumped the stone wall into the next pasture, I felt a paw clip the back of my rigger boot. I stumbled and fell but turned it into a roll. I tucked myself back into the wall as I rose. Just as I'd expected, the werewolf made the jump as well and landed on its paws. Momentum, and intention, carried it forward and past me.

'Hey!' I called out, 'You missed me!'

It came to a shaky halt and turned to face me, wobbling on its feet. The gasps were so loud I could hear the asthmatic rattle. The werewolf was not dealing well with the air.

'Breathing problems?'

I stepped forward without thinking.

'I'd say you've got hay fever.'

The werewolf glared at me again and I read that as an emphatic 'no'. The poor sod was probably so urban, and sheltered from weeds, that it had never been near ragweed or mugwort. The nettle pollen might be more usual to his human existence but not necessarily in these truck-load quantities. Which meant that the asthma attack was probably what they call 'exercise induced', a result of too much dust and pollen in the air for the poor bastard's newly discovered allergies.

I had the emergency call centre on the phone in the time it took the werewolf to collapse. I'd just asked for an ambulance for a severe asthmatic when the werewolf became a smartly suited, twenty-something man.

'Shit,' I said as soon as I'd hung up, 'The bloody police are going to love me.'

Intermission

The police of Llareggub and I settled into a mutual distrust and disbelief after another, harmless interview that left me with the shakes — when there were no police around to see me shaking. It's not like I'd actually done anything to kill the hay fever sufferer or that I knew him. There was nothing connecting us beyond the fact that he had stopped 'to ask me directions, sir'.

I called by the library and sent a sulky, 'You might want to put your minions through a basic fitness test before you send them out to kill me.'

I didn't get an email response. Which gave me plenty of time between visits to the library to kick myself over having sent it in the first place. Did I really want to sound like someone who looked forward to a decent fight? For that matter, was I *really* the kind of person who looked forward to facing off against the next werewolf?

Thankfully, such self-examination was cut off by Ben's actual response. After all, it's a fine line between introspection and angst, which is a waste of time and of no interest to anyone else but me.

So. Ben sent a response by a man in an ordinary, unmarked car who I took to be a courier. The stranger could most charitably be described as lanky, or maybe grey like the over long, untended mop of hair.

Anyway, I suppose Ben's message was technically two responses as the delivery the man brought was made up of a large, lumpy manila envelope and a small box. I opened the envelope as soon as the messenger put it in my grubby hands and a set of house keys fell out. The paperwork remained inside. Two copies of a contract and all the supporting information needed to make me the owner of the Lloyds' old place.

'This is bullshit!'

The messenger shrugged. 'Nothin' to do with me,' he said in an accent I could only identify as Northern English, 'I just need to take back a signed copy.'

I raised my eyebrows. 'So you know where Ben Lloyd is?'

'The person who sent me isn't a Lloyd,' he stumbled over the Welsh 'll'. 'It's an Olsen. Foreign fella.'

I checked through the papers and found what he meant. Ben — Benjamin Lloyd — was mentioned as of the old address and then the person who signed on his behalf, a Professor S. Olsen, with an address in Norway.

'You're going all the way to Norway to hand this back?' I asked, incredulous.

The courier didn't reply to my question and I took it as a negative, a confirmation of my disbelief.

'Check the cover note,' he said.

I flicked back to the first sheet, a scrawled note in unpractised hand-writing.

'For my best girl. I make that fifteen. Consider this the level up. Feel free to experiment with the other present. I always wanted to know if it really does work.'

'Does this Olsen know where Ben is?'

The courier smiled. 'I'd assume so.'

'Can you pass along a message?'

'Maybe you'd better write it down.'

So I did. I signed the contract and I wrote an equally unpractised scrawl, 'I get the feeling I'm your only bloody girl. Your courtship skills suck.'

I tried not to be upset when the courier read the note before stuffing it and one of the signed contracts in another manila envelope he had in his car.

'You'd tell me if he was up to something, wouldn't you?' the man asked. As if it was anything to do with a simple courier.

I wondered what he'd think if I told him Ben was a werewolf and what he'd do if I said that Ben was sending me attackers.

'What's it got to do with you?' I asked.

'Nothin', I guess.'

He got back in the car and drove off. After a few moments, I opened the small box. Laughter bubbled up and made me collapse in the middle of the yard. It was the wrong kind of laughter, the crazy kind, but I couldn't stop it. Ben had sent me a small silver cross on a silver chain.

Method 17: Nail Gun

Almost as soon as I had the keys to the Lloyd's place in my hands, I moved in. I sat down and talked with Dave's parents — for all of about half an hour — beforehand but, let's face it, we all wanted our own space back. What had been manageable before Dave's graduation had got more and more uncomfortable as the months passed. Amongst other things, it was an assumption we all made that Dave and his girlfriend would never come and visit while I was living in the Williams' family home. This probably relates to the previously held assumption that Dave and I were an item and would be settling nearby, if not with, his parents. Did I say manageable? I really mean tolerable. Or at least something I could cope with.

I also talked with Mum but she'd moved on.

'That's great news, Elkie,' she said.

I wrapped my hands around the mug of tea she'd made me and wondered if she'd missed every point I was trying to make in favour of the obvious positive. 'Thanks.'

'But I don't understand why the Lloyds' boy would do that. You weren't as close as Dave.' She paused a moment, then added, 'Were you?'

She was asking about sex, about whether I'd ever had the golden boy. Oddly enough, there are times when I still wish. After all, if we'd been busy having sex, he might not have been sending werewolves to kill me.

'No,' I said.

She looked unconvinced. I wondered if my teenage years had just been recast. I was never sure if she thought Dave and I had been together before we moved into the Williams' place. Was she trying to work out whether she'd got that wrong or was she wondering if I'd been with both of them?

'We talk,' I said, 'Ben and me.'

'Oh?'

'Online.'

'Oh.'

I shrugged. 'I guess the farm isn't doing him much good and he doesn't want to sell it.'

'He's given you a farm, Elkie. You don't just give farms to people.'

Maybe I've earnt it, I thought but didn't say. No need to sound like a prostitute. 'Ben's given it to me. Maybe he'll want it back but that's no reason not to look after it.'

She continued to look unconvinced. I wondered why she couldn't be more like Dave's parents. The Williams had been too relieved to get their own space back to look this gift horse in the mouth.

'Does this mean that it's a bad idea to invite you to move in with me?'

She didn't answer and I had a mental flash of what the house probably looked like after five years of not being lived in.

'After I've cleaned it up a bit,' I added.

She still said nothing.

'Please?' I asked. I took a deep breath and admitted a truth. 'I don't think I can cope on my own.'

I wasn't sure I could cope with someone else there, either, though. Being in Ben's home made me easy for the were-wolves to find. Anyone I lived with would also be easy prey.

'No,' Mum said, and I almost breathed a sigh of relief.

'No,' she said again, 'I'm not living out in the middle of nowhere ever again.'

I did not point out that Sweet was hardly a bustling metropolis.

So I got to tear off the boarding I'd put up years before as the first job I gave myself to do on moving in. Strictly speaking, the house wasn't habitable. It hadn't been aired or cleaned since I closed up. There had been several visits from the family solicitor and removal men in the intervening period but they were neither cleaning nor airing the property.

It did count as furniture removal, however, and only the

stuff that was considered a family heirloom — and the sale thereof unlikely to meet with her client's approval — or totally worthless was still there. This meant my second job was finding a bed to sleep on.

Oddly enough, I ended up sleeping on what had been Ben's. It took me a while to drift off because I spent a lot of time thinking how Ben used to be, the golden boy athlete of our small secondary school. The boy who'd become obsessed with games had very little in common with the athlete, never mind the man I guess he must have become. Except, possibly, a drive to compete and win.

After sleeping with the idea of him, I woke up dreaming of him — which was a little disturbing considering my usual wake-up routine. The day proper started with a cold shower and swearing to any higher power that cared to listen in that I'd never do it again.

Over the next couple of weeks and in between my work at the Williams' farm, I cleaned the house from top to bottom. Then I moved on to the sheds and the barns and found out that the solicitor had been just as efficient in there, with only a few tools having survived the cull.

'Shame they didn't show the same enthusiasm for maintaining the buildings,' I grumbled.

There were a number of places where wooden beams and struts needed replacing. I'd kind of expected it as there were similar repairs needed to the boundaries, places where the fencing needed pulling up or the stone walls needed rebuilding. The kind of damage that happens in five years of no care, without even going in what neglect does to the actual land. But I had the good luck to pull a musty tarpaulin out the way and find the object of my desire.

'Okay, maybe they didn't show that much enthusiasm for cleaning up out here, either.'

Not that the nail gun was much good anywhere further afield than the yard, being tied to the compressed air cylinders, but with it and the boards off the windows, I might be able to start some repairs.

As is traditional with horror films, I started in the most

inaccessible and generally dangerous place to be. In my defence, there was no foreboding violin music playing when I chose to start in the old stable loft and the work had to be done if I wanted to keep the loft floor up. More precisely, the work had to be done if I wanted to keep a tonne of scrap metal and several decades of dust off the ground floor and, possibly, my head. But it's the kind of situation where you can see it coming. It's the worst possible moment for anything to happen and Sod's Law pretty much says something will.

So, there I was on my hands and knees checking for delicate, rotten pieces of wood that could be replaced with the slightly more robust boards I'd already humped up the loft ladder. I'd made a mental note to build or buy a slightly more robust set of stairs but it was a job for when I decided what to actually put in the stables. Right at that moment in time, I was trying to make sure I had enough of a building to make a decision about.

Before climbing up, I'd put on my climbing harness and run a rope over a secure looking beam. I'd tested it by hanging a couple of inches of the floor and then hauled myself up to the loft space. The nail gun had also come up with me and I moved it carefully around the floor as I made my progress, along with tools for prying rotten boards up and a bottle of drinking water. It's dusty work shifting all the tat around and inspecting the floorboards, after all. Basically, I was as safe as I could make it, except for a potential attacker.

I'd been counting down the days since Ben's couriered present, aware that it was only a matter of time until he sent the next werewolf in my direction. I did the best I could to make allowances — I was effectively armed with my tools — but normal life also had to continue. I couldn't afford to just sit and wait. I got on with work, trying not to turn my back to the ladder and the obvious route of attack.

I was still surprised when the deformed grey paw — I'll never get used to the shape, which is not quite hand and not quite a true dog's paw — entered my field of vision. Hard physical labour is generally absorbing and anything that requires a level of concentration will eventually block out the rest of the world. I'd forgotten to keep watch and the paw's arrival was a total shock.

I looked up from the board I was working on into the maw of a werewolf. What I could see beyond the teeth looked smug and pleased, a look that said 'You're not so special. I beat you.'

'Hi,' I said.

I reached with slow care to the side and my heartbeat measured out an aeon of time. My hand wrapped around the handle of the nail gun. My finger rested on the trigger as if the tool had been made to sit there. The designer had done a good job.

'How about you just go back to Ben and say you won?' I asked.

The werewolf growled and leant in towards me. Its breath was, well, human. Not especially bad or strong but I could smell what the man had eaten for lunch. Some pub grub washed down with a lager. The front paws shifted, the second coming into my visual focus, within reach.

'I'll take that as a 'no',' I said and slowly moved into position, 'But the intimidation tactics are wasted on me.'

As I said the word 'intimidation' I rested the muzzle of the nail gun on the nearest front paw and squeezed the trigger. The noise it made and the slight kick it gave were a jolt to the system and were my cue to move faster. I nailed the other front paw to the floor as my would be attacker started screaming in pain.

'What? You think I hadn't planned for this?' I bluffed.

It tugged desperately at its paws but couldn't bring itself to tear free, to draw the nails through its paws in order to escape. I stepped back so that I wouldn't get caught in the flailing and considered the options. It took a couple of seconds for me to decide that I couldn't do anything but finish it. A werewolf stupid enough to hunt me for no other reason than Ben sent it after me wasn't going to back off just because I'd proved I could hurt it.

I stepped back in and held the nail gun against the poor bastard's temple. It whimpered and I considered the shot again. I wasn't sure a nail gun would definitely do the right level of damage.

'Sorry,' I said, in case it didn't.

I pulled the trigger again. The werewolf twitched and then dropped. After a minute, the fur disappeared, leaving behind an attractive, middle-aged man in casual-smart shirt and trousers. Well, he would have been attractive if he hadn't been a werewolf and now a corpse.

It took me a fair amount of time to pull the nails out of his hands. The first time I tried, I ended up throwing up off the edge of the loft onto the floor below. I threw up until I was dry heaving. I left the corpse long enough to clean up and discovered I'd been crying. I don't know when I started. I may even have been crying when I was saying sorry.

I went back and tried again. I tried to do it without leaving too much blood behind on the wood but I had to give that up. In the end, I replaced the boards he'd been so attached to and burnt the originals. Best to avoid any chance of leaving evidence behind, should anyone ever have enough suspicion to investigate me.

For the same reason, I avoided disposing of the corpse itself on the Lloyds' — on my — property. I backed the Williams' Landie into the stable and, with the help of my climbing harness and the rope, got the ex-werewolf into the back. In other words, I added the body to the cache of others. I wondered how Dave coped, if at all, being so far away from the evidence and still wanting to check it was safe.

When I got back, I ran a bath. I don't know how long I was in there but the water had gone from lobster-boiling temperature down to freezing.

Method 18: Silver

'Maybe you should put some quick lime on these,' Dave said.

I'd come back to the stash within a couple of days of the nail gun incident, my paranoia about being found out aggravated by seeing an unrecognised car drive up a particular narrow country lane that few people ever used. The car, it turned out, belonged to Dave — or his girlfriend. I wasn't entirely sure about the ownership. Either way, he surprised me.

'Hmm,' I said, 'I hear conflicting reports about that.'

'Oh?'

'Apparently it makes some surface burns but actually preserves the remains. Or something.'

I shrugged. I — well, we, really — had nine bodies and several large pieces from the one that jumped into the harvester. All were in various stages of rotting. I had thought of doing something to speed up their decomposition but wasn't really sure how. With my basic understanding of chemistry, I thought there was a fair chance that the quick lime's exothermic reaction with water would at least ignite the methane they gave off but didn't want to end up then preserving the rest.

There was also a several years old, high end car and an equally high end, slightly younger car. Both could probably be sold on for cash in hand but I didn't want to be associated with them or leave my fingerprints on them. Then there were the number plates. They were traceable and would lead to names. They were bound to put the police onto some manhunt that could end up with them talking to me.

When I had time, I might drive them into one of the quarry lagoons. Maybe I would load them with werewolves and sink them all where they were least likely to be looked for. But methane would make the corpses float, right? Or at least it would come off in bubbles.

'You've got a few more since the last time I looked,' said Dave.

'Ben's back in the game.'

I didn't bother to remind him this was a joint venture. They were mostly mine, even if we'd shared the first few.

'"Game"? It's a game to you?'

I shook my head. 'No. But that's what it is to Ben.'

'He's a sick fuck. We should have killed him when we had the chance.'

'You tried,' I snapped back, 'And you failed.'

Dave glared at me.

'And it was a murder attempt,' I added.

'Murder?' Dave echoed, waving his arm at the collection of bodies, 'What the hell do you call this?'

I winced. 'Self-defence.' After a pause I added, 'And paranoia.'

Who was going to believe I put a nail in a man's temple out of self-defence? Who would believe that they were furred up man-animals when each of these corpses attacked me?

Dave snorted with disgust. 'It's not like they don't deserve to be killed.'

'Just for being werewolves?'

'They're murderers.'

I raised my eyebrows. 'Attempted murderers, surely?'

'All werewolves are murderers.'

'You've done a survey? You've seen every werewolf in existence? You've seen each and every one of them attacking anything that moves?'

Dave glared at me again and clammed up.

'That's what the studying lycanthropy is, isn't it?' I asked.

'I'm going to find and kill as many of them as possible.'

'You're going hunting? Are you insane?'

'They're not that difficult to kill,' he said, with another wave at the corpses. I chose to ignore the 'it can't be that hard if even *you* can do it' that I heard in his voice. It still rankled that at some point I'd stopped being his equal and become 'just a woman'. I also knew Dave wouldn't make it through one of my working days in his current physical state so, if anything, he had it the wrong way round.

'They're faster and stronger than you,' I threw at him, 'The odds are on their side.'

'Only while they're furred up. I intend to deal with them when they're... human,' Dave said, unaware that things didn't work quite like that.

'You mean you're going to kill people who are sent to you as patients? What if they've come of their own accord, looking for help? What if they aren't killers? What if they're trying not to be?'

I was fairly certain that none of the one's I'd seen would have come here if they weren't part of Ben's game, and looking for a fight.

'I'll only kill the real werewolves,' he said.

While they're normal. While they're relatively weak, or so Dave thought. While they're doing no-one any harm, or were trying not to.

I turned my back on the stash and walked away. Mainly, I was walking away from the temptation to add Dave to the pile. I'd never wanted to kill an actual human being before.

I couldn't avoid him, though. When I showed up for work the next morning at his parents' place, Dave was waiting for me. His girlfriend was standing at the kitchen window watching us. From the way she watched, I guessed she was still upset that I'd been more than a friend. That made two of us.

'So Dad says Ben's given you his farm?'

I nodded, part of my attention still on the tense face in the window.

'How does it feel being a kept woman?' he asked with a sneer.

I noticed he managed to keep fur out of the conversation. The girlfriend obviously hadn't been told everything about Dave's past. Like most of the world, she would consider the existence of werewolves an insanity.

'About the same as it feels being a bit on the side. Shouldn't you be up in some ivory tower of Academia?'

Dave turned his back on me, doing that man-against-all-odds stance that self-absorbed people do when things aren't going their way. His girlfriend flinched away from sight. Perhaps her fears of a relapse into a relationship had been confirmed. Maybe she thought I was trying to win him back and he was heroically resisting.

'Where is he?'

'I don't know,' I said with total honesty, 'But his shrink's apparently in Norway.'

I'd thought about chasing up the doctor, Olsen, named on the paperwork. All I had was an address and there was just no way I could afford to drop everything and fly to Norway to find him. Not with facing werewolves on a regular basis and working on the farm.

'Norway?'

Dave suddenly switched to 'alert' and I knew I'd missed something important. Something known only to students of clinical lycanthropy, perhaps. I walked away before I did some physical harm trying to drag it out of my former best friend and former lover. Imagining a bloodied and beaten Dave was getting too easy.

I was a bit more successful avoiding Dave for the rest of the week, which was long enough to check my emails and start watching out for the next attacker. For what it's worth I sent Ben a 'still here' to receive an 'incoming' within fifteen minutes of having clicked send.

Realising he must be online right at that very moment, I sent back 'Where are you?'

'The game doesn't work like that' was all I got back, though it was just as quick as the last response.

I sent 'My life is not a game.'

Ben didn't reply and there was nothing more I could do but turn and walk away from that conversation, too. So after that I just worked and looked out for my next attacker. I spent most of my time out in the fields with the animals or at the Lloyds' place, which I still had difficulty considering my own. For some reason, I found sitting in the stable loft quite comforting when I had nothing better to do.

'I'm not letting you talk to her alone!'

The strident, soprano, Home Counties' tones could only be the girlfriend. The palpable, though silent, anger that seemed to wrap around her distress could only be Dave. Before that moment, I'd never realised I knew him so well that I could almost sense him.

I sprawled over to the edge of the loft to get a view of the yard and watched them. Dave strode manfully in front and then stopped, not sure where to find me, while the girlfriend indulged in hand-wringing a few paces behind. How sweet.

'Up here!' I called.

They both looked around, not entirely sure where my voice came from.

'The stables!'

The girlfriend looked in my direction first but the look she gave the building said she questioned whether it could really be called a stables. She was probably used to something larger and in a lot better condition.

Dave strode past her and walked inside. He looked up at me and I could see the anger but wasn't sure why he felt like that. Was it his girlfriend not letting him out to play on his own?

'It's okay,' I said to her, 'I have no interest in Dave. He just wants me to answer some questions.'

She looked around the building, paying close attention to the rope that led from the beam to me — I still didn't trust the ladder a hundred percent and I still hadn't built a replacement.

'I can't think what he'd want from you.'

'Careful,' I said, 'Or you'll end up sounding bitchy.'

'Leave her alone, Elkie,' Dave said.

I shrugged and continued to look down on them from my perch. They weren't worth moving for.

'You want the address of the Norwegian, right, Dave?' I asked.

Dave stiffened and then forced himself to relax. 'I don't know if he's Norwegian.'

'I guess not. But you seem to know who he is.'

'I know of him.'

162

I waited and the pause in conversation stretched out until the other two started to shift in their discomfort.

'He's very involved with clinical lycanthropy,' Dave finally added, 'He publishes a lot of well received papers.'

'So you should be able to find where he's based without me giving you an address,' I said.

'The Institute — '

The place, the idea, seemed too much for Dave to continue with what he intended to say. I heard the capitalisation, the importance Dave and his academic cohorts put on this place in his voice. It could be a cover for a place that held real werewolves as well as those who only thought they were man-wolf hybrids. Perhaps it was the kind of place that Dave dreamed of working in himself, so that he could kill those like Ben who might end up there.

Dave tried again. 'The Institute isn't the kind of place that's advertised.'

'Up to something dodgy?' I asked sweetly.

Dave ran a hand through his hair and looked at his girlfriend before answering. 'I heard Olsen's looking after some seriously interesting cases.'

'Well, he appears to have Ben. I'm not sure 'interesting' is the word I'd use, though.'

'Who's Ben?' the girlfriend asked.

I looked at Dave's face tighten and I answered with a big grin. 'The other man in my life.'

I could almost hear Dave growl. He was only acting upset because he considered me his territory. He'd always been jealous that I'd looked on the school's golden boy as favourably as anyone else when I was supposed to be *his* friend. It had nothing to do with sex or deeper emotional involvement. It wasn't the kind of thing that related directly to any feelings I may or may not have for Ben. I guess it was just the traditional male-female divide.

'The only man in my life... at the moment,' I said. I considered also adding 'but not for the want of trying', thinking of the recently scared off Mike.

'He's a psycho,' Dave spat out.

The girlfriend spat back. 'What the Hell is it with you? Work, this bitch... Am I always going to be second best?'

'To his obsession with beating Ben and other men that represent the same thing to Dave?' I asked, 'Bad news. Yes.'

She looked at me with widening eyes, so wide I could see the whites clearly from my perch. Her anger and hatred was pretty healthy, though, all things considered. Dave's interests? Not so much.

'I'm just not that important,' I said to her, 'If I'd been a man, you wouldn't have needed to question the relationship at all. You'd have assumed I was the old, close friend. His sparring partner and sword brother, even.'

'You had sex together,' she said, as if it were a new thing, as if it were a current infidelity.

Movement caught on the edge of my vision and I saw the next attacker, already furred up and sloping towards the stable doors. It was focussed on the girlfriend. I shifted position so that I could defend her if I had to. I guess Ben just told them where I was likely to be and it was up to them to work out who I was from that. This one had worked it out wrong.

'It wasn't exactly the most important part of our relationship,' I said to the girlfriend with careful precision, 'Entertaining but not important.'

She made a noise that made it clear that sex was always important, at least in terms of faithfulness and trust. In that I agreed and that was one of the reasons Dave was pissing me off. He should have told me he'd met someone else. He should have ended things with me. I rubbed around my neck in a way that would come off as embarrassment but actually meant I could get at the catch of my silver necklace without Dave and his girlfriend noticing. That and the rope were the only potential weapons I had to hand.

'It's over,' I said.

The girlfriend pushed for more, for proof I wasn't a threat. 'And you're with this Ben, now?'

'It's a sort of long distance thing.'

Fido crept closer and Dave didn't even notice. He had no chance if he was going to actively hunt these things. But then he wasn't, was he? He was going to have them led to his office where he intended to creep up behind them, I guess. He was a wolf in a human skin, rather than the men in wolf skins I usually dealt with.

'It's funny,' I said, to cover the werewolf creeping forwards and to hide my getting ready to swing down, 'She asks me if it's over, not the man she's supposed to be in a relationship with. Tells me exactly how much she thinks of you and your opinions, old friend.'

Dave stepped forward, ready to fight me — 'Elkie!' — just as the werewolf pounced. The attacker heard my name as it jumped and realised it was jumping on the wrong woman. It didn't so much try to avoid hitting her as shift its weight so that it could leap from her to me when she was dead. But I'd already swung into the space between the loft and the girl-friend. I'd pushed off as soon as I'd seen the werewolf's paws leave the ground.

I hit Fido about the same time it hit her. I managed to get myself on its back with my right arm, my stronger arm, around its neck in a vague choke-hold. I couldn't get the right hold but I hadn't expected to. I used my left hand to hold the small cross against its throat.

'What the hell is that?' the girlfriend screamed.

'Dog,' said Dave and hustled her out of the stable while I rolled around on the floor.

The werewolf made a coughing noise and veins of dark brown human skin, or white t-shirt and blue jeans where the clothes covered, began to appear through the fur, although they spread very slowly. It thrashed around on the floor, no longer caring that I was attached; and I rolled right along with it, scared to let go in case taking the silver away stopped the magic.

Method 19: Loss of Blood

I only let go of the silver poisoned werewolf when two chunks of fur or skin came off in my hands.

'*Ach-a-fi!*'

I threw the bloody lumps back at Fido and rubbed my hands clean against my jeans.

'*Ach*! That's horrible!'

The necklace dropped from my fingers and I fumbled to pick it up. The cross was smeared with blood that was turning into solid black lumps even as I looked at it.

'That's so not natural,' I said.

The writhing werewolf had gone from whimpering to howling with the pain and the howling was starting to get the edge of a human scream. I looked and found it more 'he' than 'it'. I crouched over it, as close as I dared. I tried not to look at it, to see the painful change I had caused.

'I'm sorry,' I said, 'I never meant to actually hurt you.'

The eyes — which had always been dark brown but were now framed with human skin — rolled and then focussed on me.

'Hurt — '

'I thought it would be quicker,' I said.

There were still clumps of fur clinging to the body but it was as if the veins of dark brown skin had become rivers. Or a lake that the fur floated on. Some of the clumps had fallen away with the skin beneath, like the two chunks that had come away in my hands. Blood was trickling from the holes they left behind but it became black and lumpy as it left the body.

The werewolf tried to speak again. 'I thought — '

'You got the wrong woman?' I asked after the pause stretched out into laboured breathing and almost screams.

'He said — '

'He? Ben?' I asked but the soon to be ex-werewolf showed no recognition of the name. In fact, it struggled on as if I hadn't said anything. Perhaps it was beyond hearing me. Perhaps it just wanted to excuse its failure and gain forgiveness before the end.

'That you'd be — '

I knelt on the ground, out of reach but close enough to hear the words it tried to force out. I tried not to gag. *This has got to be the worst way of killing a werewolf I ever tried*, I thought.

'Shacked up with — '

'Sex?' I asked, catching an association, 'You smelt sex on Dave and his girlfriend?'

'Their weakness — '

'They had sex before they came over here?' I asked but didn't really expect an answer. It wasn't any of my business anymore, if it ever had been. I was just grasping at the one thing that was likely to be obvious to a sensitive nose. It was then I realised why we'd been targeted by that very first werewolf. We both must have smelt of sex, masturbation, and everyone else had identified us as a couple. How could a hunter resist such an obvious sign of weakness?

'Distracted — '

'Yeah,' I said ruefully, 'I am a bit.'

I got up and walked around the stable looking for what I needed, leaving the silver cross against the blackened skin.

'Weak — '

'What's going on?' Dave yelled from outside.

'Just finding something to cover the *dog* with,' I called back as the werewolf started to writhe and almost scream again. 'It's not a pretty sight.'

'It's still alive?' he yelled.

I heard what sounded suspiciously like a girlfriend hitting her insensitive other half and smiled a little. I hoped she'd do it again.

'It's sick and in a bad way,' I called. 'I'm going to have to put it out of its misery.'

The werewolf itself didn't react — only reinforcing my impression that it could no longer take in anything external to its pain — but I clearly heard the girlfriend gasp. Swiftly followed by soothing noises from Dave.

'Wrong prey — ' the Fido gasped out as my fingers closed around a Stanley knife I'd left in the stable toolbox I was putting together.

'You're not kidding,' I muttered and returned to crouch over it, this time close enough to touch. It was too weak to be much of a threat itself — it hadn't even pushed away the silver cross. It looked about ready to curl up and die but it was taking too long and the magical poison was causing it too much pain.

'It's okay,' I said and reached forward, 'I've got you.'

I worked out roughly where the jugular artery ran beneath the once handsome brown skin and cut as firmly as I could. Another man who would have stood out against the pasty white locals. He'd probably made an impression when he passed through, though it might not have been enough to have people notice he'd never left. As he'd turned up here in his fur-skin, it's unlikely there was anything to associate him with me directly. The police wouldn't look for him here unless they were canvassing and they would be asking for a black man in jeans and a white t-shirt. I turned away so I didn't have to see someone who answered to that description.

'It shouldn't hurt for long,' I said, horrified at the red-black lumpy lake that started to form on the stable floor.

It took maybe a minute and when that passed I threw the nearest tattered tarpaulin over the corpse and the Stanley knife. I gagged over it, almost dry heaving before I managed to swallow the bile back down.

'I need to clean up,' I said as I walked out of the stable.

'Oh my God!' the girlfriend cried out.

I tried not to wince at the casual blasphemy and got a certain amount of amusement out of the way she covered her mouth. Only her horror was at the off-colour blood that clung to me rather than her choice of words. I looked down at the solidifying black gunk and forced a shrug.

'A stray. Covered in some kind of dirt.'

'The poor thing must have gone mad,' she said.

She reached out and almost touched me. I walked away before I found out whether she intended to or not.

'Don't,' I said. 'This looks like it's going to be horrible to clean off.' I took a deep breath and ignored the jar I could hear calling my name from one of the kitchen cupboards. If I started eating chocolate spread, Dave would know I was upset. 'You two want a cup of tea?'

There was a moment of silence as they both digested my question then, 'How can you be so callous?' the girlfriend spat out, back on fighting form.

'It's over,' I said.

She was right behind me. If she got close enough, I have no doubt she would have pushed me or slapped at me. She was in an exceptionally aggressive mood, considering she'd only recently had sex. Maybe Dave made all the women in his life want to kill him.

'It was an animal. A living thing,' the girlfriend said.

I nodded in agreement, 'was' being the operative word as far as I was concerned. I considered the past tense while I scrubbed up and started off the brew. I had a few notes to send off to Ben: Silver is not a way to go, and Dave and I will no longer be smelling of sex. At least with each other. Oh, and please don't get his girlfriend killed. They deserve each other.

'If you give me a month or so,' I said to Dave, 'I should be able to go with you.'

'So you're not going to give me the contact details for Olsen?' He asked, incredulous.

Had he really expected everything to go his way? I set him straight, or started to. 'All I have is an address and I'm not having you charge in there half-cocked — '

'Oh, please,' the girlfriend interrupted, 'Dave is a highly qualified psychologist who merely wants to talk to another highly qualified psychologist.'

I snorted. 'It might be just what he needs.'

They both glared at me.

Then I corrected the girlfriend with more precise wording. 'Actually, I think you'll find it's a postgraduate psychology student wanting to pump a more highly qualified and more experienced practising psychologist for information.'

The girlfriend blinked as if she'd just walked in on the household pet downloading porn off the Internet. There is no other way of describing finding out that someone is a little more gifted in an unexpected area than your world view allows for. Her world view did not include farmers knowing anything about academic structure — not even the most basic details of it. I wasn't going to admit I'd just run into the edge of my knowledge.

'And I want to find the man that self same specialist has in his care. I owe him. I owe Ben.'

Mainly a slap or two but I also intended to make sure Dave didn't do anything stupid. Ben saved my life, after all, and had given me his farm. And it wasn't fair on the unknown Olsen to set a potential killer like Dave on his patients.

'I'll book some flights to Oslo,' Dave said, trying to take charge, 'And let you know dates. It'll probably be the Christmas break before I can take any real time from the University.'

'And yet you're here now,' I said.

Thanks to how rarely Dave had visited during his first degree, I didn't know much about a university year but I was fairly sure he'd taken time off during the term to get out here to the back of beyond.

'Anyway, don't bother,' I said, 'I'll sort it.'

It would have been nice to force him to pay for the plane tickets but I wasn't sure Oslo would be the nearest airport to Olsen's address.

Of course, Dave ignored me. 'No. I'll organise it.'

'No, you won't.'

'I'll call,' he said and was hustling the girlfriend out of the house before she'd really finished her drink.

'I'll get the tickets,' I called out after them.

I took my time over my own cup and held on to it long after it was empty. I didn't really want to go and clean up the stables but in the end I had to. It took me a couple of hours before I managed to go back to the scene of the crime. Well, the scene of the self-defence.

'I don't suppose there's much point apologising to a corpse,' I said aloud, 'It's not like I didn't say 'sorry' when you were alive.'

I pulled the tarp aside. I couldn't believe what I saw. I pulled the tarp back over and took a deep breath.

'How...'

I pulled the tarp aside again.

'I hate magic.'

The werewolf no longer existed. There wasn't even black, lumpy blood. There was just a vaguely human shaped, loose sculpture of black flakes. Each time I moved the tarp, it caused more of the shape to distort and soften as flakes were blown away from the pile. Beside the pile lay the Stanley knife. All that remained of the blood lake was another, finer grouping of the same black flakes. I crouched down and gingerly touched some of them. They collapsed from flakes to dust.

'Okay. Maybe I could learn to like magic.'

I pulled the silver cross and chain from my pocket and rubbed off the few bits of black dust — more dried werewolf blood — that clung from earlier. Well, it might not be the best choice of weapon but it was turning out to be the best clean-up tool I'd ever seen. Ben's silver cross and a broom would solve most of my problems.

I collected the dust and tipped it into the cess pit. With the bones gone, there was nothing that would alert anyone's suspicions to human remains having been hidden in with the sewage. Even if this weird dust were still carrying DNA and chemical markers or anything else that made it recognisable as human cells.

Then I drove back to the stash with the cross and a backpack, which held a dustpan and brush, and a gallon-sized canister of petrol. I worked my way through all the corpses stored there. It was dark before they all dissolved to dust as it took a half hour to start off each corpse decomposing. I found that out by trial and error, so it was a good hour or two

171

before I even got the first to turn into black flakes. I swept it up and emptied it into the boot of the once expensive car that belonged to a dead lawyer obsessed with status to the point of almost literally becoming top dog.

I drove the older car to one of the quarries and drove it straight in to a lagoon. I didn't bother to rig up a way of driving in without me in it. I wound the driver's window down, undid the seatbelt and hit the accelerator as hard as I could. I swam out of the open window with the backpack once the car was full of water. It helped that I drove in from the quarry base, not off one of the cliffs, a thought that had tempted me for a good few minutes before I committed to action.

I got back to the Lloyd's place about an hour after dawn. I called Dave's dad and said I was taking the morning off, during which I enjoyed a hot shower and some equally hot food. It took me a few days to work up the nerve to dispose of the second car in exactly the same manner — but at a different quarry further away from the original stash.

Method 20: Bleach

Ben's response to my email was 'shame'. Whether it was his response to the performance of silver or the lack of performance between Dave and me, I'm not sure. For that matter, I have no idea whether he was being sarcastic or not. Text only conversations lack the depth and tone to be sure. So, anyway, there wasn't much I could say — or type — to that and I left the library feeling oddly deflated. Maybe I should have asked what he thought of Olsen, and whether the man supposedly in charge of him was capable of stopping Dave. But that might have made Ben nervous about why I wanted to talk to Olsen and change his game as a result.

Time limped on a couple of weeks and Dave fled back to his university and civilisation. His father and I sat down and talked futures.

'Are you, ah, still interested working for me? Now you've got the Lloyd's place?' Mr Williams asked me one morning over a brew.

'I guess,' I said. 'I guess I just don't have the experience to run it on my own, so I'm better off working for you and learning.'

He ummed.

I shrugged. 'It's not like I've got the money to restock it. The Lloyd's place, that is.'

Mr Williams ummed again.

'And it's not like you have the money to employ someone else,' I added. Otherwise there would have been someone else working down here when Dave and I were at school, never mind now.

'We've had a good year,' he said in a level tone.

'Too good,' I said back in the same tone. 'The herd has grown and we can't afford to feed them over winter.'

He sipped and made no answer.

'Unless we use the Lloyd's grass,' I said with a grin.

He looked at me. 'Partners?'

I nodded. 'Partners.'

After several years of neglect, the pasture, meadows and leys that formerly belonged to Old Man Lloyd were in serious need of topping and it would probably be a couple of growing seasons before it could be considered even half-decent again. But with some controlled grazing and small herds split over enough ground to otherwise accommodate herds three times as big, we were in with a fighting chance.

If we ran the two farms together we had more sheds, which meant we could give the animals more space when we brought them in. While we might need more bedding materials for the weaker animals — less body heat being shared — we were also less likely to get a disease that could wipe out the whole lot.

The ex-Lloyds' place — mine, dammit — also has stables, if you haven't noticed with the recently covered activity. While not huge and modern, it might be enough to get some rent from a couple of horse-riders needing livery of some degree. So Mr Williams concentrated on getting a couple of fields looking like paddock quality — even if they obviously weren't — and I concentrated on cleaning out the stables and making them look the business — even if they obviously weren't — while I tried not to think about having witnesses.

I also had a pet project. I had found parts to put together a chicken coop with a large run in the stable loft. Large enough to have four or five hens and a rooster. I was looking forward to sharing free eggs with the Williamses.

This was the positive image I used to force myself through the task of scraping shit off with a paint-scraper. Yes, you read that right. I admit I got to start with a shovel and a fork in the stables but there was some manure that was pretty much fossilised and required a more focussed and arguably more manual attempt.

I'll bet you're wondering why I didn't reach for good, modern cleaning products like bleach. The answers are, in no particular order, because bleach isn't all that modern and it isn't all that good. It just creates a smell we associate with clean. Unfortunately, what we smell is 'denatured' hypochlorite, the active ingredient in most general bleaches.

In other words, the smell is low concentrations of chlorine gas. I could never look at a bottle of bleach in the same way again when I found that out in a chemistry lesson. Mind you, I've had difficulty looking at it at all since the parvo thing.

Alternatively, just consider that the activity I was involved in is traditionally called 'mucking out'. It's called that for a reason. There's no point just disinfecting shit. You need to uncake it from every surface if you want the place clean.

It can be back breaking work clearing out somewhere that hasn't been cleaned in years. One of the reasons Old Man Lloyd had been considered so old and mean was that he'd got rid of his sister's horses as soon as she'd married and moved away. That had been over twenty-five years ago and the miserable bastard — no matter how noble and self-sacrificing in his time of sickness he might have been — hadn't even cleaned up after them. I have no doubt he reasoned it away as 'they weren't my bloody animals'. I suspect something similar had happened with the chicken coop. At that moment, I hated his long-burnt guts.

Eventually I got to a point where everything was as clean as it could be — I could even see the original surfaces — and *then* I got out some bleach and wiped everything down with a very weak mix. As far as I was concerned, the chicken coop was done after that. I set it up not far from the kitchen door on some grass and left it until I could afford to buy some hens. The stable, though, had a bit further to go. Everything needed to be painted white, if it were stone or metal, or sanded down and varnished, if it were wood. Then that was finished with until we managed to find some horses or ponies to fill the six pristine stalls.

So, I dropped a workload and went back to 'just' being the second pair of hands on the combined farms. I had enough time to go to the monthly training session for the rescue team, attend college — I'm not sure they even noticed I was missing — and check my emails on a weekly basis. I had the time to debate spending my first chunk of money on hens or an internet connection. I had the time to wonder why Ben hadn't sent me any more messages. First world troubles, eh?

It was well into autumn by the time Ben made his presence felt. He sent one word, 'Incoming.'

I sighed, relieved that the moment was finally here. While I still had to wait to be attacked, at least I knew that it would be soon instead of sitting around waiting for Ben to drop the other shoe. Or wondering if I was delusional and in need of one of those highly qualified psychologists Dave's girlfriend got so gushy about. Maybe Olsen had a room for me.

The stables had been finished a couple of weeks, the chicken coop a week longer. The paddocks looked as if the grass was okay, their stone walls needed no repairs and the wooden gates were freshly hung. There were still no horses or ponies. I did, however, have a potential customer — someone who might rent some stabling from us — coming round a couple of days after the one word email came through.

Yes, I could see it coming, too. It's not Ben that's a mastermind at timing, it's just Sod's Law. Again.

That morning started with more bleach. A bottle of the stuff used to clean domestic toilets. I used a squirt very watered down in a large bucket of water. I had the gallon containers of the more common industrial disinfecting cleaners favoured in stables, catteries and kennels all over the country but today's smell was for the potential client, not the sensitive nose of her ride.

I mopped out all the stalls and left doors and windows open to bring in light and air, and to help the floor dry out. I put my bottle of bleach on a window sill ready to take back in the house.

Around lunch-time, I came back from the Williams' farm with several bales of straw and hay. I put one of each on the now dry floor of the stall I was hoping my expected visitor would use. I moved the rest of them into the loft, carefully placing them so it looked like the traditional hay loft was being used and had plenty in store. I put out the hay net and buckets against the stall door and the tools of the trade — pitch-fork, shovel, a few other bits and pieces — by the stable door.

'Well, it looks like I know what I'm doing,' I said aloud, 'I guess.'

Then I picked up my bottle of bleach and went back to the house to brew some tea while I waited. Or that was the plan, anyway.

Thanks to Ben's gift, it looked like agriculture was the path I was going to walk through life. It crossed my mind several times to sell up and move on, where Ben's minions couldn't find me, but I guess I enjoyed it too much.

Anyway, the longer I stayed on the farm, the more often I told myself I'd get a dog. I know I probably haven't mentioned it but I was one of the few people working on a pastoral farm without one. My main reason was not wanting to see many hours of training, food and affection get eaten. However, having one would be useful for keeping an eye out for things that eat — or attempt to eat— dogs and Elkie Bernsteins.

As it is, I have a tendency to walk into their general area before I'm ready to. Even in situations where I spot them, like out climbing with Mike, I still only get a few moments warning if the werewolf isn't ready to attack.

Yeah. I walked into the werewolf.

'Oof!'

We froze and eyed each other for a moment. It's a very weird experience looking into human eyes in a furry face. I try to avoid it by not looking them in the face, as a general rule.

'This really isn't a good time,' I said.

It bared its teeth and growled at me. I carefully undid the cap on the top of the bleach bottle. As it says it's a dangerous chemical on the side of the bottle, I figured I might as well take advantage of any potential weapon I was carrying. I backed away as the werewolf stalked forward.

'Why do you idiots *do* this, anyway?' I asked.

As usual, there were no answers. I don't think the whole muzzle thing that furred-up werewolves get mixes well with speaking. If they even feel like talking.

Fido, of course, interpreted my talking as nerves. It

grinned, baring more canine-like white teeth and a disturbingly human tongue.

'Seriously, furball, go do something else. Come back later and maybe I won't shoot you.'

It paused, probably trying to work out if I actually had fire-arms readily available. I don't. More because I don't really get on with them than any squeamish, anti-hunting feelings on my part. The pause was all the time I needed to squirt almost all the remaining contents of the bottle — it had been about two-thirds full — straight in the werewolf's eyes.

It clutched at its face and howled. Then it dropped to the floor, rolling about in pain and rubbing at the burning sensation the hypochlorite caused as it reacted with biological material. I just hope I have more sense should something like that ever happen to me. I shook my head at stupidity in general and put the lid back on the bottle, now with about a quarter left.

'Come on.'

I grabbed the werewolf and dragged it into the chicken coop so it would at least be out of the way. I locked it in with the overwhelming smell of chlorine, wondering if maybe I should get something to finish the poor bastard off with. It wasn't going to be in good shape if it survived and it would be a long and painful time until I could call it either way.

I considered hosing it down and washing the bleach off but it would go for me as soon as I had it clean. Even if it could no longer see, it still had smell and hearing, and touch and taste if things went too much in its favour.

I took the bottle back into the house and carefully read through the safety instructions. Whomever had written them assumed I wanted to keep someone who'd been stupid enough to drink or bathe in the bleach alive, not help them die faster.

'Maybe I should just go cut its throat while its distracted.'

I looked around the kitchen, wondering where I'd left that Stanley knife I'd used last time. I didn't really expect to see it but I couldn't help looking while I thought about the activity.

'Would — '

'Hello? Are you Elkie Bernstein?'

I turned slowly towards the kitchen door, my immediate thoughts being something like: *I thought women couldn't be werewolves, too.* I noticed the wealthy country set style clothing and reformed my panicked ideas straight away. It could only be the potential customer — I checked the clock — and so punctual it hurt. Well, it was going to hurt the werewolf.

'Guilty as charged,' I said with a weak smile and held my hand out.

She stepped forward into my house and shook hands, her grasp firm and confident. She wasn't going to be fobbed off for even five minutes while I went and sorted out my other visitor. She would need a very good excuse if I left her for even a second. She was that kind of woman. She probably called spades 'shovels' and let the consequences fall as they may.

'Would you like a cup of tea?' I asked automatically.

She frowned, a disappointed head girl. 'I'd rather see the stables first.'

'No bother,' I said, hoping she hadn't heard anything on her way past the chicken coop, 'You can bring the mug out with you.'

She continued to frown as if expecting me to attack her at any minute. Had she seen me with the werewolf? I tried not to panic.

'A cup of tea would be lovely,' she said finally, 'Milk and no sugar.'

I made her the cup of tea and led her out to the stable without my other visitor making itself known or coming up in conversation. She checked over the stall and negotiated boarding terms. I explained that she would be responsible for the actual work and the specialist horse feed, but that I was willing to supply the tools, straw and hay along with the stall. She haggled a little. I shrugged and sipped my own cup of tea. She accepted. We shook hands and I walked back into the kitchen with two empty cups and a small but significant weekly income.

The werewolf was dead by the time I got to it. There was nothing left but a sickly looking man in a Metallica t-shirt. I think what actually killed it was the fumes. A chicken coop is not a well ventilated space and the amount of bleach I'd squirted on it created enough fumes to knock it out. I couldn't enter the confined space for a long time after I'd opened the door.

When I did get in, there were obvious and severe chemical burns to the face, particularly the eyes, and to the hands. The pain must have been terrible. The fumes had probably made some kind of chemical burn or damage to all of the breathing surfaces, like the inside of its nose and throat and lungs, but that wasn't visible damage.

I caught myself before I said 'sorry'. The werewolf might have deserved an apology for the pain and suffering but it wasn't in a fit state to accept it.

Instead, I took Ben's silver cross from around my neck and touched it to the werewolf's arm. I held it there until the body started to change into black dust.

Method 21: Broken Neck

As something of an experiment, I didn't tell Ben straight away that his latest gift — that I knew about — was dead. I've never told him exactly how I completed his missions but, this time, saying I was still alive was too close to admitting I'd left the last one alone and in pain. Even if Ben never knew I'd caused suffering — and the circumstantial evidence suggests he wouldn't care if he did — I would still feel guilty. I would still disapprove of myself for him.

The more logical explanation is to say that I was trying it out to see if it meant he'd hold off. If he did, then maybe I could manage a trip away from the farm without wondering whether a killer was after me — or people he thought were me.

So while I didn't send that email on my next trip to the Llareggub library, I looked up flights to Norway. I'm not going to name the place — and I can't think of an appropriate pseudonym — because I don't want you working out where the dangerous people are but it was pure luck that Dave and I had guessed right. The flight would require a stop in Oslo while we changed to a local flight. This regional airport was not as far north as you can get from Oslo but it all looked very out of the way. I wondered how the Welsh sticks would compare to the Norwegian equivalent as I dithered

In the end, I booked two return tickets for mid-December. Maybe not the best time to go to a country that actually knows the meaning of a 'White Christmas', but it was cheap and what I could afford.

Then I spent some time looking up various strategic games. Ben deserved a Christmas present that might wean him off the hard stuff and I deserved a battle of wits that didn't leave me jumping out of my skin every time I heard footsteps, doors closing, or basically anything sudden — including the silence that forms when animals hear something that shouldn't be there.

I also successfully avoided sending an email on my second trip in to the Llareggub library, although Ben had sent an 'Elkie?'

I imagined it as plaintive, like a small boy asking after a lost best friend or family member. The intention was probably more petulant but that still fits with the little boy image.

I found it hard to think of Ben in any other way, although I knew his body was full grown. I hadn't seen him as a full adult but sixteen was closer to a man than my mental image of him. There's just something about the way his condition had stripped away all the golden boy potential that used to shine from him on the school playing fields that also took away all my impressions of adulthood and capability.

It hurt but I ignored the electronic plea. He had to know I was alive if he heard from the werewolves he sent after me. Or, rather, he must know if he never heard back about their victory. Maybe he'd only ever heard from the ex-military one.

I ignored Ben and emailed Dave with the flight dates and times, telling him to meet me at Gatwick Airport and signed off.

Ben's next attempt at communication was more aggressive. It waited almost the full week for my attention and it didn't improve with age.

'I know you're there. I've started the next mission.'

'Shit,' I said.

Thankfully I said it quietly.

At least Ben's message meant my jumping at fireworks was almost justified. We were a fortnight or so off Halloween and Guy Fawkes Night and people, as usual, were celebrating with fireworks early. In the more urban areas it often continues through to Chinese New Year. In rural areas, it'll only be a couple of fireworks every other night but it was still enough to leave me clinging to the ceiling by my finger nails.

I guess I should have gone to the Doctors' and asked for some help. I kind of figured that my only excuse for acting like a war veteran was killing werewolves on a regular basis and *that* wasn't exactly something to go telling people in authority. Anymore than I should admit the temptation to tinker with my fertiliser supply to make explosives.

For what it's worth: Yes, it's possible; No, it's not dissimilar to home-made gunpowder; No, I don't recommend doing it. Aside from the potential danger, anything that goes bang, or should, is really an inefficient weapon. The kind of thing I reserve for mixing up on the sly if I really need to shift a tree stump and not much else. I'm sure there are people with surgical precision out there but I'll also bet they have a lot of resource back-up — like being a member of an elite military group or having rich parents.

So I have a snobbish attitude to fire-arms and explosives. So what? I just prefer the idea of things with points and cutting edges, and anyone can make use of a stick. And the police tend not to find carrying a stick quite as interesting as carrying a gun. Please note, a bow and arrow is not just a stick. They're a bit more obviously a dangerous weapon and you will get stopped if you can afford to carry one of those through town. I'm considering saving up to try it, sometime after I can afford Internet access and some hens.

I looked into bows briefly while considering Ben's latest email. It had been sitting in my inbox for six days and the werewolf could have been following me for any number of those same days. I hadn't seen a trace of it. Was this one a true hunter? Or had it just not got here yet?

I discarded my ranged weapon dreams and tried to compose an answer. Long distance weapons are good but only if you have a shot at your enemy. If this one knew how to hunt, it didn't matter whether I had a traditional yew bow in hand or not.

'Fine,' I typed, 'I'm here. I'm tired of missions. Can't we play another game?'

It wasn't so much that we used code to discuss Ben's game, we just didn't use particular words that would have set alarm bells off for anyone else. Aside from my instance of entrapment, there were no mentions of 'death', and never anything resembling 'killing', 'fighting', 'hunting' or 'werewolves'. We'd never discussed that others might be reading these or that we had to hide what we were doing. I just knew not to, like it was a game rule that had existed before we started playing.

Someone dropped a book somewhere else in the library and I jumped out of my skin, my heart thumping hard for two, three, four, five beats before settling back to a relaxed rhythm. I smiled weakly at the person who had noticed my fearful reaction and clicked send.

Then I fled, tying to control the excess adrenaline enough to keep to a smooth, quick walk.

When I got back to the farm — the Lloyds' place that I was gradually coming round to thinking of mine — I called in at the stable. The woman who had effectively prevented me from putting the last werewolf out of its misery had brought her horse round in the weeks since. I was finding the presence of the chestnut restful, although the owner had cheerfully dismissed him as a cob and a hack. I don't know enough about horses to know why this was so amusing.

'Hey, horse,' I said and rubbed my hand over the soft nose.

He wuffled at me and looked for food treats in my pockets.

'Not seen any strange men in fur, have you?'

He snorted and I took it as a 'no'. I wondered if the horse would assume a werewolf was just another human, about the usual — if incomprehensible — human business.

'Don't do anything to annoy him if you do,' I said and patted the head one last time before seeing myself into the house, 'I can do without having to explain your untimely demise to your owner.'

I got on with my day and tried to feel better about being a walking target. It's better knowing than suspecting. Actually being attacked is probably the best moment, psychologically. It lasts a finite amount of time, has a definite end, and is filled with potential, until it gets to that end. Knowing an attacker is coming is next, the waiting wears on the nerves but knowing that the end is in sight gives a kind of hope. By far the worst is the time between killing a werewolf and Ben letting me know I'm about to have a visitor. It's waiting and suspecting and paranoia and knowing you're jumping at your own shadow for no other reason than you can't control your reactions.

For example, the night before I read Ben's email. When my hairy guest out in the stables whickered for no obvious reason, it woke me from troubled sleep. I lay in my bed — still the one that used to be Ben's — in a cold sweat and with a thumping heart. I took slow careful breaths, in through the nose and out through the mouth, while I listened for further disturbance. There was nothing and I eventually persuaded my over-active mind back to sleep. The following day, the day I checked my emails in the library, was not a day when I was firing on all cylinders.

When much the same thing happened two days after Ben's message, I didn't stay in bed with a thumping heart. I got up and dressed as I listened for more disturbance in the yard. I knew there was a werewolf coming, and just because — if — it wasn't the werewolf that made the horse restless didn't mean it wouldn't be there. It could be watching, waiting, and looking for a weakness. Lying in bed panicking is a weakness so it was better to be up, and armed, and ready.

It wasn't the werewolf but I patrolled the stable a couple of times with a pitchfork in hand and that Stanley knife in my pocket before I was happy to go back to bed. I felt better having been up and doing something than I had when I'd lain in bed feeling stupid. Despite having lost just as much sleep, I didn't feel so bad the day after, either. And while the werewolf didn't come that night, it did come on a night that followed.

'I know you're there,' I said on that second patrol, trying not to sound like the first casualty in a horror film.

I hadn't felt the need to make my presence known the other night and that was when I knew my hunter was there. Perhaps my subconscious mind had put two and two together while the horse still shifted restlessly.

'Easy, horse,' I whispered, 'No sudden moves in case it decides to eat you.'

I wasn't sure if the werewolf had been the initial disturbance but it was definitely here to take advantage. I just knew it. My hands tightened on the pitchfork's shaft and I started to crouch, my stance approaching the kind Dave and I had used when hunting dragons in the wood.

There was a noise from the area I'd cleaned up to be used as tack storage and I crouch-walked over steadily. I didn't need to surprise the werewolf, I just needed to be braced for the attack that was bound to come. I would also prefer it to be out in the light, not in a darkened room.

'Only puppies chew leather,' I said.

It didn't really make any sense, and it didn't need to. I was just letting it know I was there and that I was coming. The only thing I'd wanted was to make some noise that might get a response. And something about being compared to a cute, lolloping bundle of fur was enough to make the rather more grown-up and dangerous human-who-wished-to-be-a-wolf growl.

I thrust forward into the tack room, towards the growl, fork tines first. They met nothing and I pulled back quickly. The growl took on another tone, happy perhaps even smug. I thrust again and the pitch-fork was pulled from my hands.

'Bollocks.'

I followed after it, determined to keep the pitchfork from being used as a weapon against me. Later rationalisation suggests that the longer I stood still, the more likely it was that the weapon had been reversed to point at me, or the werewolf to have moved back into unknown space again, or to have begun a charge. In reality, I just couldn't stay still, even if going forward was stupid.

I was already getting the Stanley knife in my right hand and I held out my left to balance and as a way of sensing what was around me. It fell on nothing more threatening than my guest's bridle and my fingers closed around it momentarily as I faltered, once again uncertain of entering the dark.

I shouldn't have paused, really. I was essentially standing in the doorway, silhouetted against the light of the main stable space. Not a clever idea. The werewolf took advantage, as well it might. The only surprise was that it had waited that long.

It charged me. I heard the scrabble of claws an instant before it hit and I started to duck, so I was a little out of the way when it hit. It didn't manage to get me in quite the hold it had expected and I took less of the impact than I should have done. I stabbed with the Stanley knife, aiming between the ribs but only managing to scrape the hide, and hit with my left hand, now a fist.

Actually, I hit with the bridle. My fingers had still been tight on the leather when the werewolf had charged and they'd stayed tight, a fist ready to strike, even with a horse's headband held in it.

The werewolf rolled off me and ran for the door. My left hand tried to follow and then let go of the bridle before the pull became obvious to my conscious mind. I guess some part of the leather caught on the door because the werewolf came to a very sudden halt. I heard a dull snap I assumed to be from the bridle, a gasp and the thud of a body collapsing.

I lay still and listened to the movements of an empty farm as I waited for my heart to stop thumping and the fog of a poorly aimed tackle to leave my head. I breathed in through my nose and out through my mouth, trying to push the need for fight or flight out with each lungful. The horse whickered and shifted, the smell of blood an extra disturbance but tolerated because the humans present didn't seem to be bothered by it.

When I felt normal, I stood and walked over to the corpse and looked at the reins wrapped around its throat. It was no longer furred but a man dressed in dark clothes but I couldn't bear to think of it as a man, a person. I couldn't have tangled the werewolf up in the leather better if I'd tried to. The neck and head looked at a weird angle to me and I prodded it gingerly. I don't have the medical training to be sure but I suspect the werewolf broke its own neck attempting to run while tangled with the bridle, which was also tangled with the door. If it didn't, then it probably died from cutting the blood flow to its head.

Method 22: Fireworks

I resisted the urge to go running straight back to the Llareggub library the morning after and got on with my work around the farm. During lunch, I fiddled with old fashioned notebook and pen, composing a letter to this Olsen who was (presumably) looking after Ben and who I was (hopefully) going to visit. Presumably because Ben himself could have been anywhere; hopefully because there was a fair chance I might not live long enough to make the flight. But I'd been assuming I'd die within the next week for about five years by that time, so I wasn't going to let that stop me.

I didn't want to discuss Ben sending werewolves after me — not on paper and not yet, not without knowing if Olsen knew about real werewolves. I wanted to make sure Dave's obsession with hunting down werewolves was put in print, that the idea had been shared with anyone who cared to see it. It wasn't so much the hunting that bothered me as the idea that he would kill them while they were his patients, while they were particularly vulnerable. But if I didn't want to talk about werewolves, how did I broach the subject of Dave killing them while he had them on his couch, or in a straitjacket, or however it was that psychologists might deal with vulnerable but aggressive patients?

I didn't want to tell Ben we were coming, either. I didn't want to blurt out anything that give him reason to avoid me or refuse to see me. I didn't want to miss him. Daft, really. However Ben was finding werewolves to send to kill me meant he was probably a better bet for warning about Dave's imbalance than Olsen was. But Olsen moved in the legitimate, human world and Ben was doing something shady and black market. I'd just about given up the idea that Ben was intentionally trying to kill me. I think he was just pushing me to see how much I could take. It was just a game, like the shoot 'em ups he used to play on the console. Only I wasn't a computer character and it wasn't fun.

After lunch, I stopped crossing out the garbled sentences my pen had left behind on the notebook page. It was easy to sigh and push it all away from me, as if it were nonsense and a waste of time.

I checked the horse and the stables. The owner wasn't due out until later and I liked to keep an eye on animals in my care, if only to be sure they're not getting chewed on by the latest attacker. Plus she'd said a friend of hers was after a couple of stalls and would be coming with her, so I wanted to check that my stables looked like a good bet.

I stopped by the chicken coop and hmmed to myself as I debated the costs of a handful of chickens versus a phone line with Internet connection, or even some archery lessons and kit.

I would like to point out that I have a pay as you go mobile phone, if only so the rescue team can get hold of me, but I've never had a land line and wasn't sure I wanted one, even if it meant I didn't have to go to Llareggub to check my emails. I suppose I could have used the agricultural college computers, when I actually bothered to attend a course, but I quite liked going to the library.

So that's pretty much how my day passed, the same as ever. I managed to force another few days to go by before I had no choice but to go and check my emails in the library.

'I'm here,' I sent to Ben, before I'd even looked at my inbox.

When I looked down my list of new emails, there was one from Ben: 'Take a holiday. No more games for a fortnight after I hear back from you.'

There was also one from Dave: 'I'll be at the airport on time. Make sure you are. Heard from Ben?'

'Like I'd tell you,' I said and didn't type.

If he ever realised I kept that kind of information to myself, Dave would just think it was because I harboured unrequited lust for Ben and not because I thought Dave's obsession with killing werewolves was wrong. I couldn't bring myself to send anything back — any comment was likely to be defensive about my ability to find the UK's second largest airport — and so snarling at the computer screen was the most eventful thing in my time off.

Well, most eventful except finding some village kids with a string of fire-crackers and one of our cows. I have no idea where they got the fireworks from. I really don't want to know where they got the idea of sneaking about in the fields at eight o'clock in the evening and tying a string of them to a cow's tail.

We usually bring the cows in for winter but with the extra pasture — with the Lloyds' spread — we thought we'd try moving them into the more sheltered fields instead. We don't usually get a lot of freezing weather being to the west of the country, just lots of horizontal, very cold rain. The down side of the outdoor plan I hadn't taken into account was checking on the herd at least twice a day.

The not-so-much down side, more of the unbelievable-act-of-stupidity-of-Darwin-Award-winning-proportions side, is bored local teenagers.

'What the fuck do you think you're doing?'

I'd walked down to the dancing torchlight, my own heavy duty torch held loosely in my right and turned off. I had no wish to hurt anyone, I just wanted to frighten them senseless. I timed my question with a blast of torchlight into the face of the one attempting to tie a string of firecrackers to my poor beast's tail.

'Shit!'

The other two were already gone, their torchlight continuing to dance as they fled back up the slope to the road.

'I'd run after them, if I were you,' I said. I brought my torch up so it lit my face from below and displayed my grin. I almost laughed at the poor sod. 'Before you forget your route up the hill.'

I heard rather than saw the teenager shuffle backwards in the mud and loose his grip on the firecrackers.

'I'm sorry!'

'Only that you got caught,' I said, shifting my torch to give him some light to scramble by. 'And give me whatever it was you were going to use to light them before you go.'

He threw the cigarette lighter, an act of defiance while giving in and an attempt to save face. I swung the torchlight as I caught it easily in my left hand so that the beam lit up my hand as it caught and then the teenager's face. He looked awed and I took satisfaction in that. I even grinned some more.

'Now bugger off,' I said.

As he half ran, half stumbled away, I wondered if Dave and I would have ever done anything quite this senseless in search of rural entertainment. We were more the inventing-mythical-beasts-to-slay type. Only these days I didn't have to invent them.

'Guess I'm just too kick-ass for them,' I said conversationally.

The cow, understandably, said nothing.

It took me a few minutes to juggle everything and untangle the firecrackers. I put them in my coat pocket with a mental note to remove them as quickly as possible. I put the lighter in a totally different pocket and repeated the mental note about removing explosives from my person.

'I hate gunpowder,' I said to the cow and patted her rump. 'I seriously can't believe you didn't put a hoof in where it hurt while you had the chance, though.'

The cow heaved a sigh and wandered off down slope. I heaved a sigh and wandered up slope to the battered Landie. I did most of the driving around the fields, these days, so now Mr Williams let me keep it.

Anyway, I have to admit I enjoyed scaring the local kids that night. I was starting to unwind, no longer so convinced that every noise held a threat even though it made me jump. Retirement looked like a wonderful thing. After I talked to Ben maybe he'd let me try it for real.

It had, at that point, been eighteen days since I'd seen a werewolf and it may even have been the best moment of my life. The post-coital highs I used to get from Dave don't really count, partly because they've been soured in retrospect by Dave's stupidity. They're also, by their nature, much more temporary than the satisfaction of realising that you like your life. It was such a revelation that I had to tell the three horses now living in my stables.

'I like my life,' I said, too dazed to care that I was being silly, 'And I like being a farmer.'

The horses shifted a little in their stalls and whickered after attention or treats but otherwise ignored what I was talking about. That's about when I realised I was acting strangely.

'I also quite like scaring the shit out of the local kids, but I probably shouldn't admit that,' I added to make up for it.

I grinned again, replaying the firework scene but replacing the kids I'd scared that evening with the idiots I used to catch a school bus with. I hummed as I went in to the house to make dinner and a cup of tea. But I was out again in about five minutes when I heard the horses continuing their version of begging for attention.

'Well, I know it isn't your owners, anyway,' I said aloud as I turned the light on.

I put my hands in my coat pockets and cursed.

'I forgot to take those bloody firecrackers out.'

I took a quick look around and found no sign of extra occupants in the stable, so I turned off the light and widened my search to the yard — and cursed again when I realised I'd left the torch in the Landie. Being on holiday had made me forgetful and lax.

I walked over to the battered old vehicle and opened the driver's door. I leant in and —

A strong hand or paw lashed out from under the land rover. It caught at my ankles and pulled, felling me backwards. I landed, winded and undignified, with my toes pointed towards my attacker. The furred-up werewolf clambered out from under the vehicle, keeping close to the ground if only because of the lack of clearance. The movement was not particularly graceful but that isn't important when you're busy being menacing.

'Oh, for fuck's sake,' I whispered hoarsely when my diaphragm managed to finally pull air into my lungs.

Without me really thinking about what I was doing, my hands closed around the objects in my coat pockets, lighter in one and tangled string of firecrackers in the other. The werewolf stalked forward, so close I could imagine its hot breath against my skin even through my clothes.

It grinned as if it knew my imaginings, a wolfish, rakish grin that wouldn't have looked out of place on a lover teasing his way up my body. Except a werewolf is closer to a rapist by the simple lack of consent. But it was the fur and the teeth that set the grin firmly in the horror rather than the romance section of my personal library.

This is going to take therapy, never mind chocolate spread, I thought.

Fido paused when it got high enough up my body for our breaths to mingle, the white water vapour merging in a way that made my mental detour even more disturbing. I pulled my hands from my pockets and tried to push the werewolf away, my clenched fists weak against what had once been human shoulders. It remained immovable, laughing silently down at me.

'Get off me!'

The fists flailed, although I was careful not to disturb the cradled firecrackers too much. In my distrust of all things explosive, I didn't want to find out if the black powder was set off by that level of friction. The laugh became more pronounced, the jaws wide with self-satisfied amusement.

I made my planned movements as quickly as I could. It didn't matter if they didn't happen all at once, only that they were accurate. I thrust the firecrackers into Fido's mouth and lit the fuse. As the string took the flame, I slammed my knee into the groin and swung my forearm into the inside of an elbow joint. Fido collapsed sideways and I swung out of the way.

'Oh man, I hope they're not enough to take the Landie,' I whispered as I ran for the stable.

I'd managed to curl the string up enough that all the firecrackers were close and likely to go off all at once but there was a long fuse before they did, perhaps thirty seconds. The kids had planned on not being too near the cow when they set it off. Which meant I got to look back and see Fido was still busy clutching at its balls while trying to de-stuff its mouth.

It had managed to get the knot half out of its mouth but once they went off — after the horses panicked at the loud noises and I started screaming apologies to them — the jaw was no longer there. My screams to the horses were interrupted as I turned to one side so I didn't have to see the damage while I threw up.

There's little more to say about what happened. I got to send Ben a 'still here' and wonder what he made of fireworks these days. As kids, I guess we'd all loved them, the noisier the better. Most animals are terrified of them — my equine lodgers being no exception — because of their much more sensitive hearing. And, probably, their lack of reasoning ability that means they don't associate the actions that went before with the explosion.

I couldn't work out whether a werewolf would find the sound of fireworks too much. Still, Ben would probably never be able to look at them the same way again if he knew I'd taken someone's face off with a string of firecrackers.

Method 23: Antifreeze

It took a while for Ben to get back to me. I didn't get an email for just over a fortnight, a drawn-out period that stretched my nerves. Had Ben not bothered to announce it? Was that snapping stick the first sign of an enemy? The restless horses in the stable? The firework that broke the rural idyll?

The slow slide from late autumn to early winter is a quiet time on a farm with little more than animal feeding time-tabled. There are other tasks, as-and-when tasks, but there is no hurry. There's the whole winter ahead of you. There's nothing, really, to distract from fear and waiting. Except possibly starting to worry about going to another country to meet a stranger who may or may not be involved with real werewolves on purpose.

In case you never noticed, winter doesn't start on the stroke of December twenty-first, just because the calendar says it should. It usually starts when your car breaks down in the middle of nowhere and you've forgotten your coat or when you have to pull a sheep out of a bog or some other activity that would be slightly better without horizontal rain or quite so low temperatures.

This particular year, it was just my screenwash freezing up overnight when I had to get out — still in the dark — first thing on a mid-November morning. I stopped on the farm access lane and popped the bonnet. The screenwash in the reservoir, admittedly a hundred percent tap-water, was still liquid. The night hadn't been that cold, just cold enough to freeze the stuff in the tubes and jets.

I backed up the lane and got a kettle full of water from the kitchen to clean off the windscreen and decided to leave the engine to melt the jets. By lunch-time, I had the chance to drive down to the local petrol station ten miles away and buy some spray-on de-icer and some cleaner-plus-antifreeze to add to the screenwash.

Both were bright blue with the chemical colouring that clearly says 'don't drink me'. I understand they put bitter flavouring in, too, but have never bothered to test the assumption. There were the standard warning signs and text on the label. There was an ingredients list and one declared itself 'ethylene glycol' and the other 'ethane-1,2-diol.' It didn't mean anything specifically to me but I'm in the habit of reading instructions.

I also knew that it was bad for animals, further to the human orientated warnings. Something about it being sweet — despite the bittering agent, which confuses me — and therefore an attractive flavour so it had to be kept well out of the way of anything not aware of bright blue liquids and orange warning signs. So I left the de-icer in the Landie and took the cleaner-plus-antifreeze in the house. I mixed up what I needed, a fifty percent solution, and put the bottle somewhere safe despite my lack of children and child replacements. I forgot about it because these chemicals aren't important once you have them.

Sometime about then, Ben got in touch.

'Sending someone to see you. Think you'll like him. Let me know how it goes.'

My jumping at shadows continued but at least I now knew it might be something out to get me, not just my imagination. Only things didn't go quite as I expected.

Let's start at the beginning.

I'd decided to top up the screenwash again, a litre of cleaner-plus-antifreeze and tap-water. I dug out the bottle and mixed it in the house before I brought it outside to pour into the Landie's maw. The sound of a predatory motor-bike splashing down my lane had me banging my head against the bonnet as I raised my head to look.

'Shit!'

I wasn't sure what got me most upset: that I was so jumpy, that I'd spilt most of the screenwash or that I'd just injured myself.

The big beast of a motorbike stopped, the rider putting

down the stand as he took in a dishevelled me, a battered Landie and a crumbling farm. I say 'he' because the rider was clearly male. From the shape I could see in the biking leathers I would bet on a gym fit body underneath. The black, faceless helmet cocked to one side and I couldn't quite stop myself from wondering what he looked like. What can I say? It had been a while.

'Elkie?'

The voice was a deep growl that made me blush, even as the Irish lilt it held made me want to smile. It was a vibration that I wasn't satisfied with hearing through my ears. Instant, unrequited lust with graphic mental images.

'Who's asking?' I asked through my haze.

The rider unstrapped his helmet and shook out black hair that curled around a tanned, thick neck. The face the neck carried made me blush even harder, even though I knew what was going on. No-one came down that lane asking for me. The only normal people likely to would probably ask for 'Ms. Bernstein', strictly business.

'So you'll be Ben's friend, then,' I said.

He turned slightly, perhaps to display the backpack he wore, maybe just checking out his surroundings. I knew his fur-skin would be in the bag and probably not much else, depending on how far he'd ridden.

'Elkie,' he said and this time it wasn't a question.

I nodded.

'I'm Diarmuid.'

'Wrong side of the water?' I asked.

Idiot, I thought to myself, *frustration's no reason to sound like a bigot. And an idiot one at that.*

He frowned at me as if the words didn't quite make sense, because they probably didn't, and I shrugged off my self-disgust. He was everything that modern fantasy would tell you a werewolf should be. Tall, strong, handsome. Possibly not the sharpest knife in the drawer but who needs brains when you look so edible?

'Um. Cup of tea?' I forced out.

The frown broke into a dazzling, charming smile and that deep rumble came back as a laugh and then a 'sure'. But the rumble was drowned out by another vehicle coming down the lane.

I sighed. 'Getting crowded round here.'

I didn't have to worry about another werewolf turning up but I wasn't really happy with having my daydream interrupted. If Diarmuid hadn't made himself known with full fur and teeth bared, I figured this was one mission that wouldn't end with me shovelling black dust into my cess pit. It might even be enjoyable. Possibly rewarding.

'Who's that?' he asked.

I tried to stay objective about the way he stepped between me and the oncoming threat, reminding myself it was all about males defending territory. This did not make it feel less significant and I mentally hugged a happy glow.

I looked over the oncoming car and sighed again. 'Looks like Dave has dropped everything to come charging into the wilds again.'

In his girlfriend's car. Again.

'Dave?'

Diarmuid turned his head to look at me, though his attention was on the approaching car. The sharp tone made me wonder if he knew who Dave was or if he just didn't like the sound of another man's name.

'My business partner's son,' I said, only covering a small part of the connection.

Diarmuid nodded as if it was all he needed to hear. I considered writing a glowing email to Ben about how wonderful the new entertainment or guard-dog or whatever Diarmuid was intended to be was. A woman can dream.

The dream came to a swift end as Dave stomping out of his girlfriend's car. The girlfriend was slightly better behaved and didn't even slam the door.

'I don't think she allows him out on his own, these days,' I said.

Diarmuid smiled and I surprised myself filing the shared moment away for posterity. I obviously didn't get out enough and was getting too attached. Maybe that's how Ben expected to win.

'Problem?' I asked Dave.

He was glaring at both of us. 'I just had time to come up and discuss the trip to Norway.'

Behind Dave's back, the girlfriend crossed her arms and glared at *him*, the impact of it only slightly marred by the way she was also eyeing up my werewolf. Yes, mine. I was ready to growl, too.

'That's what phones are for. Or email.'

Dave had the grace to look embarrassed. The girlfriend smiled at some personal triumph and stepped forward with her hand out to Diarmuid. I saw his nostrils twitch, just ever so slightly, as if he was taking in her smell more than the sight of her.

'Ben?' she asked sweetly, 'I've been dying to meet you.'

He smiled and I was pleased to see it made someone else flush, too.

'No, ma'am. I'm Diarmuid.'

Her eyes widened and she tried to turn to look at me but her eyes couldn't quite leave the beautiful face any more than her hand could let go of his. Dave turned very red and looked ready to explode.

'Um. Elkie?' she asked.

'A change in personnel,' I said with a smile, 'Ben's always been a long distance thing and we're apparently on a break.'

I laughed a little and Diarmuid's rumble joined in. He winked at me and everybody present was now clear that I no longer held any interest in Dave. It was interesting seeing the girlfriend finally relax towards me as I was no longer an obvious threat. It was amusing to watch Dave try not to hiss and spit like a small kitten faced with a tiger — or a werewolf, for that matter.

'Tea?' I asked again and hustled everyone indoors.

Diarmuid shrugged off his backpack and he seated it carefully next to him. I flicked a look at Dave and saw he'd noticed to.

'I need to clean up first,' I said, looking at the dirt I'd got on my hands from just opening up the bonnet and trying to get into the screenwash reservoir.

'It's okay,' Dave said, 'I'll sort it.'

I raised my eyebrows.

'I don't think that's a good idea,' his girlfriend said, more sensitive than Dave to my unease.

Diarmuid just watched with dark and interested — although slightly puzzled — eyes. He must have known I didn't want Dave taking charge but I guess he had reasons for not trying to himself. Like not knowing where the kettle was.

'Nonsense,' Dave said, 'I'm practically family.'

'Yeah?' I muttered in Welsh, 'Then there's a nasty little word for what we used to get up to.'

I came back, we drank tea, we limped through basic conversation. Things like the girlfriend asking, ever so sweetly, 'So, Diarmuid, how long are you here for?'

He shrugged and looked at me.

'As long as he wants,' I said.

'And Ben doesn't mind?' Dave asked, stirring more than his drink.

'Ben sent me to look in on Elkie.'

Dave smirked. 'That's... convenient.'

'About as convenient as the girl next door,' I muttered, this time in English.

Both Dave and Diarmuid looked at me. The girlfriend was still too caught by my werewolf's beauty to have eyes for anyone else. I'm not entirely sure she heard me properly. Diarmuid flicked an eyebrow so it raised slightly in Dave's direction, a question. I nodded, *yes*.

'Well, I guess Elkie's so sweet Ben wants to make sure she's well looked after when he's not around to do it himself,' Diarmuid said smoothly.

I had a mental itch on that one, the implications of shared ownership — of me, no less — not exactly the romantic nonsense a woman wants to hear. Diarmuid became a bit less dreamy and a lot more real. The girlfriend was jolted, too, her admiration interrupted by an echo of her relationship; Dave was here over his own shared interest in me.

'So,' Diarmuid needled, 'You two old friends are planning on going to Norway?'

He smiled and winked at me. I shrugged, trying not to grin back. It was an instinctive response to the expression rather than his words, automatic and not to be trusted.

'I thought we should go see Ben,' I said.

The girlfriend gave a brittle laugh. 'I have to admit I was a bit put out by them leaving me behind but they're going to be reunited with another childhood friend. I'm sure I'd only be a spare part.'

Diarmuid's laugh was surer and more relaxed. 'Oh, I'd say Dave's virtue is safe with Elkie. But I'm going to do my best to persuade Elkie to stay with me.'

Within half an hour, Dave and his girlfriend drove off and I figured I'd be collared the next morning for whatever it was that had been bugging him before he turned up. I was still trying to work out what had happened to his anger at Diarmuid that seemed to have vanished by the time he handed me my cup of tea.

'Another cup?' I asked Diarmuid.

'Sure. Why not?'

I brewed up a second round just for us two and wondered what was wrong with the kitchen. Something was nagging at me.

'How many sugars?'

'Two, please.'

I looked at the counter by the sink and noticed a distinct lack of blue.

'The shit.'

I heard Diarmuid push his chair back. I felt rather than heard him come up behind me, a mix of his body heat and sheer attraction on my part.

'Do you feel okay?' I asked.

'What's wrong?'

'Dave's just poisoned you.'

I searched through the cupboards, looking for where he'd hidden the remainder.

'Was your drink hot or cold when he made it.'

There was a pause before Diarmuid answered. 'He put something in the bin. And it was hot, just not boiling.'

The bin held the bottle, and not that much was actually gone but then there isn't that much liquid in a tea cup.

'Here, hold this,' I thrust the bottle at Diarmuid, 'Drink this,' the latest cup of tea in the hopes it would water down the bad effects, 'and get in the Landie. We're taking you to A and E.'

How much was necessary to kill a man? How fast would it work? If I found someone who knew, would it still hold true for a werewolf? Magic hadn't played that large a part in the deaths I'd been involved in, aside the unexplained powers of silver and Ben and Old Man Lloyd catching canine parvo-virus, but most of them had involved laws of Nature not poisons.

'I'm fine. I don't need to go to hospital.'

I shoved him out of the door and locked up.

'You've been poisoned with antifreeze,' I bit out and the big man flinched, 'And I'm not going to let you die of it.'

He rallied and growled back, 'I'm not going to hospital.'

'You're a werewolf. Not immortal.'

There was a strange kind of comfort with how worn and familiar the argument seemed, like a long-held affection, even as I knew I had to get him to someone who knew what they were doing. If I'd had a phone line and an Internet connection, I could have looked this all up without involving people who shouldn't know about werewolves. Not that I'm advocating taking medical treatment into inexperienced hands.

Diarmuid grabbed my shoulders and dragged me forward. My breath caught in my throat as I looked into those dark eyes.

'I came to kill you,' he said.

'But — '

'Just because I'm here to fight you doesn't mean we can't talk like civilised people first.'

Talk? Just talk? Sod's Law, I thought.

'Civilised people don't fight,' I said, not really grasp-ing what he was getting at. The only thing that was going through my head was, *And they probably don't go at it like hyper-active bunnies, either, but I know which I'd prefer to do.*

'Elkie, why don't we just skip the hospital trip and get on with things?'

There was a slight slur to his voice by the end of the sen-tence and his eyes were starting to show that slightly erratic eye movement associated with drunkenness. As there was no alcohol involved in brewing tea, I could only assume it was symptoms of the poison starting to show.

'I don't want to fight you,' I whispered.

He leant forward and his forehead touched mine, the smile on his face as beautiful as our shared breath was exciting. It was on the delicious end of 'compare and contrast' with the past, similar occasions I'd experienced with other people and werewolves.

'I don't think you're in a fit state to do anything,' I added softly.

'Dizzy. Headache. Fast bloody hangover, this.'

He kissed me, clumsily, as if he wasn't entirely sure who I was and what we were doing, as if he had just found himself standing there leaning against a woman and it was the obvious thing to do. It was stupid, probably sexist and several other -isms, but it was also sweet and soft and warm.

'How about I put you to bed,' I said.

I knew I'd be spending the night watching Diarmuid die — if only because he was too heavy for me to get in the Landie on my own — and knew I couldn't afford to save him if he was determined to kill me.

'The perfect end to the perfect night,' he slurred, 'So good I already don't remember what happened.'

I wasn't sure if he was joking or if his confusion was real.

'So, what's your name, beautiful girl?'

'What does it matter?' I asked, still not sure if he were serious, 'You won't remember it in the morning.'

He laughed softly.

Intermission

I started the next morning — I mean morning proper with daylight and the rest of the world showing signs of being alive — with breakfast at the Williams' place. I walked straight into the kitchen. Dave's mum almost spilling the boiling water over the counter instead of pouring it into mugs.

'Elkie! This is a surprise.'

It wasn't something I'd done since moving into my place.

'Yeah, I just thought I'd drop in for breakfast before starting work,' I said with a shrug, 'Dave said he wanted to talk to me and now is as good as any time.'

Dave wasn't around yet, though. Too used to city hours, he was enjoying a lie-in. Lucky bastard. 'Bastard' being the word I'd emphasise. Both his parents were up — I briefly considered asking them if they were actually married, just to confirm my opinion of their son — and the girlfriend was looking sleepy eyed at the table. Up until I mentioned coming in for breakfast. Then she looked behind me expectantly and back at my face.

'Is Diarmuid here?'

'No.'

She continued to look expectant.

'He's about but not coming over for breakfast,' I clarified, wondering if floating in a cess pit really counted as 'around'.

Dave's parents raised eyebrows and exchanged a look as the girlfriend looked disappointed. I have to agree with her, a healthy Diarmuid would be a wonderful way to start the day. One way or another, I probably wouldn't have made it to work if it had been a viable option, though.

'Diarmuid?' Mrs Williams asked.

'A friend of mine and Ben's,' I said as if it explained everything and the Williams nodded as if they agreed it did.

I'd thought about bringing his dust over and pouring

him into Dave's morning cup. One of those ideas that had occurred to me as I'd held the dying body. In the end, I decided the Irish werewolf didn't deserve to end up as part of the Welsh nut-case.

'I don't think Dave'll be up any time soon,' the girlfriend said with an indulgent smile.

I looked at the stairs and thought about charging up them and pulling the duvet off his comfortable, sleeping, *living* form. The only thing that stopped me was having no energy to deal with the girlfriend's response.

'I can wait,' I said, 'The animals were sorted out hours ago.'

I'd knew I wouldn't be able to sleep once I'd swept up Diarmuid. I figured I was better off working. It had been more like the end of the working day than the start of the next one.

'You had help,' the girlfriend said with a knowing smile.

I shrugged.

'I bet Diarmuid looks gorgeous doing manual labour,' she said with the wistful tones of someone who'd never tried it. 'All rippling muscle and dark looks.'

I considered the image she was painting and liked it. It would have been better if it could have been real. Not that farm work at that time of year is ever quite as sexy as she'd put into my head.

It took Dave another two hours to surface. Work having been dealt with for the moment, I spent the time discussing plans for the farms and the houses, the old cottage included, with his parents. The girlfriend chipped in occasionally with comments, some of which were even constructive, but otherwise glazed over with disinterest.

Dave took one look at me and smiled. As ever, he knew me better than anyone else in the room. Well, when he thought my emotions were important and bothered to pay attention.

'Diarmuid okay?' he asked.

He wore a grin that made the girlfriend double-take. I don't think I've ever seen a person do it for real other than that. Not that it wasn't justified; Dave is not a morning person and this happiness — no, this gloating — had apparently come from nowhere.

'As well as can be expected,' I replied evenly.

Dave knew what had happened with those words. If I'd treated Diarmuid decently, like a human being or even one of the farm animals, I'd have taken him to hospital. I'd have mentioned that there had been time in A&E if only to account for any comments that might come up later. Business as usual meant non-committal statements that could mean almost anything. Business as usual meant a dead werewolf to be hidden.

I ignored Dave's thinly disguised triumph. If he knew he'd upset me, that he had some level of control over me and my future, he would forever have me marked out as his territory. I was no longer his friend and occasional lover, I was a lamp-post to be pissed on and used to send a message to passing werewolves. All because he'd been attacked a few times in his teenage years.

'What was it you wanted to talk to me about?' I asked.

Dave shrugged. 'Oh, you know. Flights to Norway. Meeting up at the airport. Times. The usual.'

'Didn't we talk about that yesterday?' the girlfriend asked.

Which was sort of true. As well as the stuff I've bothered to mention, we'd passed a few inane comments about the planned trip to Norway over a cup of poisoned tea.

I ignored the girlfriend and asked, 'And for this you drive all the way from London?'

'I want my plane ticket.'

Dave sipped at his morning cup. I considered whether it was possible to poison a normal human with screenwash and not get caught. Well, biologically or magically normal as opposed to a werewolf. I'd already come to the conclusion that Dave was not normal in a few other, equally important ways.

'It's an email, Dave. I ordered them online.'

'So give me a printout.'

I raised my eyebrows into exactly the same expression his parents had worn when the unknown-to-them Diarmuid had been mentioned.

'How about you just remember to meet me at Gatwick and we leave it at that.'

I didn't want him to go without me. I didn't trust him not to try. Just because I couldn't think of it didn't mean there wasn't a way for him to leave me behind. I was fairly sure he didn't want me with him.

Dave smiled. 'I thought you might not want to go and find Ben now.'

His smile was echoed by the girlfriend in her own, slightly envious smile — no doubt convinced that Diarmuid was more than man enough for any one woman. And so they came to much the same conclusion from different angles. At least Dave had a chance of realising I didn't want to travel with him because I considered him a murderer. He just also happened to think I was deluded because werewolves shouldn't exist — I assume they're also not supposed to have relationships with his ex — and it was only a matter of time before we had a 'you're just like me' conversation.

'I still need to talk to Ben,' I said evenly, 'If only to say thank you for the farm.'

Dave shrugged again. 'That's what phones are for. Or email.'

I burnt with rage at him stealing my words, at him killing someone who might have been a friend or more, at him wanting to kill someone who was already worse off than he would ever be. I stood up and spoke as calmly as I could manage.

'Some things you need to say face-to-face.'

I left the room before I started using kitchen utensils to dismember someone who had been the other half of me, even before we'd been lovers. Then I betrayed him as he had betrayed me.

I finally composed a workable letter to Olsen. I started with telling the unknown, unseen professor that I had booked flights and on what date. I said a friend of mine and Ben's was coming with me. I said we'd pick up a suitable rental car at the airport. I didn't mention real werewolves or killing but I mentioned that Dave was interested in clinical lycanthropy 'to the point of obsession'.

I hoped Olsen would ask Ben about him. Not that Ben knew a huge amount about Dave, even before he was taken away, but he could say that Dave knew about werewolves, and that Dave had tried to kill him. That would at least lay some groundwork for me.

I typed the letter up on a library computer and looked at it for a while. I let other program windows cover it as I checked my emails and checked flights and maps. I looked at the last email from Ben several times.

'Sending someone to see you. Think you'll like him. Let me know how it goes.'

I turned back to the letter when I found tears in my eyes and my finger tips brushing the individual words of the email. Had Ben known I'd like Diarmuid, that I'd find him attractive? Probably, although I doubt he had intended for me to be anything other than amused by the Irishman's charm and good looks. He wouldn't have expected me to consider it more than a passing entertainment, to want to hold on for a while. He hadn't planned for me to have this dilemma, had he? He wouldn't want me to have to kill something I lusted after and maybe could have loved, right?

I tried to believe the answer was 'no'. But if Ben had known Diarmuid at all, he would have known that the other werewolf fully intended to carry out the 'mission' of attacking me. After years of being played with, Ben would expect me to defend myself, to pick the 'mission' over anything other distraction. Which is what I did when, in the end, I ensured my own survival and freedom when I had the opportunity to save my opponent.

I came back to the words that rubbed in my guilt and shame as much as they reminded me of the instant, inappropriate connection I'd felt.

'I can't do this anymore,' I said aloud.

People looked up from computers and books to look at me, then away again. I guess they saw the tears that started to leak from the corners of my eyes. But I really couldn't cope, so I decided to betray both Ben and Dave on the same day.

'Diarmuid is lush,' I sent to Ben, 'And we've postponed the mission indefinitely. Thank you for this.'

On its own, that wasn't the betrayal. That would come much later. I was simply taking a chance that Ben wasn't the kind of person to hold a grudge over my apparently hooking up with Diarmuid. No matter how child-like he might seem at times, no matter how petulant, Ben didn't stamp his foot or throw his toys out of the pram. He probably wouldn't care — right up until he found out I was going to use Olsen's authority to make him stop playing with me.

Basically, I guessed he wouldn't send other werewolves to attack me — and the assumed Diarmuid — because I'd disrupted his game, if only because he couldn't be sure the game would come out in his favour. A known werewolf killer and a werewolf standing together against another attacker? I know which side I'd put money on in those circumstances. Even then, I wasn't convinced that killing me would be an outcome Ben considered in his favour.

My gamble worked because I received an email within the week.

'Let me know when the game resumes. I doubt I can find a mission to beat you both together.'

I didn't see or hear from werewolves, friend or foe, after that until I got to Norway. A month off from being attacked was a divine gift, if only because someone had bought it for me with their life.

Method 24: Icicle

The Dave-and-Elkie show started in Gatwick. Him in carefully put together suit and long beige coat. If it weren't for the smart leather shoes, he would have looked like he was trying to copy the Tenth Doctor. As it was, he just looked like he was trying to impress at a job interview. I don't suppose it helped that he got to sit next to me, who looked like a refugee from a duck shoot, but with trainers. I was expecting cold and potentially wet at the other end of the journey and had dressed appropriately, more or less.

We barely talked on the flight to Oslo and the only comments we made on the bounce into the regional airport were in reference to the depth of snow and the size of the field versus the size of the landscape. We weren't prepared for any of it, despite my best efforts.

Nor was I prepared to be met by the man I'd assumed was a courier when he'd delivered Ben's gifts. He wasn't there with a name board or anything. He even just seemed to be in my eye-line by chance but, once he was sure I'd seen him, he nodded and stepped forward. He took the brown paper wrapped parcel I'd brought for Ben from my hands.

'Nice to see you again, Elkie,' he said.

Despite the fact that I hadn't expected to be met, I was grateful there was someone there to diffuse my anger at Dave, so I didn't make any objection. I just smiled and nodded back.

'And you,' I said.

'You must be Dave Williams.'

The greying lanky apparently-not-a-courier held out a hand to Dave. Dave shook it. The other man's nostrils twitched a little and he looked slightly disappointed. I cast a quick glance over him, looking for a bag that would give him away for sure. There was none. To balance out, I caught him eyeing the briefcase and suitcase that Dave carried but he seemed to disregard the possibility of fur as soon as his nostrils twitched. Dave didn't smell like a werewolf because he wasn't one. The other man probably did but I didn't have the nose to confirm it.

'I'm Conn,' this other man said.

Dave smiled but the look was strained. He expected more than first name introductions. 'Conn ... ?'

There was a shrug. 'Just Conn.'

Dave's mouth became a thin line.

'Olsen sent you,' I said.

Conn nodded. 'I'm to drive you to the Institute.'

'Not a courier, then.'

He smiled and there was something about the way he shifted that stopped me thinking 'dangerous'. It was more 'sheepdog' or 'watchful'. 'Nah. I do... odd jobs for Olsen.'

He moved to stand between Dave and me and gestured towards the exit. 'Shall we go?'

Conn got us to the car without ever stepping out from between us. I could have done with pumping information about exactly what 'odd jobs' entailed but daren't in front of Dave. Because I knew it would be werewolf related and I didn't want to get Conn killed. I felt like I was watching an approaching iceberg, fully aware that what I could see was not the bit I needed to know about.

'Do you ever help Olsen with his cases?' Dave asked.

'Not particularly. I'm just a layman,' Conn answered.

Dave prodded some more. 'Are you interested in clinical lycanthropy?'

There was a pause and then an amused 'Not so much'.

It was enough to make me give a mental 'ah' but apparently not enough to flag reality up for Dave. But then, Dave had met fewer werewolves and had yet to realise that there was more to some of them than just being outright killers. Not all of them, just some of them. Or maybe he knew and didn't care to differentiate. Or maybe I was reading too much into Diarmuid's attempt to 'talk'.

'You'll have to forgive Dave,' I cut in, 'He's obsessive about his speciality.'

They both looked at me sharply, Dave with a glare and Conn with puzzled frown.

'I am *not* obsessed,' Dave snapped.

Conn smiled again. 'I've met worse.'

We made it to an estate car full of furry warm bodies. Five mixed breed dogs, to be precise, incarcerated in the boot.

'The Hellhounds,' Conn said.

They panted and barked at us happily, unconcerned with our tensions. I took it as a sign that their owner — their pack leader, I suppose — was equally relaxed.

'Did you collect these back home?' I asked, 'Or did you find them here in Norway?'

Conn grinned as he settled into the driver's seat. 'Aye.'

Dave hurriedly helped himself to the front passenger seat, leaving me to get in the back. I put my hand against the metal grid that held back the pack, introducing myself before I stuck my fingers in.

'Both?' I asked, trying to work out which dogs might be from where. A couple looked fluffier than the others, as if they had thicker, more insulating layers of fur. Were they the natives?

'Aye,' Conn said again. He added, 'I tend to take in strays I come across and find them new homes once I've got them civilised.'

I looked at him in the rear view mirror, watched him carefully join the traffic in the white winter weather.

'Have any that wouldn't mind life on a Welsh hill farm?' I asked.

He raised his eyebrows and shot me a look. 'Maybe.'

I wasn't sure if we were still talking dogs or if we'd moved on to werewolves.

I looked out at the piled up snow and ice. There's no arguing that I was in a country that dealt with it better, with cars still running on the road even if they were slower than most Brits would be happy with. I thought about farming out in weather like this. I doubted much got done until spring once the snows came.

Somewhere about the time I came to that conclusion, one

of our tires burst. Conn drove skilfully out of the skid and then brought the car over to the side of the road.

'You've done this before,' I said as I braced against the seat in front.

Dave had gone pale with fear and shock, not used to anything more than normal, safe driving.

'A bit of off-roadin',' Conn said without any apparent effort. 'And the ice round here is always fun.'

'I'd prefer to have the Landie.'

Although my problem was usually skating or getting stuck in mud, depending on how fast I'd been going when I hit it.

The car came sedately to a stop, and I took the time to give the dogs a head count.

'Dogs and passengers all fine.'

'That bloody death trap is nothing more than a rust bucket,' Dave spat, 'And I am not fine.'

'You're just shaken up,' I said.

Conn looked at Dave with something getting close to surprise. 'Rust bucket?'

It wasn't a fair description of his estate car.

'He means the Landie I use.'

'My *dad's* Landie,' Dave ground out.

'The company vehicle, if you're going to be precise.'

Dave glared some more, mostly just upset because we'd seen him scared.

'We're business partners and I do most of the driving around the farm these days, anyway,' I added for good measure.

I got out of the car, shaken enough to feel the need to stretch my legs. I looked around and noted the trees close to the road — a near miss, really — and watched the few slow cars driving past.

'Any of those likely to stop and help?' I asked Conn.

He was letting the dogs out of the boot, all on long, slender leather leads, so he could get the tools and spare wheel out from underneath them.

He looked up at them and seemed to consider before answering, 'I shouldn't think so.'

'Norwegians not very helpful?'

'Nah. Not that. They'll just think we can cope unless we start flaggin' them down. Anyway, we're not far from home.'

'I'll take the dogs,' I said and took the leads.

'Don't go too far.'

I raised my eyebrows. 'Why? Something out there out there more dangerous than the ice?'

Conn gave me a level look I chose interpret as 'don't be stupid' and I also chose to ignore the look and the advice.

I walked the dogs away from the road for something to do. It was cold and I knew my feet would get wet with walking into the snow with only trainers on but didn't care. To a certain extent, I was just happy to be properly outdoors after being cooped up for so long. It was also pretty amazing to see things I rarely got to see, like several feet of snow and icicles that were almost as long as the snow was deep.

Dave followed me, catching at my elbow.

'You really think you can impress this Conn by putting me down in front of him?' he growled.

I pulled my arm from his grip and watched the dogs sniff around or try to tie me into a leather knot. I'm not convinced that animals aren't sentient enough to cause mischief on purpose.

'I didn't say anything that was a put-down. Or, at least, I didn't mean to.'

Kind of a lie. I hadn't meant to be particularly aggressive about it but I had no interest in backing down for Dave. I never had.

Dave couldn't come up with a response and he just glared at me. Perhaps I'd sounded too reasonable for it to lead to the fight he was spoiling for.

The dogs all pulled to a particular spot and sniffed around. I ambled along as good-naturedly as one can when tied up with leather. Dave followed with less happiness and more growling.

'What do you plan to do when we get to the Institute?' Dave asked.

I shrugged. 'I just want to talk to Ben. I guess I'll have to talk to Olsen first, but then he's all yours.'

I was hoping a professional — is that a psychologist or a

psychiatrist? — would be able to spot that Dave needed more than a word or two. I wasn't sure what Olsen *could* do with him but I was sure it was more than I could. After all, Dave's corpse wouldn't just disappear, no matter how tempting it was to lose him out in the snow. I eyed an icicle and remembered hearing about them being the perfect weapon. Very tempting.

'You really think he'll point you in the direction of werewolves?' I asked, 'I mean real ones, not deluded humans.'

I tried not to look back at Conn. Too many hints might give away Conn's nature, assuming Dave hadn't worked it out already.

'He's arguably the best in clinical lycanthropy.'

"Arguably'?'

'He's not the establishment, shall we say?' Dave practically purred, enjoying the opportunity to prove he was better than me. His character had really gone downhill since he'd gone to university. But, then, he had decided to become a part of Academia, which tends to thrive on proving yourself the most intelligent and knowledgeable. I assume that leads to a high percentage of smug bastards.

'So other experts disagree with him even though he's 'well received'?' I asked sweetly.

Dave ignored me. 'Anyway, even if he's never knowingly met a real werewolf, he's bound to come in to contact with them. If I work with him, I'll find them.'

'Only the ones that get caught,' I said.

Dave smiled and it wasn't pretty. 'Like dear old Ben.'

I turned my back on him as much as the dogs' mêlée would allow.

'They're all killers, Elkie. They deserve to die.'

'For the sin of killing? Or before they get the chance to sin?' I asked.

Conn didn't look like he would kill even in self-defence. Did he deserve to die? Admittedly, he was the only werewolf I'd met who didn't definitely have blood on his hands — or should that be fangs and claws? Even Old Man Lloyd was guilty of conspiring, seeing as he'd basically sent the lawyer werewolf after us.

'Oh, come off it,' Dave spat, 'It's not like you don't kill them yourself!'

'Only the ones that attack me.'

He gave a sharp bark of laughter. 'Like that makes it better. 'Thou shalt not kill', Elkie.'

'Self-defence,' I said, 'Although I'll bet there's a whole foot-note on how many ways it's morally acceptable to kill in that bloody book.'

Dave sneered and I stopped feeling bad about betraying him. He already thought I was against him, he just hadn't worked out how to justify getting rid of me. Or a method of doing so that sat with his personal philosophy of life.

One of the dogs chose that moment to give voice to the bell-like bark that's not quite a howl, the one that hunting hounds give when they've caught the scent of quarry. It and its companions tugged against the lead but they stopped pulling when I gave a swift yank and a firm 'no'. They all looked in the direction the first had sounded in, though, aware of something there that they thought shouldn't be.

Near to a home that holds werewolves, I reminded myself.

'We better get back to Conn,' I said.

Even with five dogs, I had no interest in hanging around. Of course, I'd left it too late, or the werewolf was riled by the dogs' noises. It charged out of the snow — it would have seemed like it had come out of nowhere without the dogs' warning — and into view. It crouched as soon as it realised it was outnumbered and bared teeth at the dogs that growled back. They also wagged their tails, so I wasn't sure what their reaction was intended to be.

I leant backwards against the pull of the leads and took a mental note of the werewolf's green eyes. If I hadn't known about werewolves, I would have marvelled at a beast with eyes of such an unusual colour.

'Dave. Walk slowly back to the car.'

I didn't dare take my eyes from the dogs and Fido. I wasn't entirely sure what Conn would do if I took his dogs back in pieces. I wasn't entirely sure I could do much without sacri-ficing them.

I heard running footsteps and a hand grabbed the leads

— enfolding my own hand as it did so — and joined me in pulling the pack back.

'Leave, lads, leave!'

The dogs' eagerness for battle or play seemed to lessen, or at least the pull towards the werewolf did.

'Elkie, let go. I've got them.'

I did as I was told, my attention more on the potential attacker than the inevitable physical contact with the dogs and with Conn as we disentangled.

'And get behind me.'

I did as I was told — Conn was another werewolf while I was just a human — and quickly looked around for Dave.

'Shit!' I said when I realised that he'd disappeared. Then I muttered, 'Well, at least I don't have to worry about Dave trying to kill you.'

Conn's 'What?' was understandably distracted as he marshalled his pack into something like calm.

The werewolf stalked forward. If the joints had been put together in a less human manner, if the proportions had been that of an animal that usually walked on four legs, I would have called it 'cat-like'.

'Dave's not a fan of the real thing,' I said quietly, 'And has plans to kill as many as he can.'

Conn threw a quick look over his shoulder before returning his attention to the current problem.

'It's okay,' Conn said as if he were soothing to a scared animal, 'You don't have to fight.'

Fido snarled, clearly not convinced. I thought there was an element of recognition and dismissal of Conn's words, perhaps some long-standing disagreement. The action was enough to distract me from the figure creeping up behind Fido, not quite as stealthily as the actual werewolf managed, until the last second.

Three things will forever mark Dave's final step into what can best be described as insanity for me. The flash of winter light on ice as the werewolf began its turn to face him. The howl he gave that was totally inhuman, ripped from his throat as he stabbed with the icicle. Then the red of blood on the snow, flowing from the throat of a werewolf that might not have been about to attack us.

Dave stood over the body, panting with adrenaline and effort, as the fur was absorbed back into the body. The man beneath was older than I'd expected, slightly overweight, slightly pink with exertion where his skin could be seen through Norwegian winter clothing. If he had an intact throat, I would have expected him to be bending over his legs as he gasped for breath. I walked over and closed the staring green eyes.

'You haven't had an inmate run away from the Institute, have you?' I asked Conn.

'Olsen doesn't like the term 'inmate'.'

Dave threw me an 'I told you so' look of triumph.

I stood over the human body for a moment and felt where my silver cross lay beneath my clothes. This one would need to be accounted for. I didn't need to sweep up.

Method 25: Pulling The Plug

Dave watched Conn and the lack of surprise. My former best friend and lover said, 'The only good werewolf is a dead werewolf.'

I groaned. 'Not only insane but prone to cliché.'

'Oh, like you're any better!' Dave spat, 'Why don't you tell him how many you've killed, Elkie.'

At least he didn't act aggressive. He just stood there with the bloodied, partially-melted icicle in hand. I guess he hadn't realised that Conn was a werewolf, too, or he might have made another attack.

Conn walked off, turning his back on us. He pulled his pack of dogs away as he took a mobile out of a pocket. He didn't speak to us or tell us what was happening. With less than werewolf or canine hearing, neither of us knew — although I could make an educated guess given the letter I sent.

'Just get back in the car, Dave,' I said.

I rubbed at suddenly tired eyes and wondered if Olsen could make any of this better. Maybe we'd all end up locked up tight in his Institute.

'And leave the icicle.'

Dave dropped the icicle, the hand that held it white. I'm not sure if that was just because of how cold it would have been. I followed him as he walked back, hunched over with his hands under his armpits. There would be blood on his coat and suit and shoes, fine droplets that forensics would love. There were probably the same traces over me and Conn, too.

I managed to switch seats with Dave without any complaint and fingered the locking mechanism on my door.

Conn caught the movement and, after a sideways look, locked the rear doors.

'I just want to talk to Ben,' I said softly.

'So he *has* been up to something and you didn't tell me,' Conn said just as softly.

'Are you talking about me?' Dave demanded. 'Stop whispering.'

'We're talking about Ben,' I said.

I looked at Conn, the image of a capable former boy scout if ever I saw one. I looked over my shoulder at Dave, listening intently and wondered if it mattered what he knew anymore.

'I thought you were just the courier,' I said to Conn, 'I didn't realise you were the dog warden.'

Conn smiled as if I'd been amusing, although I hadn't intended to be. It was just the best description I could come up with for the way he seemed to be bent on redeeming strays. I took a chance I suspected was wrong, if only because the stray in question hadn't been so redeemed.

'Was Diarmuid one of yours?'

Conn went very still and quiet, with allowance for driving on an icy road. Then he asked, 'What happened to him?'

Dave kicked the back of my seat.

'Dave, you're not a toddler,' I threw over my shoulder.

Conn's hands tightened on the driving wheel and I wished I could tell him it had all turned out okay but lying wouldn't help any of us. It wasn't like there was a world out there where Diarmuid had survived and was waiting for me to come home. I chose to stick with silence and the silence chose to stick with us until Conn pulled up in front of the imposing stone building that could only be our destination, Olsen's Institute.

I unloaded my backpack and parcel as soon as we'd stopped. I wasn't sure whether to make a grab for Dave's to reduce any possibility of it being used as weaponry if what happened next was vaguely as I expected. Conn beat me to it and picked up the two cases after releasing his dogs in a swirling mass. Dave just accepted that someone else would carry his bags as if he were born to it.

'Home, sweet home?' I asked Conn with a nervous smile.

He smiled tightly and looked up at the Institute's less than welcoming face. 'For some.'

The dogs sniffed and charged about happily. One or two cocked legs to leave messages about passing through their territory.

'Let's go in, shall we?' Dave asked pointedly.

He blew on his hands, already cold from stepping out of the car and its controlled temperature.

'Eager to meet Olsen,' I said.

'Yes,' Dave said.

Conn gestured with the hand holding the lighter briefcase. 'After you.'

Dave ran lightly up the steps as if he knew what he was doing. I hung back by Conn and said quietly, 'Me, too?'

I was a killer, too, and I wasn't sure what kind of invitation or greeting I was about to get.

The pack whirled around us for a moment and then parted as Conn strode after Dave. 'Not as far as I know,' he said.

I took a deep breath and joined the pack if only because it was difficult not to move with the five active bodies.

Two men in white — I guess they're called 'orderlies' or the Norwegian equivalent — had flanked Dave, although they didn't hold him. Instead of moving away from them or fighting, Dave looked at Conn and me with big round eyes.

'What's going on?'

He sounded like a child, although he'd never really been that bewildered or out of sorts.

'From Elkie's description of you, we thought you might have been a special case, so we already had security ready for you,' Conn said. 'Now you need to be held in a secure facility while the murder is investigated.'

He otherwise ignored the scene and went straight to the reception desk with Dave's bags.

'Have these put somewhere safe, please. And have Mr Williams taken to a secure room.'

'He's one of the... special cases?' the woman behind the desk asked.

Conn shook his head. 'No. We're holding him until the

police investigate a murder scene just down the road and have time to pick him up.'

'It wasn't murder,' Dave said. He moved forward, not quite a thrust but more active than his artificially bewildered approach, and the orderlies finally laid hands on him. 'It had it coming!'

"It'?' Conn asked with raised eyebrows.

I could see he was performing for the staff's benefit, too. Probably going for 'this man is totally insane and will be left here for eternity'.

'If he says anything about werewolves,' Conn said to the orderlies, 'Just ignore him. The police should be here in about an hour to interview him.'

The staff exchanged looks and nods. I wasn't sure whether they knew about actual werewolves or not. I did know they would be doing a studious job of making Dave look like here was where the police should be leaving him. Although I assume courts would be involved at some point.

Dave also seemed to get the same idea because he started pulling at the arms that held him. Thankfully, two men were enough to hold him back.

'You can't do this to me! It was a killer! It deserved to die!'

'Giovanni never laid a hand on anyone,' Conn bit out.

I wasn't totally convinced. There had been threatening behaviour on the werewolf's part. If it were a dog, that would be enough to have it classified as dangerous.

Conn turned and walked away from Dave, who was still pulling against his new minders. The orderlies stood there and let him rant. Moving with him would just have increased the chance of losing their grip on the squirming new inmate.

'Elkie?' Conn called and I ran to catch up.

'You bitch!' Dave screamed after me, 'You did this to me. Just because of that fucking Irish animal!'

'That would be Diarmuid,' Conn said when I caught up.

'Yes.'

'What did Williams do to him?'

I noted the way Conn's hands clenched into fists with white knuckles and decided it was a very good thing that

222

someone else was restraining Dave. Perhaps the warden knew enough about himself to have arranged it that way.

'Put screenwash in his tea,' I said.

Conn stopped suddenly. 'Screenwash? He poisoned him?' I nodded.

'Shit!'

All things considered, that was a very restrained response.

'I thought — ' Conn took a deep breath and started walking in the maze of corridors again, 'I thought Diarmuid might actually be able to make a go of it.'

'Being part of human life again?' I asked and smiled sadly as I thought about the things that might have been had Dave's victim been prepared to try human life again, 'Probably not. He had every intention of — Well, I guess it would have been a duel.'

'A duel?'

'I'll explain it to you when we're with Olsen,' I said, 'No point in going through it twice.'

I received a long, hard look and then, 'True.'

He gestured me into an office and pointed to the older man behind the desk. 'Olsen.'

The professor was busy at a computer and he paused, looking distracted, when he heard his name. Seeing there were people in the room, he stood and held out his hand to me.

Conn introduced me. 'Elkie Bernstein.'

I looked at the tall, slender man for a moment before shaking it. The suit was too reminiscent of the one Dave wore but otherwise they clearly had little in common.

Olsen released my hand and sat down quickly. After an initial once over, I got the impression he didn't want me or my presence. I had been judged and found... uninteresting.

'Thank you for your letter,' he said, his attention returning to his computer already.

'We thought Williams might be another werewolf from your choice of words,' Conn said, as if prompting.

I thought back to the receptionist. 'A special case?'

'Exactly.'

Olsen had little time for this. 'But Conn has confirmed that Mr Williams is just a human being — '

'Just a human being?' I interrupted, 'The boy is certifiably insane. He's a fucking murderer!'

Diarmuid and the late Giovanni were evidence of that.

Olsen looked at me briefly and then looked back to his screen. 'Let the professionals decide about his sanity.'

'The men he murdered were werewolves,' I said. Maybe it made a difference to this distant, sketched in character.

Olsen froze. It's not like he didn't know already — about Giovanni, at least — but I had my first glimpse of something other than possible interest and definite disinterest. And what I glimpsed wasn't pretty. His lip twitched in to a growl that never made it into the even voice.

'Mr Williams will find himself part of a murder investigation for his recent actions.'

There was an unspoken 'and he will pay' that sent a chill up my spine. I wasn't sure whether it was because Olsen himself scared me or because part of me really hoped Dave did pay. I looked at Conn but he remained quiet and contained, somehow separate from the emotions despite obviously having been upset about Giovanni and hearing about Diarmuid.

'I'd like to talk to Ben,' I said.

'Conn can show you,' Olsen said and permission to stand in the presence was revoked.

'Is he always like this?' I asked Conn, not shifting from my spot in front of the desk. I had more I wanted to say, things I wanted Olsen to do so that I could go home and farm in peace. If he'd deign to talk to a mere human.

Conn shrugged.

'I have important work to do, Miss Bernstein.'

I raised my eyebrows at Conn and he said, 'Olsen's obsessed with proving werewolves are valuable members of society.'

'Whereas you're just obsessed with making them members of society,' I said.

But the continued use of the word 'obsessed' was catching my attention. Werewolves focus too much and these two were no exception. One spent too much time being a super professional and the other spent too much time saving strays.

'Actually,' Olsen said from around his computer, 'We generally assume Conn was obsessed with his bitch.'

Conn flushed but didn't deny it. Perhaps his interest in strays was to prove that he was still a functioning member of society himself.

'Lucky woman,' I said, mentally transposing Conn with Diarmuid and the unknown woman with me. It didn't work as the image slipped a little to my old crush on Ben.

'Well,' I said to cover my own blush, 'It kind of explains how Ben can have more success with finding werewolves than you two do.'

'What?' Olsen jerked as if hit. He focussed on me immediately. I might be a mere human but I'd brought something new and werewolf related to his attention — and had gained some associated importance.

'How many have you found... Oh, I dunno, since Ben moved here? Or just the last six months?'

Olsen looked at Conn, who shrugged.

'Ben's sent me ten werewolves in about six months.'

'Ten?'

Olsen was standing again, shock written all over his face. I noticed how pale it was from all the time indoors and felt my lip curl like his own had moments before. Imagine having the strength and power of a werewolf at your command and spending all your time driving a computer. But I suppose age has something to do with that as well as career choice. Olsen looked to be of Mr Williams' generation, perhaps slightly older.

'You let him go on the Internet again about then, right? That's when he started our game again.'

'Game?' Conn asked.

'The duelling thing. He sends werewolves to kill me.'

'You talk them out of it?' Olsen looked incredulously at me. I doubt my skinny frame was any more inspiring than his slightly better proportioned but ageing one so the fact that I fought and won probably didn't occur to him.

'No. I survive them.'

'You kill werewolves?' Conn almost growled.

'Only the ones stupid enough to attack me.'

I thought back over the twenty-two werewolves I'd seen die and considered what passed for a score.

'And I haven't actually killed all the ones that came to me. Dave got a few of them. As you know.'

Conn repeated himself in flat tones, 'You kill werewolves.'

'I'd rather not,' I said.

Conn and Olsen watched me as if I'd just become the most dangerous thing in the room. Perhaps I was.

'And if you let me talk to Ben, or if you stop him playing this bloody awful game with my life, I may never have to meet another werewolf again, let alone kill one.'

My voice cracked at the end of that but no-one else seemed to hear it. I took in a deep breath.

'Ben Lloyd has been contacting werewolves and sending them after some girl in the English wilderness?' Olsen looked incredulous again.

'Welsh,' I said. 'Not English.'

'Same thing,' he dismissed.

Both Conn and I looked at him as if he'd just crawled out from under a stone. Although Conn isn't the three-headed monster Welsh folklore would have me believe an Englishman should be, I still don't want to be classed as English.

'Some untrained child has sourced werewolves for some game — '

'Maybe you should just teach him a new one,' I said, fed up of the self-righteous disbelief, 'Like search and rescue instead of search and destroy.'

Olsen didn't really hear me. He was too busy trying to adjust to an obsessed game player being better than an obsessed professional, if only in one key part of his plan.

Conn shook his head. 'Sorry. We get a bit too self-absorbed. Let me take you through to Ben.'

'You think you could see your way to pulling his plug until you've worked out his new game?' I asked.

'Maybe you should play this new game, too,' Conn said lightly.

It was my turn to shake my head. 'I've had enough of playing with werewolves.'

'Not even if I find you a well behaved one to live on a Welsh hill farm?'

I thought of Diarmuid and shook my head. 'Almost tried that. Didn't work out.'

'Sticking with dogs, then.'

'The real canines,' I confirmed.

'What about Ben?'

I shrugged. 'I haven't seen him in years. On the up side, I don't have an Internet connection. If he ever decides to come home.'

'Come home?'

'Well, it is his house.'

'That's not what the paperwork says,' Conn reminded me.

He took me to a corridor that required a pass through some full on security. My backpack ended up being held by one of the guards, the parcel was allowed through with me and Conn — after I carefully unwrapped enough of it to show the game inside.

'We have another corridor like this for the ones who are dangerous to others but only think they're werewolves. Olsen really does specialise in clinical lycanthropy.'

And his interest in them probably faded as soon as he realised they didn't carry fur-skins. Underlings and co-workers probably dealt with them.

'So the real thing's just an absorbing hobby?' I asked, trying to keep most of that assumption to myself.

Conn gave me a level look and I looked down the corridor. There was enough glass — well, probably Perspex or something similar — fronted cells to keep a Hollywood director in wet dreams about award winning horror films for life.

'How many are here?'

Conn shrugged. 'Ben, Philip, Alejandro, Eric, Simon. Me and Olsen.'

'And Giovanni and Diarmuid came through here.'

'Diarmuid was our first success. Or so we thought. Giovanni came willingly and then left.'

'So not all Norwegian.'

Conn spread his hands. 'Of European extraction is probably the best way of putting it. Although werewolves are a North American myth, too.'

'I met a few, what's the term, of colour,' I said. Precisely two, in fact, and I was never in a position to ask details about their racial identity or genetic background.

Conn shrugged. 'It seems to be something to do with European traditions. Maybe people with other traditions have something better to do.'

'Do other places have other men-animals?'

He shrugged again. 'No idea.'

We walked passed a furred up werewolf rocking in his room, a sign of a disturbed human mind that even I recognised. I wondered what he had done to make him so upset with himself.

'Alejandro.'

The next was another older man, somewhere between Conn and Olsen in age. He leant against the front of his cell, nose pressed up against a handful of holes that allowed sound and scent to pass through. He whimpered slightly as I passed.

'Philip,' Conn said, and he looked away as if he couldn't cope with looking at that particular inmate.

The third cell was Ben, who sat at a desk with a number of computers. The one he played with was a straight forward games console. There were three other flavours of console there and a PC that was plugged in but turned off.

'Ben,' I said quietly.

He sprung to his feet and was up against the vents, his fingers searching to find their way through the holes.

'Elkie! What are you doing here? Where's Diarmuid?'

I put a hand out and matched fingertip to fingertip, although the material was too thick for us to actually touch through the holes. I could see the child I always imagined him to be these days in his eyes, desperate for attention and to be part of something. I would guess the need was almost stronger than his obsession with playing games after years of being confined. Or maybe it was something to do with the game playing all along. The Deity knew Ben wouldn't have had much game playing and simple fun when he was a child. Not with Old Man Lloyd.

'I need you to step away from the door, Ben, while security let us in,' Conn said.

Ben edged nervously back towards bars I only just noticed existed with his movement. The room was more like a kennel run, with two distinct sections in order to protect the Institute staff.

'Do I have to get back in the cage?' he asked.

Conn shook his head and Ben relaxed again.

'Diarmuid ran into Dave,' I said, answering the earlier question.

Ben watched me as we walked into his room. 'I'll miss him. Diarmuid.'

'Me, too,' I said lamely and held out the brown package. 'I brought you a present.'

Ben stepped forward as nervously as he'd stepped away from us in the first place. I guess six or so years of incarceration knocks the confidence out of anyone, even golden boys.

'What is it?'

It was hard not to smile at the child-like question. My smiling made Ben smile back.

'Open it and find out,' I said.

The child-like behaviour continued as he fell on the cheap brown paper. It was probably the first gift he'd had since leaving home at age sixteen. Sixteen might be old enough to be a teenaged, pretend adult but it isn't old enough to have learnt how an adult truly behaves and moves through life. I have no doubt I'll look back in five or more years time and say the same about twenty-one.

'Chess?'

'I thought we could play a less dangerous game.'

He looked at me as if I'd turned English.

'Please, Ben. I can't cope with this anymore.'

'But you're so kick-ass!'

I rubbed at my temples, wondering if he was even on the same planet. 'I'm tired of it, Ben. I don't want to fight. Or kill. Or maim.'

He looked at me in silence.

'It's not a fun thing to do, Ben, and I want to get on with my life.'

'No games?' he asked and the plaintive tone I'd attached to a few of his emails was there in person, 'You don't want to play?'

'I do, Ben. I want to play. Just something else. Like chess.'

Conn cleared his throat. 'And I've got to take away your Internet connection.'

'You can't do that!'

Ben jumped at Conn and out of habit I put myself between them. Ridiculous as Conn is a werewolf and at least as used as I am to getting into fights. Neither were furred-up, so I guess they weren't really up to killing speed. It was doubly ridiculous because I hadn't done it for Giovanni. I guess I have some unresolved feelings of responsibility for Ben.

'Ben, leave it. There are other games. You don't need to send werewolves to kill me.'

They both looked at me.

'Let him pull the plug, Ben. You'll get it back soon enough.'

'Will you stay and play chess with me until I do?'

I sighed. 'I have a farm to run. I need to get back to it.' *If Olsen and Conn will let me.*

'Just for a while?'

Ben looked at me, full of childhood potential that had never been reached and might never have the opportunity to try again. Behind him, crouched over the cables for the PC, Conn also watched me. I thought about him and this mysterious woman of his. I thought about Olsen and his blind determination to prove his magical species, not just himself. I thought about Dave and his all too human intent to rid the world of an apparent threat.

'Okay,' I said.

Foxspirit.co.uk

'After nourishment, shelter and companionship, stories are the thing we need most in the world.' Phillip Pullman

Skulk: *noun* – a pack or group of foxes

Fox Spirit believes that day to day life lacks a few things, primarily the fantastic, the magical, the mischievous and even a touch of the horrific. We aim to rectify that by bringing you stories and gorgeous cover art and illustrations from foxy folk who believe as we do that we could all use a little more wonder in our lives.

Here at the Fox Den we believe in storytelling first and foremost, so we mash genres, bend tropes and set fire to rule books merrily as we seek out tall tales that excite and delight us and send them out into the world to find new readers.

With a mixture of established and new writers producing novels, short stories, flash fiction and poetry via ebook and print we recommend letting a little Fox Spirit into your life.

 @foxspiritbooks

 https://www.facebook.com/foxspiritbooks

 adele@foxspirit.co.uk

Made in the USA
Charleston, SC
20 March 2016